TURNING POINT

TURNING POINT

Edd McNair

www.urbanbooks.net

Urban Books
1199 Straight Path
West Babylon, NY 11704

ISBN-13: 978-1-60162-040-8
ISBN-10: 1-60162-040-3

First Printing January 2008
Printed in the United States of America

10   9   8   7   6   5   4   3   2   1

This is a work of fiction. Any references or similarities to actual events, real people, living, or dead, or to real locales are intended to give the novel a sense of reality. Any similarity in other names, characters, places, and incidents is entirely coincidental.

Submit Wholesale Orders to:
Kensington Publishing Corp.
C/O Penguin Group (USA) Inc.
Attention: Order Processing
405 Murray Hill Parkway
East Rutherford, NJ 07073-2316
Phone: 1-800-526-0275
Fax: 1-800-227-9604

TURNING POINT

Chapter 1

"Coming Home"

The street in the one-way-in, one-way-out projects was crowded. It was summer time, and everybody was hanging out. The grey Intrepid with North Carolina tags pulled into Oakley Park, one of the most notorious projects in Norfolk.

Russ jumped out the car. "Call me later, muthafucka," he said to his childhood friend, Vic. He threw his bag over his shoulder. Russ looked like he'd been eating weights. His chest was bulging through the wife-beater, making it a tight fit, and showing every cut in his defined body, and his arms seemed to have gained another two inches.

Neighbors watched in terror as the five-foot-ten, two-hundred and thirty-pound monster walked up to his mom's door, his Timberland boots untied and his Dickies jeans sagging halfway off his ass, revealing his striped boxers.

"How long you gonna stay home this time?" his mom asked, pulling on one of her Newport 100s at the card table and reaching for her Budweiser.

Her company smirked out loud.

"How long you gonna keep smokin'? How long you gonna stay off your motherfuckin' knees gettin' money? Better shut yo' ass up."

"No, you better shut *yo* ass up or find somewhere else to hang your clothes, smart-ass bastard."

Eighteen-year-old Russ had just been released from the Tidewater Detention Home for boys and was used to his mom shitting on him.

Since he was eight, he'd seen her doing every scam possible to get dough. She'd never made an effort to get out the projects and just dug a deeper hole for him, his brother, and sister. She'd always tricked, but only to chosen cats. But in the last six years, she had gone from chosen ones to whoever offered her an open promise. He knew most of the young hustlin' niggahs had fucked his mom, but nothing was ever said in the presence of him or his brother.

Russ loved her, but lost all respect for her when he walked in to find her sucking Drake's dick in the living room. She thought they were 'sleep, but he'd heard Drake's husky voice. Drake was a six-foot-one, two-hundred and ninety pound, big, sloppy, nasty-ass-looking man. He had her by the hair as she sucked his dick, his pants down around his ankles. She was so high, she never noticed her son.

Drake looked over at Russ and began pumping his dick in and out of her mouth. "Lick these balls." He grabbed his dick and pointed it at Russ. Then he pushed Marie to the couch face first, making sure she never looked up to see Russ. He pulled her dress up to pull her panties to the side, but she wore none.

Drake took off his shirt, revealing titties and a big belly that hung down and almost covered his dick. He took his hard, thick dick and stroked it, showing it to Russ. Then he turned and shoved it in Marie, shoving her head first into the couch hard as he could without breaking it. He slapped her ass until she grunted from the stinging pain. Then he grabbed her by her little ponytail and pumped hard, sweat dripping from his body, until he came.

He pulled out, turned her over, and threw his dick in her mouth. She gagged as cum ran out her mouth and onto her chin. He grinned a wicked smile and threw his shoe at Russ, hitting him in the back.

Russ hurried back to his room, fighting tears from the blow with the steel-tipped boot, but the pain and the confusion of what he'd just witnessed made tears fall.

Unsure of what he'd just seen, he tried his best to stay clear of Drake, but Drake continued to do trifling shit like that. Sometimes he would have sex with the door open, knowing Russ, his brother Cadillac, or even his baby sister Precious could walk by. Their moms used to be so high and drunk, not to mention scared that he might beat her ass, that she kept her mouth shut, just so he would pay a few bills.

Russ walked inside. He had been locked down for two years this time and hated coming home to this bullshit. Living like this was worse than being locked, he thought.

Drake sat on the couch, in his boxers, no shirt or shoes, revealing too much of himself.

"My little sister don't need to see your shit. Why don't you cover up?"

"Carry your ass, young punk. Just keep your ass out of trouble, and don't bring none of that jailhouse shit up in this house."

Russ ignored him and walked upstairs past his sister's room. Fifteen-year-old Precious was his heart. He wanted better for her, and she knew when Truck was home, there wasn't shit to worry about.

Russell Gonzalez got his nickname, Truck, when he and Cadillac used to play ball at Lake Taylor. He played full back and used to open holes like a truck. His friends always said once he got going, he was impossible to stop no matter what defense they had.

Precious hung up the phone and ran over to hug him. She loved Cadillac, but Truck was her favorite. He took time with her and showed her a lot of love. She was the only one he put before himself.

"Where Cadillac?" he asked.

"He gone with some girl. I'm so glad you home, Truck."

"Me too, baby." He squeezed her. "Don't go downstairs. That nasty, fat son of a bitch down there damnnear naked."

"He do it all the time. Him and Mommy have sex all loud, then he come out naked going to the bathroom. He know my door open, and he'll look in here. I started closing my door."

Russ was ready to explode. Drake had to go.

He walked in the room he shared with Cadillac. He went to the bed, turned the mattress, and checked the hole, where he and Cadillac always kept their weed for easy access. But now instead of weed, it was "hard." He pulled out the small rocks and looked at them.

Cadillac had only gotten home two weeks before him and was doing dirt already. He came running upstairs.

"What up, big boy?" Cadillac punched Russ playfully.

Seventeen-year-old Cadillac knew two things—money and rumbling. He had been locked up for everything: robbery, grand theft, and distribution of narcotics. If

money was involved, he was in. He had just done eighteen months in the Pines Juvenile Detention Home in
Portsmouth for real bad kids, one step from the penitentiary.

His style was that of a laid-back niggah, but he had a
temper that kept him in trouble. In a split second, he'd
change from a laid-back type fellow to a menace. At six
feet and two hundred pounds, his body was chiseled with
much definition, but not a lot of size. Anthony Miller, aka
Cadillac, got his name because of his smooth, but powerful, tactics.

"That fat-ass bitch still on the couch?" Truck asked.

"Naw. He standin' across the street drinkin' with those
other bum-ass niggahs."

"Time for him to go. We put up with him long enough.
I know I can take him now."

"Gotcha back," Cadillac said. "We might end up getting locked up again."

"Fuck it! I only been home a day. I ain't used to it yet."

Truck went in his mom's room and put all of Drake's
shit in a bag. He told Cadillac, "Take this outside and
throw it in the street in front of him."

As Cadillac walked outside with the plastic bag, his
mom jumped up.

Precious grabbed her. "Chill out, Mommy," she said.

"Better get the fuck off me!" Marie replied.

"Yo, leave 'im alone; not today, I mean it Mommy, don't
fuck with them today or I'm gonna test you." Precious
stared her mom in the face. Tired of Drake's nasty ass,
she didn't know if she could beat her mom, but she was
going to find out today.

"Precious Moniese Baldwin, you better get it together."

"Talk to the hand."

Cadillac threw Drake's shit in the street. "Carry your bitch ass," he said, tossing it.

Drake came charging, and Cadillac began throwing a fury of blows to Drake's face.

The crowd grew bigger. They were used to the family wilding out against any and everybody in the projects.

As Caddy bust on Drake with lefts and rights, Drake kept coming, absorbing every blow. He grabbed Caddy and slammed him to the street.

Then, out of nowhere, Truck came across his head with a shovel, and the blood poured.

After several licks with the broken shovel, Drake still stood strong. He charged Truck, but Truck bent down and, in one quick motion, scooped the entire two hundred ninety pounds of man and slammed him to the concrete. Drake then felt the old faded Timbs stomping his head to the pavement, leaving him shaking in the street.

Soon the ambulance came and scooped Drake up, but by the time the police arrived, Truck and Cadillac were gone, and nobody knew nothing.

Chapter 2

"Getting Back"

Truck and Cadillac had made it to the Hardee's on Campostella Road. Vic pulled up, and they were out, headed to Virginia Beach to rest at Vic's house—a two-bedroom townhouse that he shared with his girl.

"Y'all niggahs got problems. And you just came home today. Haven't even seen your P.O. and already fuckin' up." Vic looked at Truck.

"Fuck you, niggah," Truck told him. "Don't get your jaw broke."

"Niggah, what?" Vic smirked. "You must think I'm one of those bitch niggahs you was locked up with."

Truck knew he could fuck Vic up, but it wasn't about that. He knew about the .357 revolver that Vic always kept close and wasn't worried about Vic shooting him. They had grown up together, and Vic was always in his corner, right or wrong. But if he hit Vic, there was no telling, so he knew that wasn't gonna happen.

"Y'all niggahs been fucked up in the system since I can remember. But now it's penitentiary time, y'all gots to chill."

They rested at Vic's crib for a day, then moved into a hotel. Vic let them use his girl's car for a couple days.

Cadillac and Truck hit the streets, moving the rest of the shit Cadillac had.

Vic was a serious businessman. He had good shit, high prices, and always a steady flow, if your money was right.

Truck knew he had to get his weight up to be able to fuck with his own man. So, until then, Cadillac scored from a niggah he'd befriended while locked up one of the many times. He'd met Pablo at the group home in Norfolk.

Pablo was living with his grandmother in Huntersville Housing, where Cadillac's grandmother lived too. At the time, they were just thirteen and doing a lot of wild things young boys do. A lot of the young boys in the projects were sniffing "boy" (heroin) because everybody else around them was doing it. Sniffing soon became a daily thing, and it wasn't long before they were being sent away because of the powerful drug.

When they got out, Pablo went back to his mom's in Northridge, a low-income housing development in Virginia Beach.

Four years later, they were still holding each other down. Neither ever stayed home long enough to build any real money, but whoever was up—most of the time it turned out to be Pablo—always helped the other.

Now Pablo was feeding him ounces. In a minute they'd be ready to buy four and a half. After a couple of weeks, they got enough to buy a '90 Honda Civic and a '91 Chrysler LeBaron. Even though the cars were ten years old, they were happy. They also got a two-bedroom apartment in Cambridge Manor in Chesapeake, one mile from Oakley Park. Things were flowing. On a break-down, they were paying thirty-eight hundred for four and a half, bringing back sixty-five hundred and splitting twenty-seven hundred a week. Cadillac was content. He just wanted to live, but Truck wanted a lot more.

They jumped out of the Honda and headed to the apartment. Truck pulled out the scale, so Cadillac could weigh the "work."

"This shit is on point as always," Cadillac said, jumping up, leaving the drugs sitting on the scale.

"Better be, 'cause I'll ball that fat muthafucka up."

"Chill the fuck out, Truck. That niggah a'ight."

"Fuck him. You see the bitch in that niggah eyes, always talking that "what-he-did" shit. That bitch niggah has no idea how I get down."

"Kill 'em then, niggah, talkin' all that shit." Cadillac went to his room. "He's just our connect."

"Don't play. Vic keep asking when I'm ready," Truck said, sitting at the table with a razor and small bags.

Cadillac returned with his sweats and cut-off shirt. "I'm headed to the gym."

"Shit, I'm going too. Let's get this shit right now. Then I'm going too."

"Precious birthday Thursday. She'll be sixteen," Cadillac said.

"Yeah, turning into a lady. I was hoping she didn't grow up so fast. But seeing all she'd seen, what the fuck would I expect?" Truck shook his head.

"She gonna be a'ight. She's street smart, but she also book smart. She having a get-together at her boyfriend's house."

"That little-ass niggah she fuck with got his own shit?" Truck asked.

"Hell yeah. She was driving his Lexus. Little niggah got a GS300 sitting on twenties. He just bought a townhouse, and might as well say she living with him."

"Yeah, I saw her the other day. She called me and we met at Piccadilly. She had a bad little bitch with her. I can say dude make sure her ass go to school. She said he just graduated last year from Booker T. Washington. She say the little niggah cook up shit for some Carolina niggahs and he's getting it. He even taught her. I told her she don't even know the skill she got. Lil' bitch just laughed."

"He better make sure she a'ight, 'cause I will break that niggah's muthafuckin' neck," Truck said, steady bagging twenties.

"So we goin' to her shit?"

"Yeah."

"You plan on gettin' Pablo?"

"Most definitely."

Pablo was leaning on the green tank sitting on the right side of the entrance of Bayside Arms. He watched closely as his young team served the fiends that drove in and out of the Virginia Beach project. He pulled out his cell and called his man. "Yo, Darius, what the deal?"

"Nothing. Niggahs gettin' it, though," he said pulling on the blunt.

"I'll be around there in second. Take a ride with a niggah."

"Waitin' on you." Darius hung up.

Pablo yelled at Brit, "Come on, man, I'm out."

"Hold up, niggah. I'm up. Breakin' these niggahs," Brit said.

Pablo walked over to where they were shooting dice. "Y'all niggahs only shootin' with two dice?"

"Hell yeah. Fuck that New York shit. Three dice, niggahs always want to put shit in the game," Brit said.

Everybody started laughing, including Pablo. He looked at Brit with his new Timbs, Rocawear jeans, jersey, and bandanna. Always clean with new shit and always keeping niggahs laughing. Brit was his rolling partner. He knew how to get money, not trouble, so he got along with everybody. And the bitches loved him.

"You niggahs got to go," Brit said, counting niggahs' money in their faces. "I'm gonna carry y'all shit to the mall." He laughed.

Everybody laughed, except for two of the guys who had lost.

"Don't laugh, niggah. Fuck around and you won't leave the park," one guy said, referring to the one-way-in, one-way-out projects.

"Fuck around and you won't leave this, bitch," Pablo said with the burner to the niggah's temple. "Fuck you talkin'."

The guy stood still, his body stiff.

Somebody's mother came out the apartment across the street and saw what was going on. "In the name of Jesus, young man," she said, "in the name of Jesus, put it away." She threw her hands up.

Pablo put his burner back in his pants. He didn't want a murder charge, but he didn't want his peoples fucked with.

Brit was from Lake Edward, but he always hung out at Bayside Arms, North Ridge, and The Lakes, his home. But his girl he'd been with for a while lived in Bayside Arms with her mom and his little girl, so he was out there every day. And Pablo made sure nobody fucked with him.

They climbed in Pablo's black Mustang and turned up his sounds and burned rubber.

"You need to slow down, son," Brit told him.

"I know. Sometimes I just snap and think about it later," Pablo said as he turned into Northridge.

"Sometimes niggahs just be talkin'."

"And sometimes they don't."

Pablo respected Brit, who had been in the streets since he was nine. His sister had raised him and his little brother because his mother worked nonstop, trying to take care of them. He fell into the hustling scene automatically, especially when the spot was his back yard in one of the back alleys of Lake Edward. He started hustling when he was fourteen and used to run with real niggahs who had Lake Edward on lock. He made money, smoked trees, ran hos; when he had his kid, he'd contemplated getting out but never followed through.

Months later when he heard that Bo and his brother Rome were found cremated in his truck, that was the last straw. That situation drained him, he was between scoring and decided not to. Instead he brought a ring for Leah and asked her to marry him. He opened a car detailing shop and allowed his money to work for him. People who didn't know him, still thought he hustled, because he still carried himself the same way. Seeing that all the hustlers out on the beach came to his detailing shop, he was still well connected and associated with everybody.

They pulled in front of the townhouse on Harrier.

"What the deal?" Darius gave Brit a pound and a hug.

"What the fuck rollin' out here?" Pablo asked.

"This niggah askin' shit like somebody work for him. You work for this niggah, Brit? You work for this niggah, Javonne?" Darius looked at the guy he was with. "Who you think you is? Nino Brown?"

They started laughing.

"Wouldn't be out here if I wasn't looking at the big picture," Pablo said seriously.

"So what's the deal?" Darius asked.

Pablo walked down the sidewalk, and Darius followed.

"I got to serve those niggahs in a sec, Caddy and Truck. They been scorin' four and a half for a minute, but for some reason I'm feeling funny. Before it was nothing, now Truck be real edgy. I don't even really like fucking with him."

"I thought you were still serving them cats ounces. They comin' up, huh?"

"They keep a clientele. Question is, how long they gonna stay home to serve 'em?"

"Tell 'em to come to the house. Fuck servin' a niggah all that in the street."

"You right." Pablo knew that, but needed to hear Darius say it. He walked back to his car. He had four and a half sitting in the stash. He knew it was Cadillac's time to score. He jumped in the Mustang to drop Brit off.

When they arrived at the detail shop, Pablo saw the Suburban, BMW wagon, and 300ZX. He knew those shits belonged to Poppa, Dundee, and Javonne.

"I see your Lake Edward fam up in this bitch," Pablo said.

"Yeah, you saw those twin Escalades on the side, didn't you? And the S320 Benz? You know who those shits belong to, right?"

"Ain't that Trent and Van?" Pablo asked.

"Yeah, and they little cousin, niggahs from out Bridal Creek and niggahs be gettin' it. Every week they gamble upstairs, and those niggahs always got mad dough. But you know them LE niggahs always come with it."

"They used to. A couple years ago everybody knew LE was where the true hustlas came from, but now I don't know," Pablo said.

"LE will always be the shit, because you can't shut it

down. But niggahs tired of gettin' locked up, so they not shinin'. Lake Edward niggahs grind now. Niggahs have realized, money first. Nothing like having money stacked. Fuck all them cars and jewels and shit. Get a dependable whip, roof over your head, and stack that dough. We young, but we can buy houses. We can invest in real estate. Fuck that hustlin' shit. Niggahs can't do that shit forever."

"They makin' dough like that?" Pablo asked.

"Don't ask, son. You know how much Trent and Van makin', right?"

"Yeah. That's who I score from, Trent."

"For real? Well, Poppa probably make three times that."

Pablo looked at him in disbelief.

"You remember Black?" Brit asked.

"Yeah. His brother used to fuck with my cousin. That's the niggah that got killed on the motorcycle."

"That's who Poppa connected with."

"Goddamn! Maybe that's who me and Darius need to be fuckin with."

Brit never responded. He didn't have any plans for playing middleman.

"Holla!" Brit got out the Mustang and gave Pablo a pound. "Don't forget my wedding in May. Shorty workin' hard on shit."

"That's gonna be the wedding of the century. Bayside Arms girl marrying a grimy-ass Lake Edward niggah! What?" Pablo hollered. "How many groomsmen?"

"You know I got my team—Poppa, Reese, Black, Lou, Derrick, BayBay, and Prince, my best man. I told her match 'em up."

"I heard that, all LE niggahs. Y'all ain't shit, niggah." Pablo laughed.

"Shit, all those bitches she got from Bayside Arms and

Northridge, except for my sister. Yo, niggah, be safe," Brit said giving him a pound. He ran up the stairs of the detailing shop to rest in the studio where niggahs were gambling.

Pablo was headed to the mall when he got a call from Cadillac. Him and Truck was trying to score. He told them to meet him out Northridge, as he got off the interstate on Brambleton. He turned into the 7-Eleven shopping strip and parked in front of Kappatal Kuts. He walked inside to catch a cut.

Niggahs knew Pablo as a baller. He went in and sat in Rick's chair. Rick had been cutting his shit forever.

He started talking to the neighboring barbers about local deals. Cats started coming in selling CDs, DVDs, and clothes. Bee, one of the neighboring barbers, pulled out his clothing line and spread it out, something he did every time somebody else came in with clothes.

Pablo's phone rang as Rick was cutting him up. He reached from under the red cape and put the phone to his ear.

"We headed your way," Cadillac said.

"Hold tight. I'm getting a cut. I'll come cross the bridge when I finish."

When Rick was finished, Pablo gave everybody a pound and headed out the door and over Campostella Bridge. He called Cadillac and decided to meet him behind Be-Lo in Campostella Plaza.

Pablo pulled up where Cadillac's Honda was parked.

Cadillac jumped out and climbed in the car with Pablo. "Where Truck?"

"With a trick; I told him we been doin' this long enough. We safe." Cadillac gave Pablo a pound.

"For sho, niggah." Pablo smirked.

Pablo hit the stash and gave Cadillac four and a half ounces, and Cadillac handed him a bag.

"Be easy, baby." Cadillac got out the car.

Pablo opened the bag and saw the bundles of note-book paper wrapped in rubber bands. He looked up and saw Cadillac's shiny baldhead in front of the car. He couldn't wait to put a bullet in it.

He grabbed his gun and turned to open the door, but Truck and the double-barrel shotgun that he stared into, sent a chill through his body, as his bowels broke and piss ran. Then he heard a sound that sounded like a can-non, the glass shattering in his face and the buck shots tearing the flesh from his neck and chest.

Things got dark. The next shot made things silent.

Truck jumped in the Honda, and they took off.

News hit Bayside Arms, Northridge, and then Lake Edward before the morning. If you rolled through Bay-side Arms and Northridge, you could feel the loss on the streets.

When Darius caught the news, he ran to the detailing shop. Brit was catching the news as Darius came in the door.

"You heard what they did to my niggah, Brit?" Darius asked with tears in his eyes. "You heard that shit?"

Brit just stood there in a slight daze. He'd lost several of his childhood friends to this shit, and it never got any easier. "I just heard. You got to calm down," Brit said.

"Fuck that! I know who did that shit."

"Do you? Come upstairs." Brit signaled for Darius to follow him upstairs.

Javonne came in the detailing shop, acting hysterical. "Prince, where Brit? Darius here?" he asked, not giving me a chance to answer.

"They upstairs in the studio," I said.

Javonne rushed up the stairs, hitting the door.

"How you know we were up here?" Brit asked.

"Your little brother." Javonne pointed at me.

"Don't let nobody else up here."

"A'ight," I replied.

I sat downstairs knowing these bitch niggahs was crying to Brit. Darius was talking shit, but he wasn't no killer. His bitch ass wasn't gonna do shit, especially against Cadillac and Truck.

I was twenty and just came home from a two-year bid in Indian Creek Correctional Center, one of the many times I'd been away on tour. Up to five years ago, everything I'd learned about the streets I learned from my big brother. These last five years had been my own teachings. I was supposed to be my brother's best man in the wedding. I was his best man, period. I loved my brother with all my heart, but I wasn't givng up this shit for nothing.

He gave me everything when I was younger, but now he wanted to stop and open this bullshit detailing shop/barbershop/studio. This muthafucka ain't makin' no money. I kept this shit open, paid the bills, paid for the Acura 3.5RL that Brit drove, paid for the house he lived in. I took care of the entire family and did it out of love.

My mom, sister, and brother always kept money on the books, and I always showed my appreciation, even if it was my money. Whenever I got locked up, I always left my brother money to keep the business going, his life going, and Momma's.

Two years ago, I'd left three hundred grand stashed. I came home to a hundred and ten grand. I been home five months, and I had three hundred and sixty grand put away in this business, couple bitch houses, and a stash house.

We had a house we shared that nobody, and I mean nobody, came to. Brit tried to live right, but this was my life and I never wanted him crossing the line again. I was from Lake Edward, but I was one niggah who'd learned the value of money early. I also realized that the more niggahs you knew, the better your chance to make money. As long as you kept your shit on the low, your association short, and sorted out the real niggahs from the fake you was good. And real niggahs faked it to get along with project niggahs who were about money, so I made sure that when Lake Edward was battling with Bayside Arms—another project a mile up the boulevard—I stayed on the scene.

When I got locked up and sent to group homes, I remembered the niggahs I met and where they were from, especially cats from Norview, Campostella, Brambleton, and Atlantis. That way I could travel anywhere in the Seven Cities and always know somebody.

Me and Brit never hung. We used to, but he lived a straight life now with his fiancée, Leah. I didn't fuck with none of Brit's peoples, and everybody looked at me as Brit's crazy little brother. Everybody knew me, but they didn't know my pockets, because I never showed off. Only Brit, Kendu, and my niggah Chris knew I was getting this money from every corner, back alley, and empty building in the entire Hampton Roads, from Newport News projects to Tidewater Park downtown Norfolk.

I rocked Timbs every day—I tied them up because I was ready, willing, and able to stomp the life out of a muthafucka—and wore jeans and a white T-shirt. Sometimes I showered, sometimes I didn't. If I was on the grind, I could go two or three days of nonstop hustling. Fuck a shower and fuck these bitches. I had the mentality that if you owed me, you had to pay me. Fuck with me and I'll lay yo ass down.

I was five foot nine and two hundred twenty-five pounds. Nothing gave me more pleasure than getting money and rumbling. I'd spit in the face of any muthafucka who stood up to shine on me, then tear into his ass like London and Honcho, my Rottweiler and red pitbull.

I ran with two niggahs, Kendu and Black Chris. Kendu was from New York, and Black Chris was from Norfolk. Both had money-getting skills and wouldn't hesitate to immediately terminate any muthafucka who came between them and that paper.

Kendu first came to VA from Baltimore. He said he went to Baltimore to get money, but he ran into some real cats and ended up catching two hot ones. When he got well he decided to go to Norfolk. He'd fucked with a couple of Norfolk niggahs, until he came across Speed, God bless the dead.

Before Speed's death, he'd caught Kendu coming out the sports bar and kidnapped him. He took him, stripped him, and took pennies out of burning grease, then dropped them on his back, butt, and dick. Then he left him naked and tied up in his car.

That fucked him up for a while. When he returned on the scene, he had a nervous twitch—his head twitching to the right two times every few minutes. He had linked in with some Carolina cats and decided to take that slick New York shit to the Carolinas.

To this day he'd been making more money than me and Black Chris. Black Chris, on the other hand, was from Roberts Park, a Norfolk project off Princess Anne, known for producing some of Norfolk's most notorious hustlers. He was a cool, laid-back, black-ass niggah that bitches loved. Permanent gold fronts and an athletic body, he stood six foot two inches and had skills on the court that could get him to the NBA if he was recognized. He had a scholarship to Norfolk State, played two years, and was convinced by his agent to sign up for the draft. His agent was from Georgetown, a section of Chesapeake known for producing good ballplayers, Alonzo Mourning for one.

Corey, the sports agent, had been responsible for turning two kids from Norfolk into millionaires through their ballplaying skills, and Chris was hoping Corey could do the same for him. Until then, the streets of Norfolk was going to help him live and look like an NBA star. So they, in turn, made sure he became a millionaire. Even with an asshole full of money, he was still always at the neighborhood social and holiday parties just chilling. He was always sure to roll up and jump out the truck, cup in hand, and a fifth of Hennessy in the cut.

Chapter 3

The sun was nowhere in sight, and the skies were dark like there was going to be a heavy downpour any second. Everyone stood motionless as they lowered Pablo's closed casket into the ground. His family screamed, and his baby mommas cried as they squeezed his kids.

His mother knew people had shown up just to see what he looked like—the double-barrel almost removing his head from his shoulders and leaving his face totally disfigured—and she didn't want the funeral to be a freak show.

Darius put his arm around her and walked her to the car. Darius gripped his mother's hand as she followed close behind them.

Pablo's mother turned to Darius as the rain began to fall. "Darius, are you gonna continue to wrong your momma?"

"No, ma'am."

"Do you want your mom to feel like I'm feeling? I can't stop crying over Pab. He was my baby," she said crying.

Darius hugged her. He then turned to his mom.

Brit strolled up with Corey and BayBay. "Sorry, Ms. Carolyn. If you need me, please call." Brit gave her a card.

"Thank you, Brit. Take hold of these boys. Brit, show them a slower and calmer life. Settle down and stop running wild. I love all y'all younguns." Ms. Carolyn hugged Darius's mom. The two had been friends for a long time and had prayed many times together for something like this not to happen.

They got in their cars, and all left the site.

The Expedition and Cadillac pulled up to Darius's house in Aragona Village, a section of single-family ranch houses separating Lake Edward from Bayside Arms, and everybody walked in.

Darius counted, "Trent, Van, Brit, and Corey. Grab six cups, Javonne."

"You takin' both these bottles in there?" Javonne asked.

"Yeah. Niggahs need a drink."

They walked inside Darius's closed-in garage. He handed the Hennessy to Trent and Van, then took the cork out of the Belvedere and poured himself a big cup.

Corey and Brit had turned on the PlayStation and began playing NBA ShootOut 2000.

"So did they get the niggahs who did this?" Van asked.

"Naw. They have no idea."

"Shit will be handled in the streets," Darius said.

"Told you to chill with that," Brit said.

"Fuck that! Niggahs got to pay."

"So go do them niggahs," Trent said.

"Yeah, go do them, asshole," Brit said. "You can't, because it's not that easy. Man, these niggahs don't roll like that no more. These young niggahs about self, nothing more. You'll be fighting a losing battle by yourself," Brit said.

"Fuck Caddy and Truck," Javonne said.

Trent, Van, and Corey darted their eyes toward Javonne.

"That's who did that shit?" Corey knew Truck and Cadillac as monsters on the field in high school, and that their monstrous acts also went beyond the football field.

"Get your hands full," Van said. "Them niggahs terrorizin' cats."

"*Terrorizin'* ain't the word," Corey said.

"Nobody's worried about shit them niggahs do, but there's a time for everything," Brit said.

"True," Corey added.

"Where your brother, Brit?" Trent asked.

"He coolin'. He don't fuck with funerals," Brit said.

"Yeah, right! He could of came though," Javonne said.

"We talkin' about Pablo," Darius added. "Damn!"

"Niggah's right," Corey said.

Brit stopped playing the game. "Fuck y'all niggahs talkin'? I fuck with y'all, I fucked with Pablo, not my brother. If y'all want to know my brother exact words, they were, 'Fuck that niggah. I didn't fuck with him like that. He knew the game,' " Brit said slowly. "So if you got a problem with him, he up at the shop snortin' coke with his man, Kendu. You talkin' shit, but my brother and those Lake Edward niggahs are about the only niggahs who could even possibly fuck with them. So you need to rethink your plan. You damn sho ain't got the ass to do nothing, Darius, Javonne, Corey." Brit stared at them.

"I ain't in the shit no way," Corey said. "I work, gots me a j-o-b and a family."

Van and Trent sat quietly drinking, taking in the drama, but everyone present knew Van and Trent would burn those niggahs' asses up if they even thought their lives were in danger.

Darius's phone rang. He talked for a second and slammed the phone down.

"Caddi and Truck just ran up in the house out North-ridge."

They all raced over to Northridge, only to find two workers shot up.

"Goddamn, niggahs done shot Young Twon and Pete over ten grand,"

"What the fuck!" Darius said. He covered his face, hating the fact that the only niggah who could put a stop to it, his ace, was dead.

Satan followed Truck as he walked in the house. Throwing the money and drugs on the table, Satan said, "Damn, niggah, I'm glad you called me on this."

"Who else I'm gonna call?" Truck loudly stated. "All these bitch niggahs out here scared somebody gonna catch 'em alone and get 'em."

They both laughed.

"I ain't wanna shoot the niggah," Truck said.

"Me neither. They all right. We didn't shoot to kill. They got shot for being hardheaded. I hate a hard-headed-ass niggah," Satan said.

"For real."

They gave each other a pound and sat down to count the money and split "the hard."

"Niggah, you sounded just like C.O. Promise," Truck said.

"Hell yeah. Niggah used to say, 'Satan, I hate a hard-headed muthafucka. I promise yo' black ass this, I promise that.' "

"Sound just like that niggah. Muthafucka used to tell me, 'Truck, I promise you I'll scoop yo' chunky ass up, make you play bitch.' I say, niggah, you out yo' goddamn mind, talking 'bout he was state champion for three years straight from Green Run."

"Fuck them Beach niggahs. Pretty-ass, money-gettin'

niggahs," Satan said with an attitude. "But this triflin'-ass Portsmouth niggah name Satan got y'all ass today." Satan smiled.

"Fuck, yeah! In broad daylight too. Bitch niggahs never seen it comin', cryin' over that dead muthafucka. He gone and not coming back. Let his momma cry, keep fuckin' goin'."

Truck looked at Satan. He thought about the twenty pounds Satan had put on. When he'd met Satan while locked up in Indian Creek, he was a skinny-ass, black, grimy-looking niggah known for being a livewire. But now he had a thick, muscular body and no facial hair, just smooth flawless black skin. He was wild when he came in, and he left thicker, wilder, and smarter to the street. He'd learned to slow down, creep low, do his dirt, get paid, and stay away from the stupid shit.

"Where your brother?"

"Coolin' with his punk-ass friends. Niggahs work hard for him, but I know they soft. Might get they ass one day." Truck laughed.

They gave each other another pound and finished their business.

"Yo, man, call me. If every time was like this, we'd only have to work four times a year."

"No doubt. It's you or my brother, and you know he a fighter, not a killer. And I only run with killers and gorillas. Give it up or I'll take that pussy, niggahs," Truck said, showing his gold.

"If they don't know, send them to *P*-town. Show 'em how the grimiest niggahs in the Seven Cities do it."

"Hell yeah!"

Satan gave Truck another pound and a hug and made his exit.

Now we got enough to fuck with Vic and get nine. It's time for me to come the fuck up. Fuck this bullshit. One flip and two weeks of grinding and we got new trucks, he thought, getting in the shower.

He came out and dried off. *What bitch am I gonna call to go to my sister shit?* He threw on his new FUBU dark blue jeans and dark blue leather Timbs. He flexed in the mirror. *Fuck those bitches. It might be some hoes there.* He threw on his wife-beater and new white T-shirt.

It was ten-thirty when Truck pulled into Georgetown townhouses. His phone rang. It was Cadillac wondering where he was. He pulled up and looked at the black Q45, 5-series beamer, and the sweetest baby blue Quest van sitting on twenties, which let you know that the niggah who owned it was a true baller.

He pulled up behind the GS300. Gripping the steering wheel, he sat still as the hate raced through him. *Fuck these niggahs. How they living better than me? I'll kill every one of these country niggahs*, he thought, as he noticed the North Carolina tags on the cars. The Suburban and the 929 Mazda with VA tags was the only indication that his sister had peoples there, besides him and his brother's raggedy shit. He walked up to the door and knocked kinda hard before he realized it.

His sister opened the door. Precious hugged her brother and he hugged her slightly, handing her a small slender box.

"This is my brother, Russ," she said, using Russ because these niggahs might've heard of Truck. And that might not be good.

"What's up?" Truck said to the six cats standing in the living room.

Clean-cut, laid-back, rocking new shit, from throwbacks to Timbs to some nice jewels, these country niggahs didn't look country or wild.

The littlest niggah spoke up. "Knockin' like you the muthafuckin' police," he said, pulling on the blunt.

"Wanted to make sure you heard me coming," Truck came back, standing his ground, letting him know you don't just talk to him any kind of way.

Tension grew in the room.

A guy a little taller than the other guy came out of the kitchen with a bottle of Remy Martin. "Yeah, but you ain't got to tear my shit off the hinges."

Caddy, seeing that shit was getting ready to go down, stepped up before Truck could say anything. "He was letting you know it was time to show some respect in this muthafucka."

The black-ass niggah stood up. "Respect who? You come in my cousin shit disrespectin'. Cuz, you need to get your bitch before she catch one of these hot ones by accident," the guy said to his cousin, who was Precious's man.

Precious's heart dropped. She knew it had gone past calming down. This guy had just threatened her family's life. Her mind began to blank out as she watched Caddy's fist rip through the guy's jaw, shattering his teeth. Blood flowed, but it meant nothing as the combinations dropped his ass.

Truck pulled the .45, and Caddy had a .380.

"Get flat, niggahs."

They all laid flat at Truck's demand. Truck wanted it all, now that it had escalated to this. He picked up the phone and called Satan.

Satan showed up in less than fifteen minutes, came in, and played his position. "Who own the BMW?"

One of the guys fessed up to owning it.

Satan had already gone through it and found sixty grand and two kilos. "Do you have anything in your car?" he asked.

"No, nothing, man."

"I just got sixty grand and two kilos. I know cars. Why you lie?"

"I'm sorry, man."

"Who ridin' with you?"

He pointed. "Brick, big dude."

Pow! Pow! Satan shot both of them execution-style.

When he asked the others, they quickly gave up what they had.

After going through the house and all the cars, they accumulated four hundred grand and six kilos.

Precious and Caddy stood by the door and watched as Truck put a bullet through her boyfriend's head and executed the others with Satan's help.

As they gathered at the front door, Satan said to Truck, "Leave, you and Caddy. Your sister lives here. She got to get fucked up. Nobody walks away from this shit."

Caddy was getting fucked up. He left out and went and got in his car and left.

"Leave me a hundred grand." Satan looked at Truck. "Usually it will be two apiece, right?"

"You right."

"Give me one hundred. You give your sister two."

Truck looked at him.

"She gonna deserve it after what I'm about to do," Satan said.

Precious's eyes widened.

Truck handed Satan one hundred thousand and left the house.

Precious looked into Satan's fiery red eyes. She fell against the wall as his fist hit her nose, breaking it. Two more blows to her eyes blackened them.

He pushed her dress up and ripped her panties, to show evidence of attempted rape. Then he grabbed the straps to her sexy birthday dress and pulled it down to her waist, took his knife and asked for more money.

She screamed, "No more!"

Satan then cut her arms, one in three places, and a nice deeper cut on the other. Then he placed his hands around her neck and began choking her.

"You were tortured and raped during a robbery. You were laying here when you heard six shots," he told her, making sure to leave prints around her neck.

Another blow to her head knocked her out cold.

When the police came, she caught more sympathy than she ever expected.

Truck and Caddy were upset about how Satan did, but Precious bounced back with the one hundred and fifty thousand Truck gave her.

Truck then gave Caddy fifty thousand and kept one hundred thousand for himself, and the police never questioned them or Precious again.

Chapter 4

I was in the studio talking with my brother. I could see he had shit on his mind. "So what's up? Nervous?" I asked.

"Naw, man," Brit replied.

"You and Leah all right?"

"Hell yeah! She's what I want, that's no question. No matter what direction my life goes in, as long as she by my side, I feel like I can get through anything." Brit smiled.

"Heard that shit. I'm gonna have to find me a bitch to make me feel like that," I said.

"Don't front, son. You'll lose it if Zaria left your ass. And you'll go to shit if Tee Tee stop fuckin' with you."

"Picture me fallin' apart, niggah, over hoes. Always in pimp form, niggah, always," I said, knowing damn well that I'd do time behind those two.

I'd been with Zaria for four years, and she was the mother of my three-year-old son. She'd graduated from

Ocean Lakes High School at seventeen, and by the time she'd turned twenty-two she had already earned her master's from Morgan State University in Baltimore.

We'd met at a go-go club in DC, and used to have conversations on the phone till the late hours. Soon, I was going to Baltimore or DC every weekend. I was only sixteen, so I told her I was into music, to explain my cars and the money I was making.

She was from money and felt like Lake Edward was the worst place, but once she got a taste of this LE niggah, she fell in love, and I fell in love. And we made a son out of love and called him *LP* for *Little Prince*.

When he was born, I wanted him to have my last name. It meant everything to me, and I mean everything.

She was for it, but her family was against it. She looked into my eyes and said, "I will always be here for my two *Princes*, and he will have your name."

I told her, "Forever my girl. You are mine forever, all mine."

I wasn't making a whole lot then, but my street game kept her ass guessing.

Now she worked as an RN at Virginia Beach General Hospital. We owned a three-bedroom, two and a half bath condo with a garage in Virginia Beach, where we lived with our son. She'd bought the house in her name, since she had the job and credit, and I had the down payment. Soon after we closed, she put my name on the deed.

She was there for me anytime I needed her, in every way, so I couldn't begin to tell you how Tee Tee made her way in the picture.

*   *   *

I had known Tee Tee for a while, but through another friend. We'd clubbed at the same places, and our circles sometimes clashed.

One night we were at a party at Wesleyan College, a party thrown by this old-school cat named Pig. He'd made so much money in the game and had done so much dirt that he had fun just throwing big parties for Lake Edward and Bayside Arms cats. He was always throwing something. Playoffs, Super Bowl, boxing, you name it, he had a party, and many couples were brought together. Even a couple of little Bayside kids were made from the after parties.

One night Tee Tee was there with her cousins from Bayside Arms. Her cousins had their plans, so I offered to give her a ride to her car. She looked fine as hell as she walked to my car in her short DKNY jean skirt, red top showing irresistible cleavage, and some red open-toed sandals.

I dropped her at her car and asked for some time.

She agreed. She knew who I was—we all knew the same people—and knew a niggah would never disrespect, so she followed me back to the Courtyard Marriot.

We got in the room at about two a.m. I pulled out a Backwoods full of hydro, and we talked and smoked.

I gazed at her soft brown skin and large, beautiful breasts. I wanted to tear off her shirt and set those beautiful breasts free, then throw up her skirt and fuck the shit out of her. I decided to make a move.

She stopped me, letting me know that she hadn't been with anybody since her man was sent upstate a year ago, and wasn't for being anyone's fuck partner.

By the time we finished the 'dro, she sat on the edge of the bed and smiled. "I'm real high," she said.

"That's that 'dro, girl."

"I don't feel right. Was something in that weed?"

"Naw, shorty. I smoke weed and I drink Hennessy. What it don't do, don't get done," I told her, since nobody needed to know that I'd been snorting coke since I was fifteen.

She began to shake and rub her hands together, with her eyes tearing.

"What's wrong with you?"

I began to get scared. *How would I ever explain this shit?* I thought of leaving her in the room, but it was in my name, and people had seen her leave the party with me.

"You wanna go to the hospital?"

"No."

At that moment, I realized that I never wanted to see her like that again. She was scared, she was confused, and her body was going through changes.

I kicked off my shoes, pulled back the comforter, turned the radio to 95.7 FM, R&B slow jams, killed the lights, and asked her to lay back.

"Prince, I'm not ready for this."

"Not ready for what?" I said, raising my voice. "I tried, and you said no. Now you got me fucked up, 'cause you actin' all fucked up off some trees. Better lay your ass down and get yourself together."

She lay back, and I got behind her, took her into my arms, and held her close.

The shaking stopped after about half-hour, and the tears, after about forty-five minutes. An hour in my arms and she was snuggling her ass all on my dick.

I didn't know if I could have fucked or not, but I had my pride. You don't accuse me of putting shit in my trees to fuck you. And I wanna fuck when I want to, it ain't no comin' off when *you* want to. *I'll show her.*

I went to sleep.

* * *

The next day when she got off work she called.

"Hello," I answered.

"What are you doing?"

"Handlin' some shit."

"Where you at?"

"Why? Say what you want. Don't ask me all that shit."

"I'll ask whatever the hell I want. It's up to you to answer. I'm hungry. I'm going home and shower. Where we goin' to eat?"

"I don't care," I said, realizing she got me.

"So what you want me to do?"

"Handle your business then come to the room. I'm in the same spot."

"See ya," she said and hung up.

We went out to dinner about four or five times a week for a year, and many times breakfasts followed.

Then I gave her a down payment on a condo and helped her get a better whip. Before I knew it, we were doing everything together, and she was getting all my spare time. I was giving Zaria her time when she wasn't working, and it worked out that Zaria worked twelve-hour shifts, six pm to six am. Tee Tee left her shop at six pm. It flowed like life, smooth sometimes, and rough others.

I talked shit, but I had love for these hoes, because if anything wasn't right with them, I was fucked up inside. If I hadn't talked with either of them, I felt funny until I knew they were all right.

The knock at the door brought me out of my deep thoughts. "Who is that?" I asked.

"It's probably Van and Trent, or Darius. Darius's and Javonne's connect was Pablo. Niggahs from uptown got

him and then got his houses. But you know these bitch
niggahs can't stop them. So I'll come in and supply, and
charge the hell out of them. Van and Trent buying a kilo a
week, and they peoples got knocked off. So I was gonna
ask you if you wanted them first, if not, I'll give 'em to
Poppa."

"I don't fuck with Beach niggahs, especially out here.
Poppa can have 'em. Make sure you tell Poppa what's
going on with Darius and Javonne. Don't pull him in the
middle of a war and he don't know shit. You ain't fuckin'
with nobody. You know this ain't no halfway game.
Leave *if* alone. Run this shop and keep your shit clean
and tell Poppa them niggahs wide open."

"I hear ya."

"Naw, for real, then step back. Don't get caught up in
this shit. You bigger than this now."

"I feel you," he said.

I jumped up, remembering what Mom had told me
earlier. "Uncle El be home Friday."

"Oh shit!" Brit smiled, knowing how El got down.

"Only thing with El is, he'll get shit poppin', then he'll
get locked up again for something stupid."

"Naw, last time I talked to him, he said it's a new
game. He's never going back. I believe these three and a
half got his ass. Plus, I heard that Dundee been goin' to
see him."

"That's some shit," Brit said.

El was our youngest uncle because Grandma had an
unexpected pregnancy late in life. He was three years
younger than Brit, and four years older than me. And
Dundee was my Aunt Mary's only child. We all just
ended up in the game. The "job" shit was unheard of, or
maybe they just didn't talk about it out our way.

Mom, Cathy, and Aunt Gwynn was grown when Papa
died of a massive heart attack. Grandma almost lost it. If

it wasn't for the Lord and the church, she would have succumbed. She stayed going to church.

The church she chose wasn't in the best part of Norfolk. As she was leaving the church one night, someone snatched her and threw her in the van. She screamed, but the force of her own Bible sent her to the seat, seeing stars.

He snatched the keys and drove to a parking lot behind an apartment building.

She began to pray, "Satan, you are a liar and the blood of Jesus is against you," she said repeatedly.

He snatched her pocketbook and took the thirty dollars she'd been selected to hold.

With no fear, she looked in his eyes. "Satan, you are a liar."

"My name ain't Satan." He grabbed her head, forcing it to the floor between the seats, and when she was pinned down secure, began punching her in the back of the head continuously.

She cried for God, but the pain was too much.

"Don't lift up again, or I'll split your head open, bitch." He reached down and grabbed her crotch, ripping her stockings and panties off.

She fought, trying to come up, but he began slamming his fist into the back of her head, and elbows into her back. She tried to scream, but the pain took her breath. She just kept praying that this would end, but it didn't.

He raped her repeatedly for two hours and left her for dead.

She ended up with a concussion, cracked ribs, and a whole lot of stitches from the tearing of her body. She went through a lot of therapy.

She got pregnant from the incident and refused to have an abortion.

Then she began to drink a lot. Every day she drank, in fact. She never went back to church, but as soon as she got drunk, she'd begin praying for hours.

Somehow Uncle El came out healthy. People called him a miracle baby, because he survived mad alcohol.

Chapter 5

"Exit 15B, Newtown Road. What, muthafucka? I'm home." El yelled sticking his head out the window of the dark green Pathfinder. He asked Dundee, "So what the deal, fam?"

Dundee hadn't said much during the ride. He sat back listening to Jay drop the bars on his new *Blueprint* CD. "You know how I do," he said. "I got my spots, and my dough's flowing well. I ain't complainin'."

"Give me the rundown, Mike-Mike. This niggah act like he scared to talk," El said.

Mike-Mike took a sip of the Grey Goose that he had sittin' between his legs. "I'm gonna tell you the truth."

Their bodies jumped as Dundee flew over the bump crossing over Virginia Beach Boulevard.

"Poppa runnin' shit, makin' all the money. Dundee and everybody else workin' for Poppa and he taxin'. Then you got them Northridge niggahs, Darius and Javonne, who been comin' Poppa way since Pablo got done up and he really taxin' them. Brit still don't fuck around, still gettin' ready to get married, and Prince still Prince, you know how he do."

"Prince goin' to stay shinin', hustlin'-ass little niggah, and he got trained by the best. Who got West Hastings?"

"Nobody. Poppa said leave it alone. Some shit was going down with some robberies and shit, Norfolk niggahs, so he said shut down shop," Dundee said.

El wasn't trying to hear that shit.

"Norfolk niggahs got them shook, El," Mike-Mike said smiling.

"Fuck that, and fuck Poppa. How Poppa gonna run shit and scared to do shit 'cause he worried about what's gonna happen with those kids? Niggah can't run LE," El said.

"Check out this shit here." Dundee put in a CD. "This is the hottest niggah on the street right now."

"Who dat?" El asked

Dundee and Mike-Mike looked at him like he was lost. "Fifty," they both yelled at the same time.

El was into this new niggah, 50 Cent, out of New York.

They turned into Lake Edward. They pulled onto East Hastings Arch. The streets were congested with kids on the sidewalk, hustlers on the corners, and the police making rounds.

Dundee pulled in front of El's momma's row house.

She came out as they stepped out the truck. "Welcome home, Larry," she said, hugging him, tears in her eyes.

He could smell liquor on his mother. There were no shoes on her feet and her wrinkled clothes let him know that nothing had changed.

Guys from the corner walked over, many showing love, some just came to get a closer look at the two-time felon who went away a 210-pound fat boy and returned a 245-pound thick rock.

"Come on in this house, Larry. Get away from these hoodlums. They on their way where you just came from."

Nobody paid her any attention. Everybody grew up waiting for Ms. Gwynn to get drunk and cuss out anybody in her path. She was still loved.

Larry was headed in the house when he heard the horn of the Acura as we parked. Me and Brit jumped out.

"What up, El?" Brit said, hugging him.

"What's up, fam?" El snatched me and we embraced.

I knew my uncle El was as real as they came. He believed in living rich on the street. If he was gonna be broke, he might as well be locked the fuck up.

El smiled. "So what's going on, nephew?"

"You know me, stayin' the fuck out of Lake Edward, gettin' mine elsewhere."

"Some things never change. Where shorty at?"

I knew who he was talking about. "Both of them fine. Shorty be here in a few. I gotta get a cut, and we gonna get something to eat."

"Shit, I'm rollin'." El rubbed his head, which desperately needed to be seen by somebody at Kappatal Kuts.

We walked off from everybody and entered the house.

"I'm gonna move in on Northridge. Then I'm gonna set West Hastings back off."

"Do it," I said. "Niggahs out there don't have the weight or the ass. Niggahs gonna keep robbin' them. But you know you got to see Poppa before doin' shit on the other side."

"I ain't gotta see nobody. Why everybody on Poppa dick? Fuck him."

"Naw, El. Niggahs know you ain't scared of Poppa, but things are going smooth. You know he will eventually give you yours."

"Right, I hear you," he said.

I knew he really didn't. El was gonna do what he wanted.

I was standing outside under the dark skies. It was about five o'clock, but the skies read nine. The wind was blowing heavier than usual due to the hurricane that was about to hit the coast.

Me and El was on the corner of East Hastings and Lake Edward Drive. The backwoods burned slow as it passed from Uncle's hand to mine.

El was staring deep in the dark skies when the ring of my phone rudely disturbed him.

I looked at my caller ID. It was Zaria, so I figured I'd hit her back. She called again. *Unusual*, I thought, *she knows not to blow my shit up.*

Then her name came up again. I ignored it as my phone kept ringing. My mind started to race, but I knew my shit was tight. I know I didn't slip. Prince don't slip.

"Hello," I said slowly, waiting for Zaria's response.

"Why you got bitches callin' my house?"

"What?"

"Fuck you mean, Prince? *What* is all you can come up with, Prince? Yo' bitch Tee Tee just called. Said y'all been fuckin' for two years, you got a key to her house, and all that shit. She even said she met my muthafuckin' son."

I only called her whole name when I was upset with her or when I was in some shit. "Zaria Ann," I said, "listen, baby, it ain't even like—"

"Fuck that! Come get your shit and leave your muthafuckin' key. I'm tired of your shit. You ain't gonna keep puttin' me through this shit. Fuck you! I hate your ass." *Click!*

I looked over at El just as my heart fell to my stomach. I thought he was going to have to catch me. The ring of the phone snapped my head back, it was Tee Tee.

"What? What the fuck is wrong with you?"

"Nothing! I called you ten times, and you never answered.

"So you call my baby moms, for what?"

"I needed you and—"

"And what? You have no idea what you've done. Now that bitch gonna put me through hell to see my son. You fucked up my world. And you know the most important thing in the world to me is my son. Fuck all y'all bitches when it comes to him. I don't believe you did that. How you get her fuckin' number?"

"Out your phone," she said, like it was nothing. "I love you, Prince, but we need to talk."

"On the real, shorty, you just fucked my world up, and I'm not pressed to talk to you. That was some bullshit. You know how I get down. You don't have to fuck with me."

"You didn't say that shit when you were fuckin' and eatin' me last night, or when I bought those three-hundred-dollar jerseys. You got DCs and Timbs still in the fuckin' box that I bought in my closet at my house, muthafucka. You ain't gonna play me and get away with it. You better keep whatever you got on clean, because your shit is fucked." She slammed the phone down.

I stared at El again, as if he could tell me how to handle this.

"My shorty called my baby moms, I'm in some shit, and all my real gear at shorty crib.

"My baby moms don't even let me see my daughter. If I call her house, she'll call the police and say anything. I got to go to court just to get visitation. Don't let shit get that far," El said as he pulled on the Backwood and passed it.

"I got to go. I thought shit was calm before the storm."

"Yo, pimp, handle your shit, but don't get in trouble.

Don't forget those hoes hurtin'. You just got caught slippin'. Handle your baby moms, then Tee Tee."

I jumped in the whip, doing about fifty up Lake Edward Drive and turned right on Newtown Road. When I reached the Boulevard, I realized I had no weed. I knew when I got to the crib, it was no getting out for a couple days. I made the U-turn and called my man in Newpointe, ran inside, and peeled off a hundred twenty for an ounce of that "official."

I opened the bag and took a deep sniff of the top-of-the-line weed just before paying for that expensive-ass hydro. I got in the whip and headed up Newtown toward Zaria's house.

The faster I drove, the more the car kept pulling its way toward those six throwbacks, four authentic Mitch & Ness, eight jerseys, and ten pairs of matching Air Force Ones and Timbs.

When I pulled up at Tee Tee's house, her car, the one that I helped her buy, was parked in the front. I opened her door where I paid the rent and walked inside.

She had my Iverson jerseys in one hand and my Staubach and O.J. Simpson throwback in the other.

My first response was to shoot this bitch—we were talking about over four thousand dollars in shit—but she looked so beautiful and innocent.

Her stare was burning a hole through me, so I had to think fast. I took a deep breath and blew out, "Bitch, you fucked up some shit in my life," I yelled. I jumped over the couch at her.

She dropped the jerseys and dashed for the door, but I was on her ass.

I grabbed her, and she began swinging.

I blocked her taps and grabbed her neck. "How you fuckin' do that shit? All you fucked up was me and my son spending time. You think you matter like that?"

I knew she loved kids, even though she didn't have any, so I dwelled on my son's role instead of our relationship. I let her know how hurt I was. As my eyes watered, hers watered too.

I stared in her eyes and could see her mind racing. She knew that she should have taken a different route to make me all hers.

"Let me go before I get in trouble," I said. "I'll call you after I calm down." I left and jumped in my car. I didn't know what she would do next, but I knew my authentic shit was safe.

When I arrived at Zaria's house, my mind was fucked up. The thought of Zaria not being in my life would be a rude awakening. I walked inside to a beautiful young girl, her eyes red from crying.

"I told you I wasn't goin' through this shit with you no more," she said with a quick, open-handed slap that totally caught me off guard.

I didn't think anybody was that crazy. I stood there as she turned and fussed furiously for about twenty minutes. I listened and didn't say a word.

"Baby, it's not even like that," I said.

"How is it, Prince?"

"We just friends. I ain't fuckin' her."

"Friends, hell. That bitch told me you fucked her, and you got a key to her shit. Give me my shit and carry your ass."

"I ain't givin' you shit and I ain't goin' nowhere. So you just be mad, but I ain't goin' no fuckin' where. I love you and my son. Never would I desert y'all. Please, baby!"

"Fuck that! You need to get tested, and you'll never touch me again without a condom."

After that statement, I knew my work was cut out for me. I rolled up and listened.

By two in the morning, she lay asleep in her sweats and T-shirt, looking nothing like the sexy-ass girl that went to bed naked straight from the shower.

The hurricane had set in, and winds were blowing at over fifty-two miles per hour. I climbed in the bed easily as to not disturb her.

She felt me climb in and woke up. "Hell naw. Fuck that!" She grabbed the cover and headed out the door.

I grabbed her and snatched her on the bed.

"Let me go, Prince."

"Naw, you with me. You're not goin' nowhere, and neither am I."

She turned her back to me as I gripped her tight in my arms. She fought for about thirty minutes then settled down and fell back to sleep.

We woke to my son's cries and strong rain and winds, and spent the day doing family things.

About nine, my phone rang. It was Black Chris. "Yo, meet me off Park Avenue at the Jamaican spot, The Hummingbird."

"A'ight."

When I hung up, she just stared. She knew I had business.

As I left out the door, she said, "If I call, you better answer, or we will go our separate ways. I mean it Prince."

I looked in her eyes and knew she was serious. Very serious.

I pulled up in front of the Hummingbird. The scent of island food had my stomach jumping. I jumped out of my new royal blue Quest van and gave my niggahs a pound.

Chris and Kendu were standing in front of the check cashing place. Looking at Kendu was like looking in a mirror: Timbs, jeans, and XXX black T-shirt to hide the burners. Chris, on the other hand, was shining as always: stonewash grey shorts, black-and-grey Spurs basketball jersey, black Reebok basketball sneakers, and a white gold chain, bracelet, and watch.

"So what up, my niggahs?"

"Ya know how we roll," Kendu said.

"I'm all right. Always gonna be all right, son," Chris said, hype as always.

We all walked inside to talk business. I ordered an ox tail, Chris, jerk chicken, and Kendu, curry shrimp. We sat down to kick our plans. Them things had just came in, and it was time to work.

After eating and putting down the plans, we came out and jumped in Chris's new white Yukon Denali. We made our way down Princess Anne Road, past all the projects we all had investments in, and went straight to the duplex that sat at the end of Arkansas Avenue.

We had rented a duplex and busted down the wall so the units would be joined, turning it into a four-bedroom. You wouldn't believe the inside. The back of the duplex went back to a train track, which gave us access to an exit neighborhood if necessary.

We walked inside and Chris turned the television on to videos, and then walked through the open passage and turned on the other big screen, which had the PS2 hooked up. Him and Kendu continued their ongoing battle of the recent John Madden that had just dropped.

I walked in the office, stepping around the T-shirts that had just came off press and hadn't yet made it to the urban stores. I threw in some Maxwell and tossed in the disk, which gave me all my data about my graphic design business. I had a natural talent for going to Publisher, a designing program, and creating cards, flyers, posters for any occasion. Actually I found it mad relaxing. I would take orders through an answering service, design the shit, and get paid. Then I would play middle-man. Take niggahs' orders, send them to my printer on line, add on my cut, and count my change.

Kendu and Chris had a T-shirt business. They'd come up with a logo, set up the screen, and started printing T-shirts. Shit was going slow, but they had some young cats on the streets pumping hard. Any big event, they were there, or should I say, we were there.

"Yo, Prince, you up next?" Kendu yelled.

"You know I don't fuck with that shit, son. Got better things to concentrate on," I said, rolling some of that offi-cial. I walked to the other side. "I got next. Y'all niggahs got me fucked up. But we playin' that NBA shit. I got the Sixers. Let Bubba Chuck fuck y'all niggahs up."

They laughed. They knew I was a fuckin' joke when it came to that video shit.

A knock at the door wiped the smiles from our faces. Chris put down the game, stood up, reached in the drawer, took the .357 automatic off safety, and put it between the couch where he sat.

My nose twitched. It was time for that grimy face, and with that came a grimy state of mind. I stood there still smoking, the .45 automatic that sat in the middle of my back and the .38 that rested on my right side gave me the reassurance that I was all right.

Kendu was Kendu—black, sweaty, raggedy beard, hair looking like he don't give a fuck and wearing the same thing he had on two days ago. This niggah was real. He hit his waist, just to situate the 9mm he had tucked away. I had mad love for this cat, or should I say respect. He stood strong and let you know he wasn't about games.

He opened the door and two gentlemen walked in.

Kendu greeted them with his signature grin, his gold fronts.

"What up, Kendu?"

This guy was the same color as Kendu, gold fronts and dreads, except this muthafucka was fat. Instantly, I knew I'd fuck his ass up. Straight drop his fat ass if he got out of line.

He was followed by this light-skinned kid, medium built, bald head, and neatly shaped beard. I had seen this kid somewhere, but now wasn't the time to be giving a fuck.

Kendu looked outside one glance for police, and two, three glances for uninvited niggahs.

"Fish," Kendu said, pointing at the fat man, "and Brada," he said referring to that red-ass niggah. "This my man Prince and Chris."

Fish reached out and gave Chris some hard dap and hugged him.

"Yo, Brada, this that niggah I was talking about . . . on the news, showing out on TV. Niggah hell on the court. Supposed to be goin' pro."

Brada looked back at Chris. "Wish the best, son, from the heart. Get that real money." He reached out with an open palm to show love.

I balled my fist, gave him a pound, and stared him in his eyes, so I could see where his head was.

He stared then shifted his eyes.

Bitch-ass niggah. Probably got a wife that runs his bitch ass, I thought.

Brada gave Chris a pound and came at me with an open hand.

I stuck my fist out and stared him in his eyes.

He stared back and kept his hand open. "Niggah, you know me," he said.

I stared in deep thought.

"I fuck with your girl sister," he said.

"Yeah, my niggah." I opened my hand and gave him a pound. I was asking myself where I know this niggah from? I didn't even know this kid got down. *Low-key-ass niggah.* "You cut hair, right?"

"Yeah! Come through and check me, cuz, for real!"

The *for real* was telling me something. I was definitely gonna have to holla.

Kendu walked in the kitchen and dropped both bags on the table. He reached in and pulled out one of the packages.

In a split second, Brada reached in his pocket and pulled out a blade and had that shit open. He handed it to Kendu, before I could even think about grabbing my burner.

I'd heard about this cat. Niggahs said his pants hung low because of the two knives he carried in his back pockets. But if he made another quick move like that, I was gonna heat his ass up. *Damn! That shit was fast though. I wish I could do that.*

Kendu cut the package and put some coke on the blade. He put it to his nose and sniffed.

"Give me my man blade and leave me a toot." Fish laughed.

Kendu gave it to him, and he sniffed the rest, wiped the blade on his pants, handed it to his man, and it disappeared as quickly as it appeared.

They walked out, Kendu said some words with Fish, and they were gone.

"Fat boy all friendly and shit. All on a niggah dick," Chris said.

"Chris gettin' ready to shoot my brother-in-law. Gotta go tell my momma Chris killed my sister husband."

"That's your people?" I asked.

"Yeah, fat greedy-ass son of a bitch. We paid twenty a

brick. He just walked with one-hundred twenty grand. I know he seein' at least two grand a brick," Kendu said.

"That red niggah handlin' this?" I asked.

"Yeah, I know some of them niggahs," Chris said. "They all low-key, drive cheap, dependable cars, dress regular gear, but new shit. They have parties all the time, family shit that be off the hook."

"That niggah damn-near your brother-in-law. You better go to more family shit," Kendu said.

I knew he was all about money, and he was right. *I gots to go to more of Tee Tee family shit.* "Make that call, son?" I said.

"Already have. Niggah on his way," Chris said.

Moments later, a knock was at the door.

We opened the other side, and those two guys came in and went straight to work, turning six kilos of soft cocaine into eight kilos of hard rock. They got paid their usual fee, took one kilo, and were gone as quick as they came.

We bagged our weight and was out in the white Denali headed back to Park Avenue Rolling in this phat-ass truck wasn't shit in Norfolk. Norfolk police didn't give a fuck, as long as you ain't blasting out the window or straight up killing nobody.

We arrived at the Hummingbird, and me and Kendu jumped out.

As we were hollering our last words, two guys pulled up in a black F150, Harley Davidson Edition. Windows tinted. The doors opened, and out jumped Truck and Cadillac.

They stare. I stare.

Kendu stepped around me. "Fuck is up? Where y'all niggahs been?"

"Tryin' to eat, baby, tryin' to eat," Cadillac said.

"Heard y'all niggahs eatin' real good," Kendu said.

"Fuck what you heard, niggah. Don't get this Truck going, 'cause you couldn't stop it on the field and you damn sure can't stop it now," Truck said.

"I'll stop your ass dead in your tracks and leave your brother there beside you. Ain't no bitch niggahs here. We all got guns." Chris got out the truck standing ground.

Chris stood six feet and was hell on the court and fast. He stayed in the gym, lifting and working out. Even though he had the skills to fight, he was known for being mature and smart, but always standing ground. He was respected, and niggahs knew he was going to be big. Not to mention, he was from a family of wild cats—don't-give-a-fuck type peoples—so fuckin' with him wasn't a smart move.

"What up, baby?" Truck said, showing love.

"What the fuck goin' on?" Chris asked. "I didn't even know you were home." He gave Cadillac a pound.

"It's been a minute," Cadillac said.

"Yo, moms still wildin'?" Chris said.

"Fuck that crazy bitch!" Truck added.

"You ain't signed no million-dollar contract yet?" Cadillac asked.

"Naw, any day now though, son," Chris said.

"Got a agent? You need to be fuckin' with your boy. Can't think of his name, but that niggah the shit."

"Corey."

"Yeah. He from Chesapeake?"

"Got him. He recruit here hard. I'll call you, son, let you know where the big jump off."

They gave pounds and they walked off.

I thought nothing of them niggahs. They had killed a young niggah from out the way, but he wasn't my niggah. But if Kendu would have swung on Truck, I would've had no choice but to see what Cadillac was about. I'd heard he was nice with his hands, but he couldn't fuck with this LE bred niggah and I knew it.

"Y'all, get the fuck out of here," Chris said.

"Fuck them niggahs," Kendu said.

"Yeah, you right," Chris said. "Y'all my niggahs, and we got too much to live for. So we can't be getting shot or locked up. Those niggahs in there, I know them." Chris was staring at us both, not blinking an eye. "If one of those niggahs decide to rob you, then they both will. If one of them shoot you, the other gonna shoot you. They don't give a fuck about trouble. They do bids like it ain't shit. Fuck that. Just leave." Chris jumped in the truck and left.

I pulled off behind him and made my way back to the shop, making a few stops, including going by my house and putting some money up. I'd just made $25,000 and then after the two-kilo split, twenty-four ounces of free money.

I took my re-up money, forty grand, and put it away in the house only for me and Brit. Twenty-eight thousand went to Zaria's house, and six thousand went to Tee Tee's house. The other ounce and a half was gonna be trick dope. Get a room and have a bitch suck my dick, lick my ass, until I say stop. Keep tootin', keep sucking, toot, and licking, yeah!

I was in deep thought when my cell rang. I wasn't expecting Chris to call.

"Yo, son, what's up?"

"Get to Norfolk General. They got him. I told y'all to leave. I told y'all to leave."

"I did. Kendu didn't leave?" I asked.

"Man, I don't know what the fuck happened. His peoples called my phone from his. Told me he was beaten into a coma and he in Norfolk General Emergency. I told y'all to leave, man, I told y'all."

I could tell Chris was hurting. We'd been getting money together for a minute and were tight as thieves.

Chapter 6

"That shit there was unnecessary," Cadillac said. "Fuck that niggah, runnin' his goddamn mouth like he know me."

Precious shut the door behind them. "What happen?"

They threw the twenty-eight thousand on the glass table. They'd caught Kendu right after making a sale. Evidently he had some peoples meet him up there.

Truck said, "You better be glad, because he was in your ass."

"I snatched the money out the niggah hand. I didn't even have a burner," Cadillac said.

"When I came out, you and that niggah was going blow to blow. That's why I saved you, kid. Don't worry, I love you, man. I'll always be there to save your ass." Truck grabbed Cadillac around the neck and laughed.

Precious stood there staring at her brothers. She knew they'd done something bad, but that was them. "So where can't I go now?" she asked.

Every time her brothers got somebody, she was forbidden from going to a certain area.

"Don't be smart, or I'll make your ass stay in this muthafuckin' house," Cadillac told her.

"You ain't my daddy, fool. That niggah dead."

"Your daddy ain't dead. He runnin' around Norfolk just like our daddy, still partyin', gettin' high, and givin' us brothers and sisters that he don't give a fuck about. Fuck both them niggahs. We done came the fuck off. Fuck that jail shit. We rentin' this nice-ass house in Riverwalk, in Chesapeake, away from the gutter, out of the muthafuckin' park. Not an apartment, but a muthafuckin' house in Riverwalk," Truck yelled.

They all smiled.

"We got cars and a nice-ass roof over our heads. We scorin' a whole joint from Vic now, so the money not gonna stop. I got something in the making that's gonna put us over the top, then we gonna chill," Truck added.

"Just stay away from Campostella. That niggah Kendu fucked around over there," Cadillac said.

"That's who y'all got?" Precious said. "Damn!"

"Why, you know him?" Truck asked.

"Naw. Bitches just say they got money."

"*They* who?" Cadillac asked, to see if she was really up on shit.

"Him, that boy who drive the white Denali, play ball and shit, and that boy who drive that new phat-ass Quest with rims. He own that detail shop with his brother. Think his name Prince. They all ran together, and bitches know they gettin' it."

"Well, he *had* money. We left his ass layin' in the street unconscious," Truck said.

"I was gonna rob him and fuck him up, then Truck bust the niggah in the head with a bottle."

"Man, I just reacted. Dude hit the concrete hard."

"And those boots to the head didn't do the niggah no good." Cadillac smiled.

They laughed and started counting.

"Twenty-eight thousand. You know he had some shit in the car," Cadillac said.

"Yeah, who had time to look for it?" Truck asked.

"You had time to get all that money up," Cadillac said. "Money make the world go 'round, so let's get mo'." He stood up and took off his shirt. He opened the door that led to the garage.

Truck took off his shirt and walked in the garage. They both began burning reps on the bench, one hundred and eighty-five pounds, fifteen times, until somebody gave up.

When Cadillac finally folded, Truck grabbed a towel and strolled out. He had too much on his mind to fuck with his brother. He went to his room and picked up his cell. He pressed five on the speed dial.

"What?"

"It's that time, but it's big."

"Holla at me."

"Come over. Be ready to go to New York," Truck said.

"NY? Oh shit!" Satan yelled.

"In and out, stick man," Truck said.

Satan knew this was real, whatever Truck had going. They'd made trips and got money, and most of them ended in murder, leaving bodies in Carolina, DC, B-more, but never New York. He'd been to New York a couple times and not knowing his way around made things difficult. But he knew if Truck was going, he was definitely coming back home with some money.

"See ya in a minute." Satan sat down and pulled out his bag of capsules.

No matter how much money he had stashed away, this Lincoln Park niggah wasn't going nowhere. He was comfortable in his hood and throughout Portsmouth. Niggahs knew him in Norfolk, and of him, across the water, but Portsmouth was his spot.

He took one of the capsules and cracked it open. Two hits of heroin in each nostril had him right. He relaxed his mind. Tears began to roll down his face as he nodded off in his own world.

Satan and Truck were making their way across the Delaware Memorial Bridge in deep thought, when Truck began to open up.

"I met this dude when I was locked up in Richmond," he said. "Quiet-ass niggah never had shit to say, but for some reason he was respected. I always kept to myself, and if I did fuck with somebody it was niggahs from Tidewater that I knew on the street. One day me and dude was getting visits, and a shorty that held me down for a minute out of DC came to see him. We catch each other's eye, and dude noticed that we knew each other. Couple days later he gave me a number to call shorty in DC. When I talk to her she tells me she told dude all about how I get down. Then to find out, dude got caught up in Richmond, but the niggah was well connected up top. We talked, stayed in touch on business, but now dude talkin' real shit for real money. This niggah in the industry owes this cat over a million. Street money. Two things, the niggah is a major street icon, and it's his cousin, his mom's sister's son. So he had to recruit out-of-town niggahs to come and do his work. They say the niggah stay in the studio. You know those New York niggahs, half of 'em want to be Puff, the other half Jay-Z, but they go fuckin' up real niggahs' money."

"So what's this niggah worth?"

"Fifty thousand to you," Truck said.

"What's the plan?"

"You know how we do. Don't supposed to be no more than four people there, including Star and one of the cats on our.team. He leavin' the door cracked."

"So we just goin' in and pop Star and any heroes."

"Yeah, any heroes."

They made their way into the city for work and met with "the guide" in Fort Lee, New Jersey. The guide drove to a studio in Queens, where they sat for five hours patiently, but was brought to the real world when the grey Navigator pulled up and four cats jumped out.

They watched them go inside and, like clockwork, began to count down from twenty. The car doors opened simultaneously. They entered the studio, guns drawn, masks on.

"Get flat!" Truck yelled.

"What's going on?"

Pow! Pow! Satan popped the niggah in the baby blue Rocawear sweat suit and motioned for the others to get flat.

All of a sudden, Star reached under the desk, pulling a nine already cocked and off safety. One shot in Satan's direction sent chills, but the one to his chest from the .45 secured Truck's two hundred and fifty grand.

They made their exit just as calm as they slid in. This wasn't their first score, but it sure was the sweetest. Most niggahs you kill, you know somebody they know, and you feel for a second. But when you don't know shit about the muthafucka, you don't feel shit.

They eased through Manhattan, headed toward the Lincoln Tunnel. Once on the New Jersey Turnpike, Truck decided to take 95 South instead of fuckin' with the Bay Bridge and those police that patrol the Eastern Shore.

While rolling down 264 in the black, tinted Q45, their minds began to relax as they hit Newport News.

"Back in the Seven Cities," Truck yelled.

"You home. Get me to Tidewater. Get me on Tidewater Drive and then I'm home. Fuck these grimy-ass niggahs on this side. These Bad News niggahs off the chain. Only niggahs I seen that fuck with *P-town*."

"Fuck y'all niggahs. Everybody know Norfolk niggahs run not only Tidewater, but the entire Seven Cities. We set precedent."

They started laughing at the last word.

"Fuck is you talkin' about?" Satan said.

"You know, niggah. Y'all follow us."

They arrived at the house. They were sitting, counting out Satan's fifty grand for holding Truck down.

Precious came in.

"What's up, baby girl?" Truck asked, happy to see his little sister.

"Everything's straight." She put her bag down.

She knew anytime he called in Satan, something big was going down, and the cash on the table showed something big had went down. She looked over at Satan. She still hated him for what he'd done to her, but she knew they never got caught and that meant this crazy, wild-ass niggah had some smart to his ass. All the shit he'd done, he still was running these Norfolk streets.

"Hey, baby girl," Satan said.

"Hey, Satan," she said with attitude. "It's *Precious*."

"How you doin', Precious? How's your man?" Satan looked at Truck and started laughing.

She gritted at them. "Y'all ain't shit."

Satan sat thinking about the night he knocked her out and envisioned her body laid on the floor. He wanted her then and he wanted her now.

"I'm going to the library, Truck." She looked at him. "I'm gonna call you later."

"I'll be here. I ain't doin' shit."

"Do you need anything, baby girl?" Satan knew no

other way of letting her know he wanted some time. She was seventeen and beautiful. He had to have her.

"No, I don't want anything from you."

He jumped up and approached her. "Look, shorty, that shit we went through is done and gone. The money we made, you probably fucked it up and it's gone. That car and your clothes is probably all you got to show. Now, you may think you gonna find another man out here, but you my baby girl. So you might as well accept it and play fair. Now do you have something in your pocket?"

"No." She stared at him. He wasn't fine, he wasn't rich, but he was a real niggah; a respected niggah, just like her brothers, and that she couldn't ignore.

"Here," he said, handing her five hundred from off the table. "I got business today, but call me tomorrow so we can sit down and talk. I know your brothers got your back, but I'm here. Test me."

"Okay." She knew taking this niggah's money was the start of something, but she knew niggahs talk mad shit for some ass when they sitting on top.

Chapter 7

It was day two. I was standing in the ICU and staring at Kendu, his dreads laying across the pillow, brace holding his neck still, tubes going in his nose, respirator in his throat to help him breathe, IV in his arm, and a catheter in his dick, as he lay there motionless.

The nurses said he was conscious, but when he came to, he was swinging and fighting, trying to get up. That quickly explained why they had his hands restrained.

Chris walked in. "He still ain't woke?"

"Naw, he still wildin' out when he comes to, so they keep knockin' his ass out. They fucked him up, son," I said.

"You don't know. Make me want to go shoot up them niggahs' momma's house, since I don't know where they at," Chris said.

"Naw, they'll pay. But you don't fuck with nobody mom's crib. Moms don't got shit to do with their ignorant-ass kids. Plus, they know where you and your mom's rest. Everybody know where my moms live. Mom's crib is off limits. We'll catch 'em in the street, and they will pay."

"His peoples on the way. I got to catch up with my squad. You know we in the tournament Saturday," Chris said.

"LE joint," I said, remembering the fifth annual Lake Edward basketball tournament. This was the fourth one since ninety-eight, and it had gotten bigger than Ruckers. Niggahs was coming from everywhere, and this year was expected to be bigger than ever. It was September, the last big event before going back to school. "I'm gonna hollah Prince. Let me know what's going on."

"I'm out too. I got some shit to take care of. I'll check back up here later."

We walked out in silence. This shit had our minds racing. Just to see these niggahs now would've been straight murder.

The ringing of the cell phone broke my concentration. It was Zaria fussing about me not coming home. I let her know of the situation with Kendu, and she relaxed and showed concern. I knew she just wanted to know that I wasn't with another bitch.

"Who's that in back?" I asked.

"Twana and Leisha," she said. "You on your way home?"

I knew it was coming. "Be a minute. Gots to catch up with Chris and situate some things. I'll holla in a few. Love you."

I headed to Tee Tee's crib, where I could smoke, look at BET, relax my muthafuckin' mind, get dressed in some fly shit, catch up with my brother, and go to the mall. I needed to do something. This shit with Kendu was fuckin' with me hard. This was my man. We'd held each other down.

Before me, Kendu, and Chris started clicking, we could barely buy a half a brick. Three years later, through hell and back, we buyin' six of those thangs. Big league, baby! Yeah, we seen niggahs who moved thirty and fifty bricks. They made millions and they lived stressful lives. They were on a totally different level, wearing five-thousand-dollar suits and two-thousand-dollar gator shoes, designer this, and designer that. They girls wear seven-hundred-dollar sandals and thousand-dollar dresses, and stay in the salon and boutiques spending money buying that platinum shit.

Nobody I knew could afford that shit, except Chris. And he couldn't really afford it, but he wore it because he wanted to look like the superstar. That phat-ass Denali truck, cell phone, and his rent had that niggah pumping five dollars in the gas tank and begging. I had to throw him fifteen grand on his last package because he was trying to shine.

To this day, I only know two niggahs personally that lived like that. And that's the two real LE legends, Black and Bo. Bo might've moved twenty to twenty-five bricks a month. But I know for a fact that Black was getting fifty to sixty of them things a month, because my brother used to get ten. Black and Brit were like that, but Brit still only scored from Lo. Nobody got near Black. That niggah was like a don and still getting it in Atlanta, I heard.

When I thought of a million dollars, street money, Black always came to mind because he was LE. On my level I was balling. Nice whip, nice house, nice condo, gear for every day if I chose to wear it, and if I met a bitch and wanted to do something for her I could.

I sat there just letting my thoughts explore the air as I smoked the 'dro, wrapped with a Sweet Aromatic Backwoods. Kendu was still on a niggah mind. I just couldn't shake it. I started feeling like I was responsible. Fuck Chris. I knew Kendu, and I knew he wouldn't leave. Nobody was going to make that niggah do nothing. I should've made sure he pulled off behind me. I should have been there. *Don't tell me this coke and weed got me slipping*. I picked up the phone to call Brit.

"What up?"

"Where Brit? Who is this?" I asked.

"Who the hell is this questioning me?" the voice answered. "You called here, so you know where I'm at." *Click.*

I called back. I stood up and dialed the number back. I yelled, "Fuck you talkin' to? That's my shit. You got me fucked up."

"Who dis? *P*?" The person laughed. "This El, fool."

"Niggah, I was like, what the fuck! Where Brit?"

"In back. He'll be back in a sec."

"What's up with your man?"

"Still fucked up and tubes and shit on him. Every time he wake up, he wildin' out, so they got him restrained and shit. Looks bad."

"Here, Brit," he said.

"What up?" Brit said.

"Tell me, son."

"We need to go get fitted. It's not long before my day, kid."

"We'll take care of that shit. What you doin' tonight?"

"Whatever. I'm getting ready to go by the ABC store, then head to the spot, me and El."

"I'll check you there." I knew he was talking about our spot. He was trying to chill out and see what was up. He knew if he went home, getting back out would be hell.

"You got weed?" he asked.

"Yeah, 'dro. Better call Dundee and get some 'labo,' if niggahs plan on smoking. I'm gonna stop by the hospital first. I'll check you in about an hour. Then we hittin' Roger Brown's tonight."

"A'ight. Heard about that shit. Bitches out the door."

"For sho. We there, babe." I hung up.

I was in the shower when the curtain came back.

She was naked and looking beautiful as ever. "Can I join you?"

"Sure, but I'm pressed for time. Gotta catch up with my peoples."

She shut the curtain and let me finish.

I came in the room and plugged up the iron. I threw my Azzure jean shorts on the bed and tore off the tag. *Seventy fuckin' dollars for light faded shorts. Ralph must be out his goddamn mind.* I'd met this designer several times, so I knew him personally.

I went through my jerseys in the closet. When the Carolina blue-and-white flashed across my eyes, I looked back at the shorts, tossed the jersey on the bed and smiled. *Perfect!* I reached in my drawer and pulled out a new white T-shirt and Joe Boxer boxers. I threw on the boxers and the T-shirt, slid on my Azzure jeans and black belt, with my big chrome buckle. I reached down in the closet and pulled out the Nike box with some fresh, new, white Air Force Ones already laced for quick throw-on. Tossed them on and stood up. I placed my stainless steel Breitling on my arm, my Cartier tinted shades, and turned to walk out.

Tee Tee was standing in the doorway in her robe, holding a glass of grape and lemonade Kool-Aid. "I thought we were going out?"

"I got to do some things and I'll holla back."

"Naw, you gonna tell me now."

I didn't feel like having this conversation. "Said I'll be back. Got a few things to do." I put the Nike box in the corner.

"I'm tired of this shit."

"Tired of what? Gettin' on the phone, callin' my baby moms like y'all muthafuckin' friends and shit?"

"Fuck that! I'm done with that. I'm talking about you. What are we?" she asked, still standing in the doorway.

"Yo, shorty, my man in the hospital. I got shit to take care of and niggahs to meet. Fuck this shit you talkin' tonight. I'll holla back." I took my wallet and money from my other pants and put it in my pocket.

"Prince, what I look like? I know you, Kendu, and Chris get down. I know you got your own team out Broadlawn, Crestwood, and Berkley. But most of all, I know who you ·fuck with outside of Kendu and Chris. They waitin' on you. If you take two hours, they will still be waitin'. So don't try to talk that got-to-run shit, you understand?" she said serious and calm.

"Understand what? Who the fuck you talkin' to?" I walked toward the door, moving closer to the edge to get out since she didn't move.

She stared into my eyes. "If you touch me or push me, I'm going to take the Kool-Aid and drench your mutha-fuckin' ass tonight."

I knew she was serious.

She knew the type of niggah I was. She knew if she threw that shit on me, I was gonna fuck her up. But as I stared in her eyes, I saw at that moment that she didn't care. The deeper I looked into her eyes, the more I could see the hurt. *Did I force her to not care about herself?*

I didn't know if she knew, but if she threw that Kool-Aid on me, I was going to whip her ass. I mean, fuck her up. She'd never throw Kool-Aid on another niggah. Then I thought about my hundred-dollar DC's, seventy-dollar shorts, two-hundred-dollar jersey all ruined with purple Kool-Aid. I knew I didn't have shit as sweet as I had on in the closet, and in the end I would probably catch a case.

"What is wrong with you? If you don't want to fuck with me, let me know, but right now this is how I'm living."

"So the hell with what I do? Fuck me, huh? We can go out with other people?" She stared at me.

"Do whatever you want." I shrugged my shoulders. "I don't give a fuck."

"How could you say that? That's so cold," she said, sadly moving to the side.

"That's just how I feel. I ain't with all this shit."

I got my keys and went out the door. I got in my car and took off. I did care what she did. I did care if she went out with somebody else. All I had to do was take the time and kick some pimp shit and possibly all could have gone well. But I wanted to get out in the streets and didn't feel like hearing the bullshit.

I arrived at the hospital about eight o'clock and walked in a room in the ICU expecting to see Kendu with all that shit hooked up to him. To my surprise he was sitting up with only one IV in his arm. "What's up, son?" I held my hand out.

"A'ight, babe." He reached out and grabbed my hand with a weak shake.

As I gripped his hand, my eyes watered. I had fucked up by not being there for my partner, but never again.

We talked for about twenty minutes. He didn't remember what happened, so I quickly filled him in so he'd know his enemies. I let him know to relax, get himself together. Their time was coming.

I was beginning to feel better because of his progress. The way all that shit was hooked to him before, I didn't think he was going to make it. He began dozing off from the morphine while I was talking. The doctors said he'd be there at least four days, and they would be trying to put him in a private room by tomorrow.

When his girl came in with a couple of his top workers, I showed love and made my exit.

By the time I got to the condo, Brit, El, and Dundee was there chillin'.

"What up, fam?" I gave Brit a pound, then El. Then I grabbed Dundee and gave him a hug and a pound. I hadn't seen my cousin in days. Dundee was the only niggah in my family that I would ever fuck with, because he was making a lot of money for Poppa and with Poppa.

"So what's the deal, cousin?"

"I'm a'ight, niggah. I'm always straight," I replied.

"Let me get some change, niggah, lookin' like a million bucks," El said to me.

"You don't need shit. Heard you heatin' up Hastings again," I said.

"That street belong to me. I can come and go forever. It's still me," he said.

"Those young niggahs don't know you," Brit said.

El laughed. "Y'all muthafuckas crazy." He grabbed the bottle of Hennessy.

"Everybody rollin' to the spot?" I asked.

Dundee looked at me. "Where?"

"Roger Brown's."

"I can't fuck with it," Dundee said. "I got some shit to take care of out the way."

We knew out the way automatically meant Lake Edward.

We took three Dutch Masters to the head. I didn't care for the Dutch, but Dundee rolled his own weed, so we couldn't be choosy. We waited for Brit to change and we broke out.

"Come on and roll, Dun," I said.

"I got to get out the way," he said, stressing.

"How long you gonna be out there?" I asked.

"About an hour."

"Bet. I'll roll with you, then we'll meet them niggahs." I jumped in the BMW wagon sitting on dubs. I hollered at Brit and El, letting them know we'd catch up in about an hour.

Me and Dundee pulled up at the barbershop. There was a crowd of niggahs out front as always. It was nine p.m., and it didn't mean shit. Several nice whips were out front, so we knew the money was out there.

We jumped out, gave niggahs pounds, and became part of the crowd. Mad eyes fell on the Carolina blue and fresh whites, but the platinum chain that lay across Dundee's Lakers jersey let niggahs know who was getting the money.

Thirty minutes had passed when two guys pulled up in a beige '94 GS300, tinted. Dundee ran to the beamer then jumped in the Lexus. He was gone about ten minutes when the Lex pulled back up.

He walked inside the barbershop and I followed. He opened a small brown bag and pulled out a large knot and began counting. He had just sold a big eight.

I heard all the commotion in the back, so we walked that way. Just what I thought, *cee-lo game flowing*. I saw a couple heads I knew and a few I didn't. It was about twelve niggahs around, and about six playing. We stood there watching the game for about ten minutes, trying to see who was hot.

After scoping the game and level of players, I threw two hundred dollars down when the bank got the dice back. Everybody money was down when the bank hit triple threes, making him an instant winner. He scooped up all the money.

I threw another two hundred down.

Bank rolled again. I watched as the dice stopped— two, two, six. That six made him an instant winner

I threw four hundred down, trying to win back what I'd lost.

He rolled four, four, two.

Yeah! I thought.

Niggahs began to roll. Beating that deuce was going to be hard. Niggahs know a deuce will ride and get everybody money, and so far it was doing just that. I rolled. Nothing. Rolled again. Nothing.

"Niggah ain't got shit, Skunk," some niggah yelled.

I rolled again. Nothing.

"Break these niggahs, Skunk, break 'em. This niggah scared."

I concentrated on the roll, but was wondering why this niggah decided to suck the bank dick while I was rolling. "Suck his dick later . . . after I roll," I said.

Some laughed except for the ones who was on his team.

I could feel he was a baller with the new Mitch & Ness throwback, crisp butter Timbs, and the big diamond stud.

I rolled five, five, one.

He scooped my money, and dude kept making comments like he knew me.

I looked around as bank shook the dice, waiting for all the money to drop.

After thirty minutes I was down almost two G's. "How much in the bank?" I asked.

Niggahs looked at me surprised.

Skunk answered, "Twelve thousand."

I only had a one thousand left. I looked at Dundee, who was standing beside me smoking a Backwoods.

"Fuck this," dude who was talking mad shit said. "That niggah ain't got no money."

"When I finish playin'," I told dude, "I'm gonna put my foot in your ass."

"Do it," Dundee said. "Shit come fast, go fast."

I looked at the bank.

"I got half," someone said.

I turned to see Brada, gave a pound, and yelled, "Stick it."

Everybody picked up their money.

"They ain't got six thousand, Skunk. Make him show you the money," dude said.

I ignored him and looked at the bank. "Roll, son."

He rolled. Nothing. Rolled again—two, two, one.

My heart came back up from my stomach and my fist tightened. I was holding twelve grand.

My phone rang. It was Brit. I handed the phone to Dundee and told him to tell him we were on the interstate.

It was close to midnight and this was just getting going. It was 1:00 when I finally hit cee-lo.

I split the eighteen grand with Brada, because he caught half. Then I had to split my nine grand with Dundee because his six grand was on the line. I spent all that time and only won fifteen hundred. Came in with three grand and left with four thousand, five hundred. *Damn!* I put my money in my pocket, and we all walked outside.

Soon as dude walked out the door, I caught him in his jaw. He tried, but he was young and lacked the skills. He went down quick.

His peoples stepped up, but the sound of Dundee cocking the double-barrel shotgun stopped niggahs in their tracks. Niggahs knew me as a chill niggah, unless you got me wrong, but everybody knew my cousin as a niggah who'd blast for no reason at all.

Brada calmed things down real quick. I realized Brada knew more niggahs than I gave him credit for.

We jumped in the BMW wagon and raced to downtown Portsmouth. We arrived with enough time to get two drinks, peep the bitches, and head home.

Dundee dropped me off at Tee Tee's house and broke out. Her car was there, but she was gone. I sat there thinking of our incident earlier, but I kept saying to myself, "I know she wouldn't go out with nobody else."

I called her sisters, her best friend, her auntie. Nothing. I began to get sick, thinking of another niggah fuckin' her. I rolled a Backwoods and turned on the TV.

It was now four a.m., and Tee Tee was still missing. I pictured the way she gave me head and opened her legs wide for me. Now she was out there showing her goodies to another niggah.

I went in the room and got my burner and laid it on the table. *I can't flip over no bitch. I can't get in no trouble over this girl.* I sat there trying to talk myself out of it when I heard a car door. I jumped up and grabbed the gun and ran to the door. It was our neighbors. This shit had me going. At this time I wasn't thinking about my girl or my family, just Tee Tee.

I walked back to the living room and sat down. I went in the room and pulled out an eight ball, laid four lines on the table, and tooted them up like no tomorrow. I felt as if my eyes were going to roll to the back of my head, and my left leg got numb. My mouth got numb too, so I lit the Backwoods again.

I was dozing off when I heard the base outside. I grabbed my gun and looked over at the clock—seven minutes after five. I looked out the window to see the truck turning around. I threw one in the chamber and bust out the back door.

As I came around the corner, her door opened, and she leaned toward him. I grabbed her leg and snatched her out the truck. She fell against the door to the ground, and I snatched her up by the neck, pushing her against his door.

When I saw dude move in the truck, my reflexes made me fire three shots in the truck before I knew what happened. My whole life flashed before my eyes. Two caught dude in the chest, and one went through the windshield.

Tee Tee stood there shaking and crying, her hands over her mouth.

I looked in her eyes and shook my head. The thought of letting two more hot ones go in this girl's head was the right thing to do, because I knew the rules—no witnesses. I didn't mean to shoot dude, but he shouldn't have moved. He should have just stepped on the gas.

She stood there as if she was in a trance, covering her mouth, her eyes wide, tears rolling still. "I'm sorry, Prince," was the bullshit she murmured over and over.

Sorry for what? I thought. *Sorry for fuckin dude, or sorry for shit ending up here? One niggah dead and you about to go.* I tried to raise my arm, but it seemed so heavy. I took two steps back and realized I couldn't.

I broke out at a quick pace and ended up at the detail shop. I sat upstairs in the studio and tooted damn near an eight ball. My mind and body was going numb, not from the killing, but from the thought of getting caught.

After a few, the coke had my body amped and not really giving a fuck about dude. Niggah should've known—when a bitch got a niggah, tell her to come to your spot or meet her at the hotel. Don't go scoop that bitch and go rolling all over town with her, simple-ass niggah.

But thoughts of Tee Tee was still fucking with me. I had some good times with that girl. She always gave me space. Since the beginning, she always kinda knew I had a girl. Even when she found out Zaria was not only my girl, but my baby momma, she still fucked and treated me like her own. She loved so hard that I couldn't help but to love her back.

After two years I had a baby momma still in my life, and I had a girl that I loved also, but I couldn't leave Zaria. Still there's no way in hell that bitch thought it was all right to go fuck another niggah. Fuck that! You called him, he scooped you, you wanted to give him some muthafuckin' pussy. I raised my right hand as if I was shooting her ass. "Fuck her," I tried to tell myself, but that shit wasn't working.

Chapter 8

It was ten a.m. when Brit heard the phone ringing. "Get that, Leah," he said, tying up his grey New Balance.

"Two months before the wedding and this phone is off the hook," she said. "This ain't your house. Don't worry about this phone."

"Who the hell is it? Dropp?" Brit asked, referring to her old boyfriend. "Want his baby back." He knew saying that shit got to her, and he sometimes wondered why.

"You always carry shit too far, Brit. I could say some shit smart back, but then you'll be ready to act all stupid." She answered the phone. "Hello."

"Say what you gonna say," he said. "I don't give a fuck, 'cause I'm gettin' ready to get papers on yo' ass. Then you'll belong to me."

"You out your damn mind, niggah." She went back to the call. "Hello?"

"What up, baby girl? How you?"

"Fine. What's going on, cuz? How my little cousins?" she asked, referring to Poppa's kids.

"Good, always good. You know I'm gonna always make sure of that."

"I know you are, Poppa, I know you are."

"Brit there?"

"Yeah, right here." Leah handed Brit the phone and stood right there in his face.

"Yo, this niggah called me," Poppa said.

"What niggah?"

"Brada."

"Okayyyy?"

"You know he fuck with your brother girl, Tee Tee sister?"

"Naw, I ain't know that," Brit said. "Who the hell is her sister?"

"One of those hot ass stylists and shit. You don't know her. Anyway, niggah, they say Prince burned a niggah ass up last night. Say some niggah was at the crib. Layed him out in his truck and jetted," Poppa said.

Brit snapped back. "Jetted?" He smiled. *Yeah!*

"Holla, if you need me."

Poppa words brought Brit back to Leah staring him in his face. He hung up the phone. "My brother shot a niggah last night," he said, "or this morning. Shit, I don't know. He popped somebody, and now he on the run. I'm going out to find him before the police pick his ass up."

"You want me to come?"

"Naw, this big boy shit. I'll be back. Love ya." He grabbed his grey Polo and headed out the door. He got in his Ac and called Dundee, trying to find out if he knew anything.

Dundee didn't, but he told Brit, "Meet me at the spot."

Chapter 9

Iwas sitting in the den and looking at videos, smoking
'dro when Brit and Dundee walked in. "What up?"

"Tell us, man," Brit said.

"Saw shorty with another niggah and lost it. I snatched
her out the truck, grabbed her, and dude moved like he
was getting something."

"Why he didn't take off?" Dundee said. "Niggah tryin'
to play hero for a bitch that wasn't even his."

"That's straight murder. If they tie you to that shit, you
gone, man, you gone." Brit looked sadly at me.

"I'm on the move, son. Just gonna change up, but I'm
on the move."

About this time, there was a knock at the door.

El came in. "Fuck is goin' on?" He looked at me. "You
a'ight?"

"Yeah, man, I'm straight."

"Talk to me," he said.

El had been locked so much that he knew a lot about
laws and charges.

After I ran the story down, he stood staring deep into space and pulled on the Dutch that Dundee had rolled.

"Where the burner?" he asked.

"Chesapeake Bay."

"Any witnesses?"

"Naw."

"That bitch is a witness," Dundee blurted. "I can't believe you fucked your shit up over a triflin'-ass bitch. You killed a niggah, and it didn't make a muthafuckin' difference to your pocket. You know the rules."

"Yeah, I know." My pimp status was shot.

"Just lay low and we'll see what happens," Brit said.

"Yeah! Let's see, because if shorty girl gonna tell, she'll be telling it to the 'fishees' in the bay," El said.

Dundee looked at me and shook his head. "Brit gonna have to find him a new best man. You gettin' ready to go on vacation over a bitch."

"Y'all can kill that bullshit. I'm tired of hearing it." I stood up and pulled on the Backwoods. "I don't wanna hear that shit no more."

"Hear what?" Brit yelled.

"I say what the fuck I want, niggah," Dundee said over Brit.

"Fuck is you talkin' to? You can't whip nobody ass here, nephew. And if you wanna practice, ain't shit stoppin' you." El stared at me and stepped closer. "What?"

Brit and Dundee came closer.

I found my nose inching toward my tightened lips and gritted teeth. I stared them all in the eyes. I knew damnwell I couldn't fuck with these niggahs like this. I knew what they were feeling, and me runnin' my mouth gave them reason to fuck me up for being stupid. You just don't fuck with the next niggah over a girl. Never. And if she don't choose you, then step the fuck off.

The cold eyes that stared at me let me know that the

brother, cousin, and uncle that was holding me down before, and would be there to hold me down later, at that
moment, would've fucked me up. They waited on a reason.

Desperately needing a drink, I took a step back and
turned toward the kitchen.

Chapter 10

The black F-150 pulled into Oakley Park, and Truck and Cadillac stepped out looking simple: jeans, wife-beaters and white Ts. Niggahs hanging out kept staring because they knew Truck and Cadillac were getting money. Several were hustling, but only two or three were worthy of fuckin' with Truck and Caddy. They stood in their mom's front drinking deuce-deuces of Heineken, smoking a tightly rolled Dutch.

"Which one of those niggahs can I trust to make a real hustler?" Caddy said. "I'll turn Moe into that niggah. He already got a whip. I'll put him on, front him two joints, and make all these niggahs come to him."

"Naw, man, Flight that niggah. He popular. He ain't got no car, but from that ballin' shit, he know mad niggahs, and that will get him poppin' all over. He'll be that niggah in a couple months."

Truck motioned. "Flight, Moe, come here."

"Y'all niggahs need work?"

"Yeah," Moe said, "if the numbers right."

"Niggahs be comin' at me nonstop, son," Flight said.

"What you movin' now, Flight?"

"Ounce a week."

"What about you, Mo?"

"Two ounces a week."

"Y'all ever work together?"

"Naw!"

"Naw!"

"Well, start. Y'all responsible for four and a half, and the shit is tight."

They all climbed in the truck and rode to the back of the projects, where Flight and Moe got out with four and a half ounces of hard, ready to set the park off.

They were leaving the park when Truck's phone rang. It was Satan. Satan never called him. He always did the calling.

"What up?" Truck answered.

"My peoples lookin' for that diesel. Ready to spend like twenty grand."

"For sho. Let me holla back real soon."

"Real soon. One."

"Niggah, Satan lookin' for that diesel," Truck said to Caddy. "That's that Portsmouth shit there. Fuck with that, and we'll be rich in a minute."

Truck was calling Vic, while Caddy was talking about getting rich off heroin.

"What up, Duke?" Vic answered.

"Need to holla at you about that boy."

"I'm at Magic City. Come on through."

They shot over to the strip club in P-town, jumped out the whip, got patted down, and went in the club.

One of the bitches caught Truck's eye as he looked around. He hit Cadillac.

"Goddamn, kid, that bitch phat as hell. Look at her pussy knot. I'll eat that bitch up." Cadillac reached in his pocket and threw down five tens.

She made herself comfortable, ready to give Caddy conversation. She figured if he peeled off fifty for one song, there's gotta be more.

Truck made his way to VIP, where seven girls were dancing for three cats. Vic stuck out his hand and grabbed Truck, sitting him down next to him. "Yo, this my niggah Truck." He pointed to his peoples. "This is Van and Trent."

As the bitches danced, Truck saw that Vic, Trent, and Van all had twenties and fifties stacked, and them hoes were letting them do whatever.

When Truck reached in his pocket and slid the knot of twenties across the table, two swarmed to him like a bee to honey.

As they danced, he politicked with Vic. Everything was set.

Make this move and pocket some change, Truck thought. "You fuck with these niggahs?"

"Yeah, them niggahs make good," Vic said.

Trent and Van overheard Truck referring to them and leaned over to see what he was talking about.

"What up?" Trent asked Vic.

"What up?" Truck frowned like Trent was frustrating him. "Look here, Beach boy, I don't fuck with y'all, and you don't know me."

"You right, but I heard about you."

"And what, niggah?" Truck stared him down, gritting.

"Remember, these beach boy, money-gettin'-ass niggahs run all day. And we trained to go." Trent stared back.

Truck was a big motherfucker, but the Glock 9mm in Trent's jeans, and the 9mm that his brother Van had with him, assured them that they would make it out the club.

Vic stood up smiling. "Y'all niggahs chill. Spend some of that money y'all niggahs makin'. Fuck one or two of these hoes, niggahs ready to fight over VA Beach and Norfolk, until they lock your ass up."

"We a'ight," Truck said.

Vic knew Truck, and the look in his eye said something different. He put his arm around Truck's neck and whispered in his ear, "I make a lot of money with these niggahs. All they pump is diesel. Now they buyin' coke too, so don't fuck with them, dog. A'ight?"

"Bet." Truck gave Vic a pound.

Truck talked with Satan and set things up. He was sending Cadillac with security that Satan had his back. The only thing he could see happening was Satan flippin' the script and gettin' dude, but Caddy would be straight. He dropped Caddy at his new LS400 Lexus—it was a '97 but new to him—with twenty-inch rims. You couldn't tell Caddy shit.

As Caddy was pulling off, Truck blew his horn and parked his truck. He pulled his sawed off shotgun from the back and threw it in the back of the Lex.

"Now let's go get this money."

"Hell, yeah!" Caddy said with a smile, as they headed to Portsmouth.

"Something in my gut keep telling me not to sway from what I do. Let's see what's poppin' in P-town, partner." Truck leaned back, allowing the wind to circulate through the LS 400, as the sounds of the Clipse banged through the system.

As they pulled in the Amoco gas station, people were running in and out of the store. Panhandlers stood in front begging, and tricks stood on the side trying to get work. They noticed the new Mountaineer parked by the air pump.

Caddy pulled behind the truck, and Truck jumped out and got in the back seat of the Mountaineer. He gave Satan a pound.

"This my cousin, Ty." Satan shot Truck a look to kill. "He spendin' thirty."

"Drive," Truck said. "Go left and head through the tunnel."

They headed back to Norfolk, with Caddy close behind.

"Take this first exit, make a left at the light. Make this next right."

Satan was getting a little shook now. Truck was carrying them into Berkley. This wasn't good.

"Make this left and pull in front of that house right there. Okay, turn off the car."

As soon as the ignition went off, they heard one go into the chamber of the Glock 9mm.

"Run them pockets, son." Truck put the barrel to Ty's head. He put Caddy's gun in Satan's chest.

Ty began to stutter, trying to put some shit together.

Pow! The shot to Ty's thigh made him pass Truck the bag.

"Don't turn this into a homicide, Duke. I got enough bodies for the year."

Two more shots, one in Satan's shoulder and the other in the floor, let Ty know that Satan had nothing to do with this sweet heist.

Truck made Satan get out of the truck and get flat. He ran to the passenger side and snatched Ty out and slammed him to the ground.

Ty yelled from the pain in his leg.

"Run those pockets too, niggah," Truck said, going in Ty's pockets.

Ty had a roll of at least three grand.

Truck ran over and went in Satan's pockets. Five hundred was all he had. "Don't move!" he said, heading to the Lex.

Ty was staring as they were pulling off.

"Stop," Truck yelled at Caddy. "Why you starin'?" he asked Ty.

"Because I'll see you again, niggah."

"I was lettin' this niggah live." Truck fired two shots into Ty's chest. *Pow! Pow!*

The Lex eased out of Berkley onto the interstate, and through the Portsmouth Tunnel with thirty grand of free money.

Precious was lying in the living room in total darkness listening to Jahiem's CD when they arrived back at the house. She was deep in thought and never heard them come in.

They clicked on the light, startling her. They placed the money on the table and began counting.

"Who the fuck in Norfolk would be stupid enough to keep fuckin with y'all?" she asked.

"Niggahs wasn't from Norfolk," Truck said.

"They were from Portsmouth."

They laughed.

Truck's phone rang. "Hello."

"Thought y'all were on the way?" Vic asked.

"Oooh! Had to make a detour. Get a niggah and get back."

"You got the niggah who was spendin' twenty G's?"

"You know I did. You could have made that in a month, off that cat, then made that every month."

"Goddamn, Truck," Vic said, frustrated. "You know me, I need mine today. Worry about tomorrow, tomorrow. I'll hit you later." Vic couldn't get mad. Inside, he knew his man, and shit didn't surprise him.

"Look, I was lying here thinking, every time y'all go out, I don't know if y'all even comin' back." Precious wanted them to calm down. "If y'all get locked again for the shit y'all doin', I'm goin' to be fucked up out here by my damn self. Start thinking of me. I need y'all."

Truck came over and put his arm around her. "You gonna be a'ight. Just worry about school and doin' good. I got you here."

"Stop cryin' like you some rich-ass little bitch." Cadillac stopped counting dough and looked at her. "You been through the storm. Now enjoy this shit here and shut the hell up."

Precious leaned on Truck. "I knew you wouldn't understand."

"Naw, girl, I understand. But soon as we put our guard down and try to live a normal life, muthafuckas gonna get us or try us. So if we ain't gettin', we gettin' got. Not here!"

"Fuck him!" Truck said. "He need a role model. I'm gonna get him in the big brother program if somebody take his ass."

They all laughed.

Cadillac looked at Precious. "Come here. We come from nothing. We ain't like those Beach muthafuckas, we truly come from nothing. Our lives haven't been worth a fuck to us and nobody else, but we a'ight right now. And I'll die before I let it change, okay."

"I know this, but now we got it. Can't we put our heads together and figure out how to keep it? Open a store or something. I'll work. We all can work, except Truck. He don't have no people skills," she said giving Caddy a pound. "We doin' business plans now in school. We studyin' economics. I want us to have a family business like folks on TV; sit down and eat dinner as a family, go on trips as a family. Give me a life. Can I have a life?" She walked to her room.

"What the fuck is this?" Caddy yelled loud enough for her to hear. "Phat house, phat cars, money to shop. I guess livin' out the Park was better?"

"Give me some security, asshole," she hollered from

the back. "Let me go to school and know when I come home, police ain't gonna be surroundin' the house. Let me go to sleep and know if the phone ring, y'all ain't locked up or dead. Ease my mind."

"We do gots to chill," Truck said. "I'm hearing her and if we focus on the hard, we can see five G's a week off that alone."

"Man, shut up. We said that before and then you go grabbin' the sawed-off shotgun, changin' the plan."

"Just like you changed the plan, robbin' Kendu, a niggah we know," Truck said.

"Because that's what we do—we rob, steal, and kill."

"Naw, niggah, that's what *you* do. I'm a hustler and a survivor. I take advantage of life situations and make niggahs remember the golden rule."

"And what's that?" Caddy asked.

"Yeah." Precious entered the den. "What's that?"

"Don't get caught slippin'. Don't slip or I will get your ass. I don't give a fuck where you from: New York, D.C., Baltimore, Philly. This niggah here, trained by the City of Norfolk, will get your ass," Truck yelled. "They made me, now the world got to deal wit' me," he added in a regular tone.

"Damn right!" Caddy yelled. "Norfolk City, baby! Legend Russ Gonzalez being mentioned with the likes of Stacy Robinson, Kenny Speed, Shampoo, and Black."

"The real Black!" they said simultaneously.

"My brother ain't nothing but the truth." Caddy gave Russ a pound and continued to count the money.

Chapter 11

I walked in circles around the den, jamming to the sounds of 106 & Park blasting through the fifty-four-inch TV. I was about to lose my mind sitting in this house. I felt fucked up, running and living in hotels.

I walked out to the garage. I opened the kettles and let London out. This Rottweiler was big as shit, but mad playful.

After wrestling with him for a while, I put him up and let Honcho out. Honcho was my red pit bull. He wasn't real playful at all.

He ran over, trying to tear the cage off the Rottweiler.

I was grabbing him, trying to be playful, until he started growling.

I sat my new .380 on the rack that leaned against the wall. I started fucking with him again. He was going to realize who the fuck I was, or he was going to die this day.

My hand was jumping these days. Maybe it was my nerves.

After a minute, I put his ass up.

* * *

The next couple of months on the run was scary. It took two weeks for them to issue warrants for my arrest. My mom had a stack of little yellow bags from the sheriff's department. I stayed on the low and watched my every step.

My baby moms had heard what happened from Brit. He gave her half the story, but once she heard Tee Tee was involved, whatever else was said didn't mean shit. She was hating me, and fed up with my shit.

I knew she loved me and would marry me in a heartbeat. But I wasn't ready for marriage, and she was tired of the bullshit, so we weren't talking. I figured it was for the best. Here I was wanted and my face plastered on Crime Line for murder, and I hadn't talked to her, but talked to Tee Tee.

I'd spent the last month in Suburban Lodge on Independence. I had heated that muthafucka up. I was moving weight out of that joint. Oh! I never stopped working. Staying in the streets kept you movin'. It was gonna be a long time 'fore they caught up to me.

My man Kendu was doing much better. He hadn't remembered a lot about the incident, but he was told the entire story again. He never said much about it after, but I knew it was in his head.

Brit's big day came. Damn right, I was his best man. We all stood up there like muthafuckin' kings. Yeah, them bitches were fine, but us niggahs was the pride of Bayside, standing up there in our tuxedos. And I'm gonna give it to Leah, her bridesmaids were off the hook, with their low-cut dresses hanging off their shoulders.

With a full church of family and friends, it was like a

Bayside High School reunion. Old and new. Here it was, five niggahs standing here holding my brother down as he made his vows. I looked over at them. I remembered when all these older heads hustled in the back alleys.

Now BayBay, Lou, and Reese all got jobs. Derrick just came home and was on the grind. Poppa straight because of that niggah right there, Black.

Black and Brit was always tight. I guess, deep down, I always knew Brit fucked with these niggahs, but if he ever got in a bind Black's number was programmed in his phone.

Black looked at me and smiled, gold crowns gleaming. He knew me from a little niggah, but being an LE legend from NY to VA, that's what I'm talking about.

I looked back at Brit and Leah. My heart was with him. I hoped one day to stand there with somebody. I prayed that God would bless me like He blessed Brit.

When the ceremony was over, everybody headed to the reception at Grand Affairs. As the church emptied, four plain suits walked in. They stood patiently as pictures were taken.

One walked up to me and identified himself as Detective Walsh. "We're not here to make a scene. We're not even gonna cuff you. We need you to ease out the back. We got a car right outside," he said, staring me in my eyes.

"For sure. No problem," I said.

Evidently they knew how to get me and they could have came up in the spot and got me, but they respected my brother's day and for that, I respected them.

As I eased out the back, I saw Brit getting upset. I looked at Black. "Tell Brit to chill. Go to the reception, take mad pictures, and don't fuck up that girl day. Come check me later." I gave Black a pound.

Needless to say, I didn't get to the reception. I missed

Thanksgiving, Christmas, New Year's, and Valentine's. No shorty to eat dinner with or send flowers to. This shit was getting to me. Doing the time wasn't a problem, but trying to keep my mind within the compounds of these walls was. My money, my son, and if any street shit kicked off that involved Brit, I wouldn't be there.

My court date was Monday, June 16, 2003, ten a.m., Courtroom B. I was looking at fifteen to life, and they had three witnesses. Ms. Walker from across the street looked out after she'd heard the commotion and saw me get away. Then there was Joyce, who just wanted to be nosy and involved, when she needed to have her eyes on her three kids. She was up and had to tell everything she saw.

Then there was Tee Tee. I felt like my world had crumbled.

I had gotten one of the top attorneys in the area, Broca-ferrah. He was top-of-the-line and said he had some shit he had to dig for, but it didn't look good. Then he wanted more money.

It was the Saturday before my trial. I didn't expect any visitors, so it came as a surprise when they called my name. I walked out confused about who could be coming to see me. I had already talked to Brit.

I snatched my head back when I saw Brada on the other side of the glass. I sat down and picked up the phone. He put his fist against the glass, and I touched the glass in response.

"So what the deal, playboy?" he said.

"Same shit. Holdin' it down, though."

"For sure. You from the Lakes. I wouldn't expect nothing else."

This niggah seemed mad cool. *I wonder what the fuck is up?* I knew he, of all people, knew the real story.

"Look, I'm up here for business and family reasons.

First, business, we gonna do big things. I'm waiting on your release. We talked to the old lady, and for some reason she saw nothing. And the other girl, people saying her daughter is on a milk carton," he said real low, but slowly moving his lips so I could catch the words.

"Now for family, shit happen so fast, she didn't see shit and she sticking to it. Her sister had gone and picked her up. We were at our house, we knew the niggah who offered her a ride. Look, Prince, I know her. Been knowing her a long time. She wouldn't fuck with nobody. You got her ass fucked up. She loves the fuck out of you. Since you been gone, she been sick in the fuckin' house, work, and home. She done lost weight." Brada shook his head.

"For real?" I said, thinking she was out to do a niggah in.

"She like a size eight, dude. The way she losin' it ain't good, but she look good, real good." He raised his eyebrows.

This niggah had my mind racing. I always remembered her at about a size twelve.

"I'm getting ready to burst, but I'll see you soon."

"I owe you one or two."

He smiled. "Can I collect on them both today?" he said, his smile gone.

"What's that?"

"You comin' home Monday. Tuesday I'm gonna have us suites at the Boardwalk down the beach, me and Ashante, you and Tee Tee. Family time." He smiled. "You gotta talk to her sooner or later, and I got to look like the good brother-in-law."

"Done." I placed my fist on the glass.

He stood up and responded.

I watched him walk out in his new Guess carpenter

shorts, and long white Tee, setting shit off with some crispy new white DC's. A knot came in my stomach with a look of disgust as I looked at my orange jumpsuit and light brown flip-flops.

I went back to my block with new thoughts, praying this niggah was for real.

Chapter 12

"Hell, yeah!" I said to myself as we left the court-room. I didn't give a fuck. All I knew was I was FREE.

Brocaferrah didn't only make them realize that nothing tied me to the murder, but that also whoever did it might have done it in self-defense. See, when dude leaned over in the truck before I popped his ass, his hand was on a 9mm that he had under the seat, which worked in my favor.

It was three o'clock, and the sun was shining. Down-town Norfolk never looked so good. I jumped in the BMW wagon with Dundee, straight to Precision Cuts on Baker Road.

"Goddamn, Prince," Brada joked, knowing the deal, "look like you just came home."

I laughed. "You don't know?"

An hour later we were on the interstate, headed to my baby momma's house.

"She expectin' you?" Dundee asked.

"Hell, naw. She should be at work," I said, catching an attitude, thinking about her being home with another niggah.

To my surprise her car was out front when we arrived.

"What if she got company, man? You should of called." Dundee shook his head.

"If she got company, I guess I'm going to Princess Anne this time, huh? I'll be locked in Virginia Beach."

"For sure." Dundee handed me the loaded gun.

I tucked the gun away and walked inside, using my key. I yelled, so as not to alarm her.

She came out of the bedroom. "Glad you out," she said.

"Yeah, me too."

"You need to make a move because we ain't like that no more. I got a friend," she said.

"Well, I hope your friend got a house, because you know better than to have a niggah in this muthafucka. You know all my shit here, money amongst other shit. This is our shit, and until I get my shit out, treat it like that. I don't give a fuck what you do outside of this muthafucka. Now move, so I can shower and shit."

I took off my clothes and started the shower, while she stood in the room talking about something. I came out and took off my boxers. I stood naked with my boxers in my hand and thought of asking for some ass. Then I thought of her with another niggah. I threw my dirty drawers in her face and went to the shower.

"Tell Dundee to come in," I yelled. "He in the car."

I came out the shower and went to my closet. *My shit was just as I left it.*

I got dressed, and me and Dundee was out, headed to the shop. We talked nonstop. He'd been handling my shit since I'd been gone. I ran my shit smooth, so he had no problems. I just had to make sure Kendu and Chris got along with him. He ran shit thoroughly, so I came home to some nice change. Enough to get a drop-top something.

Kendu and Chris were getting the truck cleaned when we arrived at the shop. I looked over and Darius and Javonne were detailing cars. Niggahs I used to look up to as real money-making hustlers were washing cars, working for Brit. *Damn! Just as quick as niggahs blow, they fall even quicker.*

Niggahs started catching me up on things. Found out Darius was smoking and was working for damn-near nothing. Javonne was scrambling. Child support was killing him. Trent and Van got caught up on possession and kidnapping charges, and they ain't supposed to see daylight.

And the big news, that niggah Dropp had came home from a five-year bid and had Northridge popping again. He got the same house Pab had, that Truck and Cadillac shut down. Word was the niggah had at least twenty-five grand a day coming through that bitch.

"So what the deal, baby?" Chris gave me a pound and a hug.

"You know me, baby. Know how I do."

"We know now, don't we?" Kendu smirked.

We kicked it for a while until Brit and Poppa came in. Just being around fam listening to music, and sipping on Hennessy felt wonderful. The "haze" these niggahs was burning was like heaven.

"I need to talk to you, man," Chris said.

"A'ight, give me a second." I ran upstairs and told Brit I needed a signed check. I had decided I wanted one of those new 350ZX convertibles.

I got to the phone and called Mike. He worked at Auto Nation.

"Yo, you got Mike."

"What up, man?"

"Goddamn, Prince. Somebody said you had bought your last car from me. They said your transportation was state vehicles." He laughed.

"Well, let's make them muthafuckas a lie."

"What?"

"New 300 shit."

"Yeah! 350."

"Platinum drop, fully loaded. Today!"

"I got black, ready and clean."

"Black it is. Pull my file. My info still the same. Call my credit union."

An hour later he called back for me to bring two recent pay stubs and a ten-thousand-dollar check. I knew my shit was tight.

Chris carried me to the Nissan dealer off Bonney Road. We were rolling fast, talking, and both got silent as we rode down the boulevard and the bright red "Hot" sign from the Krispy Kreme stole our attention. He made the quick right and got a dozen. He stuck around and ate hot doughnuts until the keys were in my hand and the car was in front.

"Yo, I don't like to tell shit like this, man, but you my man."

He had my full attention. "What, son?"

"I was at the Courtyard the other day fuckin' with this shorty, right, and we leavin' and I see Leah pullin' off in the beamer. I'm sittin' in the truck, smokin' a Dutch, and guess who I see come out?"

I just stared at him.

"Dropp! I ain't sayin', but you know."

He'd just turned a beautiful day into shit. I felt like shit because I knew this shit was going to crush Brit, but he had to be told.

Deep inside, I believed Brit was skeptical of that, but

prayed that, she loved him enough to forget dude. But she was with him for years, and niggahs knew Dropp had her ass open.

Dropp treated her like shit, but she would cry for his ass not to leave her. He would beat her ass, and she would cry for his ass to come back. He tore her car to pieces with a brick, and she dropped the charges. It was wild.

When that niggah went away, she got with Brit on the rebound and had a baby nine months after. The baby died two days after being born. Some say it was Dropp's, but we never knew.

Now this niggah home and gettin' it, rockin the new tinted-out Q45, new kicks and throwbacks every day, draped in jewels. The niggah was ballin', but niggahs know you don't fuck with a niggah wife. *I should go split this niggah head open, but then I'll have to burn his ass up, because him or somebody from his team will be trying to retaliate.*

Me and Chris arrived back at the detailing shop. Shit was packed. Cats were up in the studio, with the cee-lo game going on. Me, Chris, Kendu, and Dundee stood out front, catching up on everything.

I wanted Dundee there in case there were any problems, or, if they had a problem with my cousin. "Speak up now while he here. I don't wanna hear that bullshit later."

Cats started coming from upstairs, some smiling, some with mad attitude.

Corey was always happy for some reason. "What up, ba-by?" he yelled, giving me pound and a hug. "Miss ya, boy." He smiled. "Did ya man tell you I got him in?" He punched Chris.

"Don't jinx me, son," Chris said. "I ain't tell nobody."

"I got him in the camp. I can't do no more. Look,

Prince," Corey said, getting hype, not letting anybody get a word in. "I got the niggah the nicest deal waiting. All he got to do is step it up and do his thing, and he'll be getting that real money. I got Reebok waiting, I got Coca-Cola, I got mad million-dollar endorsements waiting. Muthafuckas hollerin' at me," he said in a low tone.

Oh shit! Here come that extra shit that the cognac brings out in niggahs.

"I know my niggah. He gonna do his thing," Kendu said, giving Chris a pound.

"Fo' sho, niggah," I added. "Yo, and fuck that jinx shit. Pray, man. This is your ticket, or we'll all end up locked, dead, or broke over some bullshit. Being locked, son, made me realize. You are close, almost there. Raw talent and God—who can fuck with you?"

Everybody standing around was mad serious. They knew Chris had the potential to make it and inside most of us wished for the best.

"Muthafucka better do something. Shit, I got bills." Corey laughed. He had broken the seriousness.

Niggahs watched as he pulled away in his new Expedition sitting on twenty-two's.

I finished talking with Kendu and Chris. After a few words with Brit and Dundee, I was out.

Chapter 13

Cadillac looked around MP, the Jamaican restaurant in Military Crossing. He was sitting where he could see who came in the door. His life was going fast. While Truck was beginning to be more laid-back, staying inside more and enjoying the fruits of his labor, he had a nice stash and his protégés were natural earners.

Cadillac had said Flight was that niggah, and he proved right. Moe had become Flight's right-hand man, and they were getting it. They were up to a whole brick and building. Caddy signaled to his soldiers from the booth where he was sitting. They gave pounds and got in line.

"So what's up, partner?" Cadillac asked Moe and Flight.

"Gettin' this fuckin' money, niggah." Moe grabbed his pocket then sat down.

"So I guess I'm straight, huh!" Caddy said.

"And you know that, daddy," Flight said.

"Why the fuck you keep gettin' locked up for, Moe?" Caddy asked.

"Bullshit, man. Nothing really," Moe answered non-chalantly, with a slight smile.

Cadillac stopped eating. "Check this. You been locked up two times and walked right out. You get locked up again, better make sure they keep you. Gettin' locked ain't a laughin' matter. Y'all niggahs gettin' paper, gots niggahs on y'all dicks. Time to get out the park and get your own shit. Concentrate on this paper. Let them other niggahs battle in the projects, that rough paper."

"How we supposed to get a crib with no job and we only seventeen?" Moe asked.

"For real," Flight added.

"You got money, don't you? A'ight, bring them broke muthafuckas you givin' money away to. Tell yo' aunties and cousins that borrow shit to get a spot in they name and pay them five hundred dollars or something. To a workin'-ass niggah, five hundred is like five thousand G's."

"Niggahs say you fuckin' Precious now." Caddy stared at Flight directly.

Moe kept eating as if he heard nothing.

Flight stopped eating and looked up. "Naw, when she stop over your mom's, we talk," Flight said, clearing up whatever Caddy had heard. "She mad cool."

Truck had told Caddy that Flight was fucking Precious, but he had other young hoes on his dick. They both knew Flight and Moe were prime niggahs put out there to rep them, and they knew keeping Flight close was good in a way.

"A'ight, whatever. She the one y'all need to holla at. She know dude number. Talk to her."

"Bet," Flight said and kept eating.

"Moe, I know you got peoples who would get you something in a heartbeat," Caddy said, knowing Moe had four older sisters.

"Shit! My peoples get it in they name, they gonna move in that bitch."

Everybody laughed.

"For real, though, I could live with my sister Candice. She ain't got no kids. She goin' to Norfolk State and she been fuckin' with the same niggah for about five years. Some niggah from out the Beach. He cool. Hustle out Atlantis Apartments and The Palms. Laid-back niggah. You'll never know he get down."

"That's them Beach niggahs. Clean-cut, lookin' cool as hell, like they always ready to holla at some hoes, but I can say that I've met some that be gettin' it," Caddy said.

"Like them Lake Edward niggahs," Flight said.

"For real," Moe said.

"Fuck y'all know about Lake Edward?" Caddy asked.

"My pops from Lake Edward, son," Flight said. "Me and moms stayed with him until I was nine. That was the late eighties, early nineties. Lake Edward was off the hook. But, see, my moms from the Park, so we always came out there. So I know heads out there. I hadn't seen them niggahs in years until I started ballin' in tournaments and got a whip to get around."

"I thought you lived out the park forever, son?" Caddy said.

"Niggah, you wasn't ever home. I remember you and Truck wildin' out, y'all family wildin' out, but your sister was always quiet. Then we moved out there for good. You and Truck stayed locked up."

"Why you stop goin' out there?" Moe asked.

"Long story."

"We ain't in no rush," Caddy said.

"My pops and his brothers were tied up in some drug shit. Muthafuckas came up in the crib, tryin' to rob the place. Cut moms up, hung me in the closet by my neck with my feet barely touching the ground, just so I could breathe. They did some treacherous shit behind them thinkin' my dad had some money in the house. Find out they had the wrong house. They say between my dad and uncles they had like twelve houses.

"After that bullshit happened, my moms left and never let me go over there again. She started smokin' and shit. It fucked her up. My pops fucked her up." Flight stared into space.

"Pops ain't never come check for you?" Caddy asked.

"Naw, soon after they had a big bust, they were all on the run. Then a few years back, my moms told me they were back, doin' the same shit. She told me to stay away from them because she didn't want me getting caught up in that lifestyle."

They chuckled. He was already in knee-deep.

"So your pops on like that?" Caddy said, hype.

"Naw, he got killed on a motorcycle."

"Hold up. They call your uncle *Black*? And that other niggah his brother, *Lo*."

"Naw, everybody thought Lo was his brother, but he was they cousin," Flight corrected. "They say my great-grandma raised them all like brothers."

"Yo' peoples is notorious, son," Moe said. "I know about Lake Edward because that's all my sister boyfriend talked about years ago when he first started comin' around. He used to score quarters and halfs, and he used to go out Lake Edward."

"Fuck them. I done robbed all them niggahs," Caddy said.

"Naw. Y'all robbed Northridge niggahs, not Lake Edward niggahs."

Caddy took in what Flight said and realized this niggah had been around some shit all his life. This shit wasn't new to him. He was bred for this shit. Caddy was going to pimp this niggah hard and keep him close.

Moe looked at Caddy and then his boy Flight. Now he knew why Flight was so calm about this hustling shit. If he was around it since he was ten, he'd caught some of that shit. And if he was connected out Lake Edward, then he might just have a plan, especially the way he let Caddy know he'd robbed some other niggahs and not Lake Edward. Moe could see Caddy was getting on Flight's nerves, but he knew Flight wasn't gonna try him, at least not right now.

Moe decided to go with the flow, knowing what the bottom line was. Truck had put them together, and they'd become mad tight from holding each other down every day. With Flight by his side he got money.

They all stood up and walked out of the restaurant. Flight and Moe jumped in the whip and headed back to the Park.

Things were quiet until Flight put in Jay-Z's *Blueprint* CD.

"Put in that 50 shit, son," Moe said.

"Fuck 50, niggah. I'm tryin' to think. Jigga help you survive on the street. These other niggahs help your ass get locked the fuck up, like you do."

"Hear that niggah threaten me, fam?"

"Yeah. When a niggah keep fuckin' with the police, you heat everybody up. Niggahs ain't tryin' to get locked because of the next niggah stupidity, straight up. Your brother doin' enough time for all of us. When my niggah Herb be home?"

"Next year, if he don't get in no shit."

They hit Campostella Road.

Moe could tell something was eating at Flight. "What's the deal, man?"

"Truck and Caddy front us a half a brick for twelve, five. I could easily sell two big eights for thirty-five hundred each. You could too, but all we see is fifteen hundred to split. We have no choice but to break it down further, touch more hands, take more chances, because these niggahs tryin' to pimp us."

"If you kill him, everybody out the Park against you, because they feedin' niggahs. And this little money beats nothing."

"During the basketball tournament out Lake Edward, you remember those niggahs I was talkin' to?"

"Yeah, with the Legend and Suburban?"

"Yeah, those are the niggahs I used to fuck with as kids and now they doin' it. I was just hollerin', but I can get them things for nineteen, twenty all day. We can put niggahs on, we doin' all the work anyway."

"I'm with you, dog. Just tell me the plan," Moe said, knowing Flight had a plan and he was down for the ride. "I'ma holla at my sister and Oz tonight, see if they want to go half on a spot. It's time for that."

Flight pulled in the park. "True. I'm going to find me a little one-bedroom, build this dough, and get something nice out the Beach. Get my moms some help, then move her in with me, away from all this bullshit."

Moe jumped out the whip. He looked back into Flight's eyes. "Whatever you decide, I'm with you. I'm with you 'til we bouncin' our kids." He shut the door.

Flight smiled. All Moe wanted to do was get money, play PlayStation, and rap. He didn't even sweat a lot of bitches because he was usually actin' up. But that was their environment, because when they chilled alone outside Norfolk, he was laid-back and quiet. But the .380 that remained in his waist at all times let him know that this niggah, just like all "Tidewater" niggahs who played these streets, was "trained to go."

As he pulled off, reality slipped back in. He still worked for Truck and Caddy, barely pocketing two grand a week, putting in work all hours of the day and night. For now he was going to work hard and show Caddy they needed to do better by him, and see where it went. He really wanted to give them the benefit of the doubt, but Caddy straight up threatened Moe earlier. That wasn't good. He felt as if Moe worked for him and Caddy had no right to say shit to him.

Something in his head kept saying, "Be patient. You'll get your time to shine."

Chapter 14

The bright light shining through the window of the 10th floor suite woke me as it hit my eyelids. I still couldn't believe I was free. I walked over to the window and stared out over Waterside. The view was unforgettable. I stood there enjoying the feeling of being free. I lit the Backwoods and took a long pull of the haze.

After I finished the Backwoods, I washed my face, brushed the teeth, and threw on the same shit from the night before.

I strolled downstairs to the restaurant, knowing I was going to fuck this buffet up.

I sat down with a plate full and began eating when a young lady strolled up to the line. Her black pants suit, white button-down shirt, and heels let me know she was about business. Her nails were short and manicured to perfection, eyebrows arched, and she had light-brown streaks in her dark, shoulder-length hair.

As she headed back to her table, I noticed a beautiful princess cut ring on her right hand. I found myself staring at her dark skin, bright eyes, beautiful lips, and when I spoke and she smiled, showing the most beautiful set of teeth.

"Please join me," I said, standing up before I knew it. I had never hollered at a woman. The most mature was my son's mother, and that was years ago.

"No, thank you." She smiled. "I'm okay."

"Are you here with someone?" I asked.

"No. Actually, I have a seminar I'm going to and I have to do a short presentation here this morning, but I do appreciate the offer."

As she began to walk away, I touched her arm. "My name is Prince. I came here last night because I had mad shit on my mind. I woke up feeling much better. As soon as I saw you, my day brightened, for real. Please, just a few minutes of your time. What's your name?" I asked, pulling her to my table.

She sat down, and we began talking. Her name was Anita. Found out she was from Norfolk and had graduated from Lake Taylor. Received her bachelor's from NC Central and finishing her master's in August from Virginia Eastern Medical School. Then she would pursue her PhD. She worked full-time and didn't have time for anything else.

We ate, and she went to her seminar. She was scheduled to speak at eleven-thirty.

I went back upstairs to shower and change. I threw on my new faded light-blue Coogi jeans, with a crisp new white Coogi shirt with the light-blue print, set off with the new crispy white DCs, with a light blue stripe.

On the way out, I peeped inside the conference hall. She was just going up to do the presentation. I walked inside and stood by the door. She looked at me, and I gave her the thumbs-up. She proceeded as if I gave her confidence and every so often I got a glance and I nodded okay. It wasn't for me to know what the fuck she was talking about; that was for the people there. I was there to let her know she was rocking the crowd.

When she finished, I stepped out.

She came out moments later. "Thank you," she said with a smile.

"I didn't know what the hell you were talking about, but you had the crowd's attention, and looked good doing it."

She blushed. "You crazy."

"Well, I know you have to get back to your colleagues, but I'd like to know how everything turned out, and hear about your day later." I smiled.

She knew I wasn't giving up that easy. She stared into my eyes. "You got a girl, Prince?"

"No."

She gave me her number.

I programmed it in my phone under Anita Wm. 26 (twenty-six-year-old woman). I pressed *send* and listened to her answering machine.

She was staring like, *I know he not checkin' to see if it's the right number*.

"Hello, Anita, this is Prince. Been thinkin' about you since I saw you this morning. Call me when you get in." I left my number. "One!"

"Have a good day," I said to her and broke out, leaving the ball in her court.

The valet brought my 350Z around the front. I tipped him five dollars and in minutes I was on 44, headed to the oceanfront to fulfill my commitment to Brada. I had to go face Tee Tee. I knew for all these months she'd been beating herself up with what-ifs. And if that was the case, it would explain her weight loss that Brada spoke about.

Inside I regretted taking dude's life, and if I had it to do again, I would probably stay in the house and just whip her ass. But I can't change what happened, and I faced that shit a long time ago. *Fuck that niggah.*

I picked up the phone. Anita was dwelling in my head. I wanted a smart, beautiful, intelligent woman, but I wasn't that intelligent niggah. I didn't have all that book shit, but you put me anywhere in the U.S. and I'll figure out how to get money and survive. I knew the street, shit. But I could tell shorty was aiming for more. This bitch had to understand a niggah like me. She said she was from Berkley. Goddamn, that was considered one of the worst areas in Norfolk. Can this educated bitch from the projects still understand a niggah like me? Has she been fucking with those books so long she forgot how to hold a niggah down? A real niggah who run these hard VA streets? I wanted her, but I couldn't change. I can act like I got some sense sometimes, but I can't change. Casual gear to me was DCs, sweats, and a white Tee. Dress up was Timbs, jeans, and a new white Tee.

My mind raced as I tried to think of somebody from Berkley or Lake Taylor that could give me some info to see if this girl was really worth my effort. *Damn!* I began to think real hard, then it hit me, my half-sister's first cousin. I called my sister and got my half-sister's number, to get her cousin Bam's number. Bam knew mad bitches. He was from Berkley, graduated from Lake Taylor and was twenty-four, so he had to know her.

"Bam!" I yelled into his cell.

"Who is this?"

"Prince, son."

"Who?"

I hadn't spoken to dude in years, but how many niggahs was named Prince in Tidewater? "Cookie brother, from Lake Edward."

"What up, niggah? Man, it's been a second," he yelled, realizing who he was talking to.

"Telling me. What you got poppin' these days?"

"You know me. Front me mine, I'll have yo' money on time."

"You know my motto," I said seriously. "Buy a key for twenty-three and we'll see. Get your weight up, niggah." We shared a laugh.

"Peep this, son, Anita Bailey, she from Berkley, went to Lake Taylor." I heard them say her last name in the seminar.

I heard Bam talking to somebody. "Oh, that's her. I never knew her real name," he said, talking to whomever.

"Yo, P, bitch name Dumpling," he said, laughing.

"What?"

"Naw, when she was younger, she was short and fat. One Halloween for some school shit she was a ghost. Niggahs said she looked like a dumpling. So everybody started calling her that. She was always quiet, got along with everybody. By the time we got to high school, she was bad as hell. Know who used to fuck her?" he asked.

That's the shit I'm calling for. "Who dat?"

"Sheik."

"Who Sheik didn't fuck?" I said.

I never knew him, but I seen him around. He was a well-known older hustler in Tidewater. Grew up out Oceanview. He was six-foot-two, slim build, light-green eyes, and long wavy, dark brown hair that he wore in a ponytail. Never had a thug reputation, but ran with a crew that was known to. With his pretty looks, once he got dough, and the 320 black Benz back in '96, it was over.

"He ain't fuckin' nobody now. Niggahs probably hittin' his pretty ass. After the judge handed him those fifteen years," Bam said. "Yo, but on the real, niggahs say he treated her nice. Let her push the whip and all that. She cut him off after bitches kept trying to fight her and shit. She was low-key after that, into the books. And then one day I saw her standing in front talking to R.I.P. After that dude was over there every day, she was still with him." He paused. "So what up, Prince?"

"Naw, she was at a seminar and said she was from Berkley. Thought you knew her." I was done and ready to hang up.

"A'ight, baby. Hit me when you get your weight up."

"Holla," he said.

He didn't find that funny.

"Mister R.I.P.," I thought out loud. I knew Ronelle. Papers said he was the hardest-hitting linebacker to ever come out of Hampton Roads. He had gone to Penn State and then got drafted to the NFL. This niggah was a beast on the field. Was she still with him? She had a ring on her finger, but it was on her right hand.

Shit, I liked her and I got money, but I ain't had NFL money.

The thirty-minute trip to the oceanfront had seemed short. The traffic stopped as I approached Pacific Avenue. There were tourists out the ass, muthafuckas comin' from miles and miles.

My phone rang. "Where you at, son?"

"Right here, partner, makin' a right on Atlantic."

"Pull up to the top parking lot. We'll open the door."

The strip was packed as I inched down Atlantic Avenue. I was getting mad looks. First, I thought it was because I took my shirt off and was only rocking the wife-beater. The tattoos were screaming at bitches, as my arm hung out the window. The chest and arms had gained a little definition from push-ups in the cell, but I realized they were on the 350Z, not the sweet-ass niggah pushing that bitch.

I pulled into the Boardwalk and pulled up and around and parked. I grabbed my shirt off the seat.

Just then, the door to the hotel swung open, and she stepped out looking cute as ever in her white and baby blue Baby Phat gear.

I stared in her brown eyes as she approached me.

She was beautiful, smooth pecan brown skin, small lips, small nose, and high cheek bones. Her coal-black wavy hair was pushed to the back.

I took her in my arms and hugged her.

She squeezed me tight and stood motionless.

I closed my eyes and inhaled, pulling her as close as I could. She felt good. The five foot cutie who'd lost all the weight I put on her from the late-night dinners and sweet shit was looking like perfection.

I gave her sister a hug and my man a pound, then we headed upstairs. They knew we needed to talk, so they went their way while we went to our room to catch up.

I walked in and realized why I loved VA. The view of the Atlantic was like no other. I kicked off my shoes, and threw my shit in the chair and walked out looking down at the thousands of people running around on the beach. The water had no ending. I enjoyed the slight breeze that made its way through the ninety-six degree weather.

"I had so much I was going to say. Now I really don't know what to say or how to say it. And I know you don't want to hear a whole bunch of shit."

And usually she would be right, but I had actually prepared myself to listen to her shit. We walked back inside the ice-cold room.

I sat at the table and she handed me the ashtray with a Backwoods already rolled. I lit the Back.

"That crazy shit you put me through was uncalled for," she started out. "Even after you gave me the green light to do what I wanted, I had the choice and the right, but I never did. I haven't fucked with nobody since we first went out through the years and especially for the last few months. I've realized I don't want, or have, the desire for anyone but you. You my man, and I love you like crazy. I can't picture my life without you." Her eyes teared up. "I've always been true to you and don't want it no other way. I just want to love you."

I was pulling on the Backwoods hard, taking in everything she was saying. I was feeling her, but I knew I wanted other things. These streets had me, and nothing was going to pull me out of them right now. I had to run. I had to be able to make moves, but I needed a girl I could trust, a woman I could depend on and love who would love me back.

"Look at me, Prince," she held my face and stood directly in front of me. "I love you. I want to be here for you and only you. All I ask is that you play fair and respect me. All that other shit is done and in the past, never to come out my mouth again."

I stared into her deep brown eyes. I was feeling her and her every word.

"Sorry for not believing in you. You've been there and I should have. That night is a blur, and I rather keep it like that. I will say and I promise, if you love me, I'll love you back." She smiled and leaned into my arms.

We kissed, and my lips ran down her neck. I ran my hands across her ass and pulled her closer with a firm grip. The softness of her ass had my dick hard, and the fact that she had no panty lines allowing the thong to disappear into her ass had me about to go wild.

I pushed her top up and removed it, untied her shorts,

and let them fall. I stood up and stared at this new and beautiful body. I undid my shorts and let them fall.

She removed my wife-beater and tossed it to the side. She began kissing my chest.

I undid her bra.

She reached into my boxers and grabbed my dick. That muthafucka was so hard, it was jumping. Niggahs know! That's when the gorilla came out.

I pushed her onto the bed and couldn't resist sucking those nipples, as I removed her thong. I snatched off my shorts and began working my dick in her tight, moist pussy.

Once I was in, I relaxed for about two minutes, just allowing those hot, wet walls to grip my dick. Then I began to move and stroke. The sounds her pussy made as my dick hit her wetness made me turn into a fuckin' animal. I fucked until sweat dripped from my face and chest onto her.

When I came again, we collapsed on the soaked sheets, our sweaty bodies entwined, gripping each other like no tomorrow.

We dozed off into a nice sleep, until the reaction of her soft ass touching my dick woke him up. I slid back into her from the back as she lifted her leg slightly. For about fifteen minutes I laid there and slowly stroked in and out until I came again.

She got up and started the water for the Jacuzzi that was in the room. Moments later she returned. We got in the Jacuzzi and she handed me a rolled Back. It was about six p.m., the sun was going down, and the beach was quieting. She came and joined me in the Jacuzzi.

We were friends again. She was mine again. Girl can't be mine if I ain't fuckin'. She mine now. She caught me up on shit that was popping in the street. She had been chilling, but her girls Vonia and Fee damn sure kept her up with their business and everybody else's. After about an hour, she got out and began gathering our things. Then she pulled out some black Pelle Pelle shorts and my black and white Kings jersey with some new black DCs she'd picked up. She laid out my boxers, socks, and a clean wife-beater. She'd always been like this. I was just running too much to realize what I had.

I got out the Jacuzzi and headed to the bathroom. New toothbrush and everything. By eight, we were in the room chilling, smoking, and ready for whatever.

The phone rang.

"What the hell you want?" she asked.

"Time to eat."

"Ashante said it's time to eat." Tee Tee looked at me.

"For real, I'm starving," I said.

"Brada said come over here and hit some of this good green before we go downstairs," Tee Tee said, relaying Ashante's message.

We get over to their room and kick it for a minute while finishing his Optimo. We decided on Friday's off Lynnhaven. Me and Tee jumped in the 350Z and pulled downstairs. Brada came around the corner and hollered, "Follow me," from the new two-door Lexus convertible. That shit was sweet, and it moved like that. He was driving that bitch.

We all ate, talked, drank, then raced up the shore back to the hotel.

We ended up in their room. Me and Brada stood on the balcony as he dropped his plan. He didn't care too much for Kendu's brother-in-law, so some things had to happen. Not my business. He was ready to deal straight with me and offer me a lovely price. That was the plan. I was gonna wait on him, because he had to handle brother-in-law. Whatever, I knew Kendu was with the money.

Me and Tee Tee returned to our room, not to our tub, but to our bed and our weed. I was straight for the night.

I tried to open my eyes once being awakened by the sounds of the waves splashing on the shore. I reached down to pull the sheet up. Leaving the door open to the patio was a good idea last night, but the morning breeze off the ocean made me rethink my decision. I forced my eyes open, only to fight with the brightness from the sun beaming high over the Atlantic.

I sat up and looked over at Tee Tee. Boy, it felt good waking up to the view of a woman. I leaned over and hugged her, then reached past her and got the half-smoked Backwoods. I lit it, and she woke up.

"Weedhead," I said. "Flick of a lighter is just like an alarm clock."

She smiled, got up, and straightened up the room, then headed to the shower. I didn't even give her a chance to turn it off before I jumped in.

We were getting dressed when she asked what I was going to do. She looked at me and held out the new key to our old place.

"Naw, I don't want to come back there."

She had a look like she was lost for words.

"Look, Tee Tee, go to Ashbrook Apartments and fill out an application for those new three-bedroom town-houses with the garage on Bonney Road. Give them a deposit and tell them you want the key today. If you go this morning, we'll have an answer today. Like now."

She got the picture.

We walked down, and I saw her new Grand Jeep Cherokee. "That's what I need," I said.

"Really?" she asked.

"Yeah, I got to move some shit."

She bust into a big smile as I handed her the keys to the 350Z.

"Call '2 Men and a Truck.' Tell them to move your shit to the new spot in the morning."

"Okay," she said smiling. "Where am I supposed to get the deposit, month's rent, and moving money?"

"Same muthafuckin' place you got money for this new truck." I pulled off.

I left and went by Zaria's. She wasn't home, so I gathered all my shit, money, safes, clothes, and loaded it in the truck. I was feeling fucked-up because it wasn't only about us, but also my son. As I drove to the spot and unloaded everything, I thought, *another family fucked*.

It was about four when Tee Tee called with our new address and keys. I met her over there so we could view the place and trade cars. *Give me my shit*.

For the next couple of weeks, I gave Tee Tee her time. We fixed up our spot, and spent mad hours and money in Super Wal-Mart. I was still doing a lot of running, trying to maintain shit. I was holding Chris down quite a bit, because of his out-of-town trips with his agent Corey.

My other quest those days was Anita and how she had me going. This woman was exciting and being around her put me on my toes. We'd had many conversations over the phone and several lunch dates, but she had never allowed us to be in a closed, cuddly environment. It was always an open atmosphere, out in public. My life was in order. I just didn't know exactly what I wanted, but I was happy.

Watching Brit tear hisself down every day was starting to get to me. Brit was getting fucked up every day now, not handling shit like he usually did up at the shop. He was going through something, I could guess, but I wanted him to come at me.

Anita had a break between four and seven, so I planned to meet her for dinner. I called Brit to join us. We met at Applebee's off the boulevard.

Dinner was great. Brit was impressed with the lady I was trying to pull into my world.

She had to get to class, so I walked her out after she said goodbye to Brit.

"Glad your brother could join us. He's real cool."

"Thanks," I said laughing.

"I'm serious, Prince, he is." She stopped laughing. "Prince, I want to see you later," she said with her head down.

"Okay. Where we gonna meet?"

"My house," she said.

"Call me when you get home. I'll be waiting." I leaned over and kissed her as I opened her car door.

She smiled that beautiful smile that fucked with my emotions. I realized at that point, *I don't give a fuck how old a woman is, you treat her with respect and be sweet, she'll break after a while. They all will.* I watched as she pulled off.

I jetted back in to find Brit on his third Hennessy straight, no chaser. Sometimes niggahs be havin' a good time and just exercise the option to get fucked up, but this wasn't Brit's character.

"So what's up, bro? What's going on?" I asked, slightly out of breath.

"Not a whole lot, man. Dealing with life."

"And? We've been doin' that forever."

"Naw, man, this shit fuckin' me up. Leah keep having unaccounted-for time. Supposed to be out with Daria. Daria get home at ten, she lost 'til two-thirty. Supposed to be at work, get missing for two, three hours with some bullshit excuse. This been goin' on for a sec, and I been dealing with it. But the other night she came home like two o'clock in the morning, left my daughter over her moms'. When she stepped back in the house I tried to tear that bitch head off."

"You ain't hit her, did you?" I was hurting because my

brother was hurting and it was nothing I could do for him. I knew what that pain could cause a man to do—make a mistake he'll spend a lifetime regretting.

"Man, I hit that bitch and took her off her feet. It was dark and I had all the lights out. She ain't know what was going on until she was laying on the floor with her mouth fucked up."

"So what happened?" I asked, knowing it was more.

"She called the police. I got locked but got out on my own recognizance."

"You gots to chill, son, go to the spot and chill out. Gather your thoughts. I know you don't want to hear this, but if she want to fuck somebody else, you can't stop her."

"That's my wife, *P*, my fuckin' wife." He downed the rest of his Hennessy.

I sat there sympathizing, trying to relate to his pain.

We sat and talked for a while longer, then broke back to the shop.

After making sure things were straight, I had to break out to meet Chris and Kendu at the duplex. We hadn't had a chance to chill out and really catch up on shit.

We were doing some things when my phone rang. *Anita Wm* appeared on the caller ID. "Hello, babe," I answered.

"Hey, Prince."

"Hey, Anita. You know I was waiting on your call."

"Were you?" she asked seductively.

"Yes, for sure. I have much to discuss with you."

"So why am I still here alone?"

"Tell me something."

"I live off Haygood Road. Cross Independence and the brick town homes that sit on the right. 3662 Colony Point Circle."

"See you in about a half."

* * *

When I pulled up to the section of brick town homes, I was impressed. I entered through her garage where she kept a 2001 Jaguar. Her house was about a quarter of a million.

I came in and sat down. She had scented candles burning, watching cartoons. I hated cartoons but went with the flow.

Before now, our conversation was day-to-day life and all about her, but tonight as she sipped the wine, she began to open up and let me into her world. By eleven she was relaxing in my arms as we laughed to an episode of *Good Times*. By 12:15 we sat looking at Midnight Love, and she began to let her guard down and allow the lovely woman to come out. She began talking, letting me know she only had three men in her lifetime. The first guy was a friend of her brother's and she felt he cared and they dated for a year. Then an older guy came along and strung her out like a lost girl, making her into something she wasn't. So that ended.

As she explained her most recent boyfriend, she was hesitant, talked slow and quiet, told me of her involvement since her junior year in high school. After graduation she went to NC Central, and he went to Penn State. He flew her to PA at least once a month. After getting accepted in the pros, she was by his side day in and day out. He even bought her a ring and had her set a day. She'd spent over thirty grand for her dream wedding, bought their house, a Jag, and a truck.

Three days before the wedding, he flew in, met her at the house, made love to her like he'd missed her tremendously, stood up, put on his clothes and told her he'd changed his mind about marrying her. She could keep the ring, the Jag, the house, and the forty grand they shared in their new bank account.

I sat there thinking, *this niggah left you good.*

But it meant nothing to her. She was hurt and humiliated. She said, "Fuck niggahs," she was going to concentrate on school and getting Anita together.

I looked at the sadness in her eyes and decided to take
my chance.

"I want to hold you. I'm tired. It's been a long day. I
want to climb in your bed and go to sleep. My word is
bond, love. I wouldn't start off lying. I'm trying to build
trust."

She agreed. We went upstairs and laid across her bed.

My phone began to vibrate. I ignored it. Then again
and again. It was my sister. Brit was down at Princess
Anne locked up, and Leah was at Virginia Beach General. I told her a piece of the story and broke out. She was
ready too, I thought.

I reached the jail to see about his bond, but it was a no-
go.

Evidently he'd rode by his house and this bitch had
Dropp over there. She thought a restraining order was
going to keep him away.

Story I caught was, he kicked in the door and started
flipping. After going to blows with Dropp, he ran and
pulled the burner.

Dropp burst out the door when he had the chance, not
wanting things to go too far, but the two shots that kept
ringing in his ear let him realize it was already there.

Brit took the gun and beat Leah unconscious after slic-
ing her face with a box cutter from her neck, straight
across her bottom lip. Doctors said he barely missed a
artery that would've caused certain death.

I couldn't see Brit. They didn't even want to give this
niggah a bond. I thought, *there's no way out of this. Not to
mention her peoples weren't going to take this well.*

Chapter 15

It would be two weeks before his arraignment. Even then, they tried to hold his ass and almost succeeded. The judge set his shit at a hundred grand and promised that if he went near Leah, he'd put his ass away personally.

I was standing outside talking to Keith McNair, the bondsman that worked with the honorable Frank Bo. We call him the "honorable" Frank Bo because he'd bailed out more niggahs in Tidewater than you could ever imagine. Mothers knew the name, whether they used him or not.

I'd finished signing the papers with Keith and was kicking it about being a bondsman. It seemed like a lucrative business.

Brit came out, and Keith took the time to run down his "don't-get-lost" speech.

We were making our way down the long two-lane Princess Anne Road.

We hadn't said a word, when we saw a brother walking on the narrow street, barely out of the way of passing cars.

"That muthafucka just got out too." I laughed. "Scoop his ass?"

"Yeah. See where he goin'."

We pulled up on him.

"Need a ride, partner?" Brit asked as dude reached for the door to get in.

We knew he wanted to get the fuck out of Princess Anne. Ain't nothing out there but court, jail, and white folks.

" 'Preciate that," dude said.

"No problem, man," Brit said. "I understand."

We laughed.

"Been in that bitch for six months on some child support shit," he said.

I looked at dude with his new Timbs, jeans, and white Tee. If he had dough to get those Timbs, he should have put something in the mail. "Need to handle that, son," I said. "That's some bullshit."

"Yeah, a niggah just can't get the fuck up," he said seriously. "Got to pay two seventy-five a month. I be out here scramblin'. Stay with a shorty out Bridal Creek. That shit ain't free and money ain't flowing. I need a job. Anything."

"Workin' give you dough to put toward some work. Gots to get that weight up. Can't go to a niggah beggin'," I said.

"You right, man, for real."

I could see him looking at me from the back. Ballers know ballers. He could see I was real, young, and getting it. I had Tee Tee's Jeep. She had the 350Z and was loving it. That shit was old to me. It wasn't all that. Fuck that bullshit-ass car. Naw! After Brit shit and three tickets in two weeks, for real, I say, *fuck that car!*

We were coming up on Lynnhaven, and I knew Bridal Creek projects was off Lynnhaven in the Rosemont area, and I wasn't going that way. "I'm going straight up. Where you want to get out?" I asked the want-to-be baller who couldn't pay two seventy-five a month to be free. *Damn!*

"Naw, I'm goin' to Witchduck. My brother got a spot out Northridge. He at work, but his girl should be home. I hope." He laughed.

"Bet. We goin' to Newtown," Brit said, letting me know we were going to LE and not the shop.

I saw dude's eyebrows go up. He knew. I knew he knew.

He had to ask just to confirm. "Y'all from out Lake Edward?"

"Yeah." Brit smirked and glanced at me.

It was something about being from LE. It was the only beach projects that were known all over Hampton Roads, and it really wasn't projects. It was row houses and apartments that became notorious in the late eighties, early nineties, because it was so close to the Chesapeake Bay Bridge. New Yorkers moved in and flooded it with drugs and dealers. It was an easy export to supply cats all over the Hampton Roads. It got a notorious reputation because it produced some of the biggest hustlers in Tidewater and still carried a reputation today. Maybe because today you had hustlers of every kind coming from the large LE complex.

Kendu was from New York. He used to say, "Uptown niggahs were known for getting money and hustling Brooklyn niggahs were known for robbin' cats. Queens niggahs were known for putting the murder game down, and I guess LE became the melting pot for all these type of niggahs."

"I know some heads out there," he said. He started throwing names around, "Yeah, man—Text, Hop, LA,

Hannibal, Black Jewel, Guttah," not knowing whether it could boost him or hurt him.

For Brit, if he say the wrong name, it might get him done up.

"You fuck with that music shit?" I asked, knowing that all the heads he named call themselves "Goodfellas," and they fuck with that music shit. They were smalltime hustling cats. Maybe two out the clique was making money, and carrying all them niggahs with weed money.

We dropped him off in Northridge and broke out to LE.

"So what's up, man? I know you don't want to hear this, but you need to let her go. Things happen, feelings change. But please, stay away from her," I said.

"I'm done with her, son." He stared at me. "But you need to handle getting her out of my house so I can go home. Bitch had the nerve to change my locks. That's why I had to kick that shit in."

"A'ight, I'll take care of that shit. Just chill."

I dropped him at my moms' and headed that way. I had to go by and talk with Leah. I cared for her because I felt she was a good girl, but that was my house and I allowed Brit to live there.

I pulled up in front of the house. Damn! Black Q45, green Tahoe, cream Cadillac. *Her cousins, Dropp, and whoever the hell else.*

My phone rang. *Restricted number.* I started not to answer, but decided to with all the bad shit goin' on these days. "Who the fuck is this callin' my shit restricted?"

"Me, son," must be Corey shit. "I'm on my way to the airport, son. Just got the call."

"For real, baby? Hell yeah!" I screamed. I was so hype, like *I* was going to sign a contract.

"Yo, Prince, we did it, man. All this time in the street,

all the struggles, we made it, man," Chris said. "Come on and go, Prince. I got you, man. You know how we do."

I could hear that he wanted some support. "Yo, Chris, go handle that paperwork. That's what you and Corey goin' to do now?" I asked.

"Yeah, I'll be in Cali, son. I won't be back 'til after the season."

"Where you goin'? LA?"

"Naw, Oakland. I'll call you, man, and give you the final details."

"I know you got lawyers, agents, and all that shit, but use your head, niggah. Use your head. Keep it straight and handle your business. I got shit to hold down here."

"Yo, man, be safe, Prince, and take care of my peoples. I got you, man," Chris said and hung up.

I sat there feeling happy for my boy. He was out of this game and on his way to a much larger world.

By now Dropp and a couple of her peoples were out front like they came to greet me.

"What the fuck you doin' here?" Tabby asked.

I could see why she was upset. Tabby was Leah's sister, and April their chubby-ass freakish cousin.

"Don't answer. Just turn around and carry yo' ass, because she ain't got shit to say to you *or* your punk-ass brother."

One of the niggahs standing in the driveway said, "You do need to burst, son. She don't wanna talk, and we don't want shit to pop off."

"If I was worried, I wouldn't have come. But y'all muthafuckas know me." I looked on, letting them know I ain't never scared.

"That shit was fucked up, son," Pete said. He was one of her friends that fucked with Dropp. "You know your brother gots to pay for that shit."

My eye shot over at the niggah. I had to get a perfect picture, so I would never forget his face. I'd never seen him, but his face was embedded in my mind.

I saw Leah peeking.

"Fuck all that shit y'all talkin'. I need to talk to Leah." I walked up to the front door.

Goof, one of her guy cousins, jumped out the Sequoia with a Heineken in his hand. "You didn't hear my peoples, son?"

Goof had never been locked up and wasn't known for starting trouble, but at two twenty-five and six feet of solid muscle, he wouldn't hesitate to fuck a niggah up, including me. He was into that karate shit.

"Check this. I didn't come around here for all this. But I'm glad y'all are here because she gonna need y'all help to move her shit, because this is my house and she got to go. I guess she gonna move in with one of y'all. I guess she goin' home with Dropp since he love her like that." I rang the bell. "Somebody need to find a truck because I got the sheriff coming. Her and her shit need somewhere to go."

Leah opened the door. All her peoples were looking at Dropp. They knew without him, none of this shit would've happened.

I looked at Leah. There was no trace of her beating, but she still wore the scar on her bottom cheek.

She looked at me with a "what-you-want" attitude. "Why are you here? Your brother and I are done, and his black ass is going to jail," she said, standing strong. "So don't come in here with that I'm-sorry shit for him."

I stood looking around. I could tell other muthafuckas was staying there.

Tabby and April walked in, followed by Goof.

"Fuck him," April said. "Don't listen to shit he sayin', Leah."

"I wish he get the fuck out," Tabby added.

"Tell him to leave, Leah. If he don't, I bet Goof put his ass out."

"Leave, Prince, now. Get out," Leah said.

"You heard her, kid," Goof said.

"Look, Leah, you know this is my house. I let y'all live here. My name is on this deed. If I leave right now, I'm going in the front yard to call the police and sheriff to arrest y'all for trespassin'." I pointed to her cousins and Goof. "And the sheriff will sit your shit on the curb." I pointed at Leah.

They all shut the fuck up, mouths dropped just staring.

"What you want?" Leah said with a different attitude.

"Same thing—my house—and for allowing me to talk I'll give you 'til five tomorrow instead of today." I smirked. "Y'all Brit problems, not mine."

"That's fucked, Prince, for real," Leah said teary-eyed.

"Naw." I opened the door and looked out. "I told your new man and his boys to stick around because I was putting you out and you needed some help, and those niggahs gone. That's fucked up, ain't it, Goof?" I closed the door and headed to my whip.

Chapter 16

Flight walked into his grandmother's house. The sight of it made him sick. His grandmother tried her best to keep the house clean, but with auntie's kids running wild and his uncles and moms smoking shit upstairs, it was impossible.

He walked over and kissed his grandmother. "Hey, Ma."

"I told you about those streets, DeAndre, I told you," she said from the heart, as if she might cry.

"I ain't messin' with the streets, Ma. I be hearin' you."

"No, you don't. I ain't no fool. You 'posed to be the man comin' up in the Park. I'm old, but I ain't crazy and I ain't deaf. Don't get me put out DeAndre. I'm old and rather go on to glory than be put out in the streets."

"A'ight, Ma," he said running upstairs. He pushed open the door to see his moms, uncle, and his uncle's friend sitting in the filthy room, wide-eyed as if nobody knew what was going on.

He looked at his mom in disgust. She sat there in a jean skirt that was too big and a T-shirt with no bra, her titties jiggling with her every movement.

"Let me holla," he said going to the other room. He looked back at his mom coming his way. He couldn't help but remember when she was every niggah's dream. She was skinny now but still shapely. Comparing the size three now to the used-to-be nine with the tight waist, she looked sick to those who'd known her for years.

"What the fuck you want, boy?" she asked, trying to keep her eyes to the floor.

"I'm getting ready to make some changes." He looked into his mother's eyes with shame and hurt. He gave her twenty dollars and told her, "Enjoy your last blast on me. I'm coming back tomorrow, and we gonna get you checked in somewhere. When you come out, I'll have us a new place, Chele."

He hated seeing his moms like this, but she was caught up, and he didn't see no way out.

"Okay, boy. I hear you," she said taking the twenty.

"Chele, where's my grandma?" he asked, not looking at her.

"Downstairs sitting on the couch."

"Naw, my dad's mom."

Her head snapped up. She stared at him. "Why?"

"I want to holla at my peoples."

Chele stood as if she was thinking of how much he resembled his father, except for the height, which came from her side. "I still forbid you to fuck with them," she said walking out the door.

He grabbed her arm. "You don't forbid shit no more. You ain't did shit but make me suffer since you left him. Now I'm knee-deep in this street shit and you gonna leave me out here alone when I gots peoples. I'm trying to give you some hope. Chele, other niggahs dogged you out. I'm your son. Let me bring us up and you never have to depend on another niggah again. Fuck how we livin'."

"She in Atlanta, that's all I know. And with that, you still don't know shit."

"So my uncle and them ain't connected here no more?"

"Last I heard," she said slow as if he was stupid or as if she only wanted to say it once. "Your Uncle June, dead. Your dad dead, Boot dead, Lo and Black, whatever his name is, from what I heard, he don't even call himself Black no more. After your dad's funeral they all moved to Atlanta. I don't want this for you, DeAndre."

"You ain't give me nothing to work with. I got to get it how I can. What else I got?"

She stared into her son's eyes. "You got your dad's features, but your uncle's ways. Black was hard, serious, but easy-going, as long as you gave respect. Your daddy was a sorry son-of-a-bitch. All he had on his mind was bitches. Niggah kept a ho in the cut—two, three hoes." She gave a half-smile. "I don't know what to say about him. For real, I don't know how to get in touch with your peoples, but if anybody can, try Brit. He from out Lake Edward. Him and your uncle was boys, real road dogs. He own a detailing shop out the Beach. That's all I know."

"Like brothers, huh?"

"Naw, Black and Dee had a brotherly love that I've yet to see," she said walking out.

Flight walked out hating his mom for keeping him from his family. All his life he'd heard different shit about his other half—how they acted, how they balled, how they lived, and what they did. It was everything that he wanted a part of, even when they tried to cut them down by saying the whole family dealt drugs.

He left knowing that this hustling shit was in his blood. He gripped his gun with the thought and jumped in his whip. Before he could pull out, he saw a pretty white Denali pull in the Park.

He was getting ready to back up, when the Yukon blocked him in.

He pulled the nine out and clicked it off safety. By the time the cats' feet hit the ground, he knew he had the drop on them.

"Calm down, baby," Truck said, coming around from the passenger side.

"Hope my man ain't got you livin' like that." Vic smiled. "Just like Truck. Quick to pull out your trouble." He laughed.

Flight didn't see the same humor in the situation. These niggahs been in the game long enough to know not to play like that. "Gots to be more careful." Flight threw the burner on his front seat. "What the deal?" he asked, giving Truck a pound and a hug. Then he gave Vic a pound.

He'd seen Vic a couple times with Truck. He was probably the niggah Truck and Caddy scored from. He knew Vic was getting it. That Denali didn't come cheap and those twenty-two-inch Oasis rims that were still spinning confirmed it.

"What it look like, son?" Truck asked.

"Same shit. Steady flow. I ain't mad."

"Heard that. Where you headed?"

"Pick up your sister. Got some things to take care of."

"Better take care of my little sister," Vic said, enforcing the fact that he was like family, not knowing Flight had known Precious for a long time. "Yo, kid, it's time to roll. I ain't with all this action going on around me." He climbed in the truck. "Fuck this corner shit."

"Yo, Truck, y'all got to start showin' me a little more love."

"What? I thought we were doing that."

"Man, I'm movin' mad weight now and my pockets keep gettin' missed."

"Let me holla at Caddy and do some math," Truck said, not believing him.

"A'ight, but check this, I don't know if your man was just talking or if he was trying to insult me, but if I ever see him or this truck out the park again, I'm gonna lay him down."

"Yo, this my man. He's not to be touched ever," Truck said. "Don't get that big."

"You heard me. I was gonna get him tonight, when he made that last comment, but I gave him a pass because I don't want you to have to make a choice between your man or your money. But you heard me."

Flight wasn't scared of them. The fear was gone. If he had something to say, it was going to be said, and if he wanted a niggah done, he was gonna be done.

He got in his whip, headed up Campostella Road, and hit the interstate headed to the Beach. He pulled into the LaQuinta Inn. He picked up the phone and called Precious.

"Hello."

"I got a room at the LaQuinta on Newtown. You on your way?"

"Yeah," she said.

"Hurry up. I'm waiting."

Flight was lying across the queen-sized bed looking at BET ComicView. It had been a long day. He sat wondering how his vision changed overnight. He had about twelve grand put away. He watched his money stack and was proud of himself, but being out Lake Edward and talking to cats he came up with, niggahs talked about buying phat whips, opening businesses, and investing in music and shit. Niggahs were getting money to get shit popping, and his little change left him out of conversation. But things were about to change. The knock at the door broke his thoughts of becoming VA's finest.

He opened the door to the most beautiful sight. Precious was looking like she was going to the club. It caught him off-guard. He'd known Precious since she was nine and had seen her at her worst. Now these last couple of years, she'd changed into a classy young lady.

He pulled her to him and hugged her. She felt good and smelled so refreshing.

She sat down and pulled out a Backwoods pack.

He watched her perfectly manicured hands. Even with the long nails she had no problems unraveling the cigar. He looked at the short skirt and allowed his eyes to travel down her golden brown legs to the yellow open-toed sandals to match the sleeveless yellow shirt tucked in her black skirt, showing off her tiny waist. Her outfit, the long, straight weave, and lightly applied makeup made her look every bit of twenty-one.

When she put the Back to her mouth to seal it, he realized the designs on her toes and nails matched, and when she licked the leaf, her tongue stuck out past the "oooh, baby" lip gloss, which gave him a hard-on that had to be satisfied.

He kept his composure as she handed the L to him to light. He hadn't smoked all day, and it was what he needed. It relaxed his body and slowed him down.

Instead of jumping her bones quickly and slamming this dick home, he pulled her to her feet and pulled up her skirt, bringing a bright yellow thong in full view. He turned her around, pulled the thong to the side and slowly hit her from the back real slow for about ten minutes, then real hard for two.

Ten minutes later she lay in his arms as he sent loud snores across the room. She looked at his 9mm on the nightstand. She leaned over him to turn off the light.

He grabbed her arm. "Fuck you doin'?"

"Turning off the light, Dee," she said. "I'm with you,

baby, believe me." She clicked the light and rubbed his hairless chest.

"It's just gonna take a minute. We'll get there," he said, squeezing her in his arms.

"I hope so." She smiled. "I really hope so."

"Oh yeah, find me a crib. See whoever and take care of that shit. Just let me know what I need. I can swing nine hundred a month."

"Okay." She squeezed him and closed her eyes. *Fuck that, wherever he goes, I go.* She grabbed his dick and stroked it. When it got hard, she pulled him on top of her.

He fucked her good and hard, looking down at her, and staring into her eyes. She was so beautiful, with her hair laid out across the pillow, as thoughts of killing her brothers ran through his mind.

Chapter 17

It was Thursday night, the day before Brit's court date. We knew that he was going to do some time, but how long was the question. Everybody decided to go to Donzi's. Brit met us there. He hadn't planned on staying long. He had some for-sure ass to lay on before going away.

The club was packed, so we ended up parking farther down, past the hotel. Me and Kendu walked up to the front. A line formed down the sidewalk.

As we strolled slowly past the line, I saw mad niggahs showing love. I don't give a fuck, if you gettin' it, niggahs and bitches know.

"This line long as shit, son," Kendu said.

"I don't fuck with lines," I said.

Brit came up, followed by BayBay, Lou, and Wil, in Wil's new Navigator. They valet parked. They showed love getting out the truck. Then I saw the shadows escape from a cream 745. It was the kid from the group the Clipse and their manager. This kid was well known also.

Soon they had an entourage of niggahs, about fifteen deep, trying to shine.

We stood about eight deep, trying to hold our own shine.

Girls crowded around trying to get in where they fit in. A Hummer pulled up, followed by a new Range Rover. Some kid named Plaxico jumped out with five cats following him. I heard this kid was from the Beach and had gone to the NFL and was paid lovely. The bass that shook the club was from the Black H2 Hummer sitting on twenty-four's. It was followed by two S600 Benzes and a CL500, all wearing VA tags, except for the two hundred and seventy grand Bentley GT that wore GA tags.

Everybody watched Iverson jump from the Hummer that someone else was chauffeuring. But even as they approached the sidewalk ten deep, ice blinging and money showing, all eyes were on the Bentley and the short, dark figure that stepped from the driver's side with his back turned. The passenger side door opened, and out stepped a slim-ass niggah with dreads. He was dark-skinned with eyes fiery-red from the Henny. The diamonds that glittered from his neck and wrist let niggahs know he was one of those niggahs.

The driver paid valet and turned to the crowd. All eyes were on him. Then Big El hit the LE call and these niggahs broke a smile. Every entourage that stood on the sidewalk may have been world known, but everybody knew somebody who knew Black. And he had just touched down.

He stepped up and hugged Big El tightly as if they were brothers. Then he hugged Brit real tight, saying many words that were never spoken. He looked at me, and I stared into his eyes through the tinted Cartier's.

He reached out, and the gleam from the watch and

pinky ring was killing me. Our hands met, and he snatched me to him.

I was ready because I knew Black, him, Brit, and many others had spent mad days fucking me up and fucking up each other. They taught me everything.

I was staring into the eyes of that LE legend, and he was like my brother. I had personally watched this niggah go from selling half a gram, to selling over five thousand grams in one pluck.

He hugged me. "Thought you were watching Brit," he said in my ear real low, not letting me go.

"I been tryin', man. You know him."

"Yeah, you know him too. He not built for prison, but he'll be alright." He pushed me back, looking in my eyes. "He'll be a'ight."

I smiled because I was hearing him, but a message was there that I couldn't get. By now those ballplaying niggahs and music niggahs was giving him love one by one. He had stole all the shine and he was with us, LE niggahs. Because security didn't know him, our clique was still last.

But niggahs knew the club was a banger, and everybody left fucked up. The bar was bought out, to no one's surprise. It was a night to remember. Niggahs came out and began disappearing to their cars with girls.

Me and Kendu were walking and joking with four shorties when he stopped and went into a deep stare across the street. His smile was gone. He was in a trance.

"Come on, Kendu," one girl said.

"Better check on your friend," another said.

I walked back. "What's up, man?" I looked in the direction he was staring.

"The grey Intrepid," he said with no emotion. He turned and broke into a brisk walk.

I noticed one guy sitting in the car. He was talking to a girl and the other standing in the door leaned back as the girl hugged him. Around them stood five more guys talking and joking with the girls passing by.

When my eyes finally focused, I realized it was Truck and Caddy. A knot came in my stomach, and my leg began to jump. I knew it was getting ready to go down as I saw Kendu coming up from where his car was parked.

"Yo, baby, not tonight, not now," I said, coming up on Kendu.

"Back up, *P*. The keys in the car," he said as he crossed the street.

I ran to the car and pulled out onto the street, but traffic was stopped. I pulled my .380, put it in my waist, and jumped out running to where Truck and Caddy were parked.

Just as the full picture came into view, I saw Kendu raise his gun and pump two into the back of Caddy's head. He never saw it coming as Truck jumped up, knocking the girl into the parked car.

Kendu shot her, trying to get Truck. Truck was hit four times in the side and back. Kendu turned and broke into a strong sprint between the office buildings.

I ran back to the car and drove slowly by the scene. Caddy dead, girl dead, Truck laid out motionless, but they hadn't pulled the sheet over his head. I guess he was still breathing. I rode around trying to see if I saw Kendu.

Police were everywhere, so I went home.

Tee Tee was still up when I walked in. "Heard the club was off the hook," she said. "My girl called me. I started to come out."

"Glad you didn't. Niggahs wildin' out," I said, trying to call Brit.

There was no answer. I called the house. Still no answer.

I lay down to catch some sleep. I knew Brit had to be in court by ten. I was gonna catch him there.

Chapter 18

Flight was in the gambling spot with Moe when his phone began ringing. He ignored it. It rang again. It was a "623" number. It was downtown and he knew it. He wasn't doin' no business tonight. He was going home to Precious, so fuck it.

It rang again.

"What?"

"It's me. I'm at Norfolk General," she said between hysterical sighs.

A nurse took the phone.

"What's wrong?" he yelled.

"Sir, you need to get to Norfolk General Emergency."

Him and Moe hit Monticello, leaving Young's Park. They shot up Brambleton to Norfolk General. He ran inside, scared that something had happened to his girl, but mad that he knew it was something her simple-ass brothers did.

He walked in and saw Precious, her moms, some more of their peoples, and Vic.

"They killed my brother!" Precious yelled, falling into Flight's arms.

He wrapped his arms around her. He looked confused.

"Caddy dead and Truck shot up," her mom said, tears rolling.

After a while the doctor came out and said Truck was paralyzed from a bullet lodged in his spine. To remove it would cause him to lose feeling and control from his neck down. Right now he had use of his arms, but he wasn't out of danger yet.

They all left except Precious, Flight, and Vic. Vic later decided to leave, so he hugged Precious and told her to call him. He held his hand out and gave Flight a tight grip, and hugged him.

"He gonna be all right," Vic said. "It's gonna be all right. They owed me nine off the last package. I know you owe them twelve. Pay me mine. Your price is eighteen, and I'll front you just like I did them. Business don't stop. You the man now. I'll call you, I got your number," he said real low.

He gripped Flight's hand tightly and broke out, just like that.

Muthafuckas just didn't give a fuck. It was business as usual, death and tragedy being part of the game.

Chapter 19

I arrived at the courts at nine-thirty. Moms was worried because she hadn't heard from Brit. We sat in the courtroom waiting for him to enter as they called his name. We listened as the judge issued a *capias* for his arrest. My mother leaned over and fell into my sister's arms and cried.

Leah finally sat opposite us. Even though she'd done her dirt, she still loved Brit. Her mother held her as she cried uncontrollably. She had fucked up a good marriage and a good life for her and her child, all for being weak and falling into the traps of Dropp. She threw everything away for a nothing-ass fuck. She'd been played. It had to be eating her ass up inside.

We all exited the courtroom in silence, everyone wondering where Brit was, including me. I never figured him to run, but then it hit me. I remembered Black's words, "He will be a'ight. He's a'ight."

Goddamn, Black! My eyes watered. I knew my brother was gone. He was really gone.

I stepped fast out of the courtroom and waited for my mom and sister. I had gotten myself together, and now my mind had switched to Kendu. I knew Brit was with Black somewhere down South or wherever Black sent him. All I knew was he was alright. Me and Black both knew he wasn't built for prison.

I hugged my sister as she wiped her tears.

My mom came and took my hands as we walked to the car. "He shouldn't of ran," she said. "He gonna be runnin' forever now. I did the best I could, and he do this to me. You just got out of all that mess, and now here he go worryin' me. Sometimes I wish the Lord would just take me away from all this. I'm tired, boy." She stared at me as I opened her door and she got in.

I couldn't even look her in the face. I didn't mean to worry her, and neither did Brit, but we'd made choices as men and had to live with the consequences.

I walked Tabby around the car to the driver side.

She stopped and turned to me. "Don't have me sitting around here worried to death about Brit. I am not Momma. I know how y'all do, so don't have me sitting around here fucked up." Tears slowly dripped down her face. "Tell me, is he a'ight?"

I took a deep breath. "Yeah, he alright."

"Assure me. Help me sleep better," she said directly, no tears, just a serious, stern look.

"I saw Black last night."

Her eyes opened wide, and her eyebrows went up. She knew Black just like Brit. She watched them grow from kids playing in the yard, to hustling in the alley, to having kids. She knew Black.

"He told me Brit was gonna be alright. He gone and Brit gone. Assume the best." I hugged her.

She smiled a slight smile.

"Tell Momma try not to worry. I got to go."

"Be safe, Prince. For real, be safe," she said climbing in the car. "You all I got."

"Call me," Moms yelled as they pulled off.

Two days had passed, and I hadn't heard from Kendu. His picture was on TV and in the paper. I realized life was crazy. Here I was at the duplex. Kendu had left some work, and a paper with two names and numbers. These were the numbers for his main worker and Chris' main worker. They were two cats I'd met, so I was willing to fit them into my organization. *Fuck them other niggahs.*

I wasn't that pressed for the money, and I didn't know them like that. I sat wondering where life was going. The closest people to me were gone.

I wanted my peoples to call. I really wanted Brit to call, just to hear his voice, but I knew he couldn't take the chance. And if he ran, we'd be cut off for a while.

I pulled out my Backwoods pack sitting at the table and removed both bags from the pack, and a cigar. Dumping the tobacco on the table, I laid out the leaf, broke down some of that official, and put it in the leaf. I got a piece of haze from the other bag and put that in the leaf too.

I had an idea. I ran in my room and pinched some coke off a pack and sprinkled it on the weed and rolled it tight. I lit it and took a strong pull. It gave off a foul odor that I wasn't used to, but the more I smoked, the more my spirit began to lift. I closed my eyes and pulled harder. It was all I could do not to cry. I had never been here, and I had never been without Brit.

The ring of my phone brought me back. *Unknown caller.*

I never answered these calls, but with my peoples missing in action, I pressed *send.* "Fuck is this callin' my shit unknown?" I answered.

"Chill, son," Chris said calmly. "Everybody stressed."

"You ain't here, niggah. This shit is bad in VA," I said with attitude. "You out in Oakland livin' the nice life, niggah. All this street shit behind you now. Don't call here talkin' about chill, and you don't even know what the fuck goin' on. You stressed over a jump shot, we stressed over life, niggah. Fuck you talkin'." I pulled on the Mega-mix Backwoods as things were silent on the phone for a minute.

"I met A.I., son. He was here the other week for a big party Shaq had. Once introduced and he found out I was from Norfolk, he opened up and began schooling me. We talked for about half an hour on some serious shit. And two things he told me."

"What?"

"One, he said people are going to think you changed. And people are gonna be mad and envious of you, and they are going to pre-judge you, not realizing that you never changed, just the way they look at you now has. And secondly, he said, don't argue, don't worry, but in time, your family and true friends will see the light, and that's all that matters. So I understand your ignorance and stupidity, and I'm giving you a pass."

"I hear you," I said, letting him know that I didn't give a fuck about him or A.I.

"I heard about your brother, and you know that's small. Niggahs run all the time. You learned most of the shit you know from Brit, and ain't you the niggah always hollerin' you from LE, and LE niggahs can survive and get money anywhere? Brit ain't only from LE, but he help make LE what it is."

I smirked, and a slight smile came on my face. *I do say all that shit.*

"And how did you know about Brit?"

"Not important, but I know you need to put some

work into that shop. Change it from a hangout, and make that shit produce. The studio, barbershop, and detailing shop, don't let it go. Legitimate businesses, that's where we goin', dog. Gotcha back, man," he said seriously.

I was hearing him now.

"Secondly, I need you to take fifteen grand to Robinson down on Freemason."

"Attorney Robinson?" I asked. This was the top black attorney in VA.

"I already spoke with him, and he gonna meet us at 811 tomorrow evening. Tell your cousin to meet us too, in case they give Kendu a bond."

I knew 811 was the Municipal Center downtown, 811 City Hall Avenue. "He with you?"

"Yeah, take care of that today, ASAP, and we'll see you tomorrow, man. A'ight?"

"Yeah, got you," I said. I wanted to apologize, but the words wouldn't come out.

"Yo, Prince, we gonna be straight, man. Promise you."

"See you tomorrow, Duke. One!"

I finished the "L", gathered up fifteen G's, and headed downtown. I entered the building that reminded me of a two-story old house with twelve rooms that were set up like offices. I was pointed upstairs to Robinson's office, where I counted out fifteen G's and received a receipt for $9,500.

I stared at the older grey-haired gentleman dressed in a dark grey two-thousand dollar suit, looking like John Gotti on trial.

His response was, "Chris will explain tomorrow."

"Mr. Robinson, answer this, is my man going to jail, or can he walk?"

"If he do, it won't be for long, and yes, he can walk. I

just got some work to do. I'll do my best, and usually my best is enough," he said with confidence.

I shook my head in agreement and exited his office.

He patted me on my back as I left out. "Do you go to church, young man?"

"Yea, FDCC on 26th Street," I answered.

"They say once you pray about something and it's in God's hands, you should stop worrying, or you don't believe or don't have faith. I'm like God. Once you retain me, stop worrying. It's my problem now, and I ain't worried." He smiled.

I jumped in the 350Z and headed up Brambleton headed back to the Beach.

My phone rang. It was my son's mother.

"We need to talk."

"What?"

"No, in person. We need to discuss some things."

"What the fuck you want?" I said aggravated.

She was real smart, but now she was doing her own thing. I realized she was lacking common sense, and it was wearing me down.

"Okay, I'm pregnant. I'm trying to build a life with Corey. So we need to tie up all our ends. He say he lives right and don't need no repercussions from your life. He's a graduate from Virginia Tech. He's an electrical engineer, works for a major company, with benefits for me and my kids," she said.

I was sitting there wondering why she was blowing this niggah up, like I gave a fuck. She had me fucked up when she said she was pregnant. I never pictured that or suspected it. "What in the fuck do I care! Do you!" I said and hung up.

She called back. "Don't be so nasty. Why you got an attitude?"

"Fuck all that. State your business."

"I need child support documented on paper. I need to sell this house and get another one. Then you need to set up visitation."

"This niggah is really in your head, goofball-ass nig-gah. Now you gettin' ready to have a goofball-ass baby. Whatever! Sell the house and we split shit. Anything else, take it to court, so we can have it documented, as you say." I hung up. All the shit I was going through and she hits me with this.

I arrived at the shop to the same shit. Niggahs work-ing, niggahs gambling, and some just hanging around. I walked into the barbershop area. I told the barbers that we had a mandatory meeting at closing. They looked at me as if I was crazy, except for Jamil.

Jamil was from Pittsburgh. He'd been around a while, and shining wasn't his style. He hustled hard, and Nor-folk streets welcomed him. He cut hair from nine to six every day and still found time to play ball and move a big eight a week.

I walked in the back to tell Javonne about the meeting. I walked upstairs to the studio, rolled up some haze, and sat back in one of the three booths. I tried to realize how this entire thing could be run easily.

My phone rang. It was Anita. We talked, and every-thing in my world seemed to ease as our private conver-sation unfolded. "Girl, you had me on the phone for an hour and twenty minutes."

"You're easy to talk to, Prince."

"That's good to know. Now what up?"

"What you mean?"

"What's the deal for tonight? I got a meeting, then it's me and you. Here, there, where?"

"It's up to you."

"So come up here, then we'll go to Beach Hot Tops, sit in the Jacuzzi for an hour, and sip on some wine."

"Make it Grey Goose and cranberry and we'll see."

"See you in a minute."

I hung up and called Dundee. He was downstairs chilling. I instantly jumped up feeling good about my cousin's presence. I walked downstairs to see four of the hottest bitches I'd seen in a minute, along with Jamil, Javonne, Dundee and El just kicking it.

"What the deal, fam?" I said to Dun and El. We showed love by pounds and hugs.

El directed my attention to the red bitch with the long weave, big titties, and mad sex appeal. "This Chele," he said. Then he introduced the petite light-brown, half-black something. "And this is Joss."

She was fine, just too small for my time and dick.

"That's Queenie over there talking to Lecia. Lecia the one sitting down," Joss said.

Queenie was brown-skinned, short cut, phat ass, small waist and breasts. Her shit was tight.

My eyes gazed from Queenie's ass to Lecia's eyes. How this black-ass girl got these light eyes? I couldn't take my eyes off her. Her hair was wrapped, falling on her chest, and a little cleavage showed from the white top that strapped around her neck and exposed her back. It stopped at a small waist, but her hips looked slightly wide in the black jeans and black sandals that showed her pedicured toes.

One glance showed her nails were nicely manicured, but desperately in need of a filing.

She never broke eye contact. "I'm bad with names. You are?"

"Lecia," she said, showing her pretty white teeth through those glossy lips.

"How are you, Lecia?"

"Fine. How are you?" she asked.

Before I could answer, El said, "That's my peoples, Prince."

The knock at the door broke my stare-down with Lecia.

I opened the door and hugged Anita. Her linen pants, and top, open-toed sandals, along with the well-manicured hair, nails, and toes—looking as if she had gotten them done earlier that day—had her on point. It let bitches know what my criteria were.

"Yo, I need to have a meeting. Need to clear this," I said to Dundee and El, never introducing Anita. These folks weren't important. "El, carry these hoes to the truck. I'll be out in a minute."

I walked out with El and the four girls, telling Anita she could have a seat. "Dundee, open the back garage to let me pull my shit in." I jumped in the 350 and pulled up the top.

"See you soon," Queenie said to me. "Real soon, I hope."

I then directed my attention to Lecia. Her stomach was flat, and her chest was bigger than I thought. Her ass was phat. Wide, but up and out. She had me going. Can't explain, but I almost wrecked the 350. "I'll see you later, I promise," I said. I had to have her.

I pulled in the back and put the 350 in the detail shop and locked her in. "Where them hoes from, Dun?" I asked, getting out the whip.

"I met shorty the other night. Queenie her sister, Joss they cousin, and Lecia they buddy. She twenty-two, don't got shit, stay with her peoples," Dundee said. "But the black bitch is fine, and that's her hair and eyes."

"Give me a second. I'm catching up, so go do something. Keep them hoes out."

"Bet."

We walked inside, and I informed everyone that Jamil was now the manager of the entire shop. Javonne would run the detail shop and would report to Jamil. I was going to find somebody to hold down the studio, but until then, they would sign in and pay by the hour. No more hanging out. Either you work or you're payin' for a service. Meeting was adjourned. Tomorrow was going to be a new day.

In ten minutes all lights were out, and we were headed out the door.

Nobody ever asked about Brit. These days people knew if somebody wanted you to know something, they'd tell you.

"Yo, cuz, I got some cats that can hold down the studio," Dundee said. "Let them record they shit, and they'll engineer shit for everybody and get you money. I see what you doin'. Fuck hangin' out. It's money time."

"For real." I gave him a pound.

"I'ma bring these cats through tomorrow so you can meet them."

"Set it up early. Busy day tomorrow."

"Who these niggahs anyway?"

"Streetfellas."

"Who? Guttah and Hannibal."

"Naw. Guttah, Lights, and Ashy."

"A'ight. Early," I said, getting in Anita's car.

We drove across the street to Hot Tubs, rented a room by the hour, and sat in the Jacuzzi. Going was a surprise, and her getting naked wasn't even open for conversation. She got in with her hot pink panties and bra.

I got naked. I saw the stare when my dick swung against my thighs as I climbed in the hot water.

She laughed when I grabbed it as it hit the water.

I eased down, relaxed, and we sat in silence for a

while. I closed my eyes and was in deep thought about how I would fuck Lecia, until I was interrupted by the warmth of Anita's lips touching mine.

I reached out and held her. My hands began to wander, but she stopped me and let me know she was there to be held and talked to.

We chilled for an hour then got a bite to eat, and I quickly said my goodnight.

The following morning I was awakened by the ring of the phone. It was Chris. They were on their way to 811. He was making sure I had called my cousin Keith to bond Kendu out.

I was in the lobby talking to Keith when Robinson and Chris came through the doors from the magistrate office.

"Half a million, with no proof," Chris said.

"This shit ain't no joke," Robinson said. "He got five charges: murder, attempted murder, brandishing a firearm, endangering lives, and possessing a gun, which is an automatic five years."

"You need to get me another ten grand to my office for me to continue. This is going to be a lot of work." He shook Chris' hand and mine and headed for the door after a few words with Keith.

"Can you handle this?" Chris asked Keith.

"Yeah, five hundred thousand bond. I'll need fifty thousand."

"Take a check?" Chris asked.

"Not usually, but I know who you are. Congratulations," Keith said, knowing Chris had just signed a nice contract with the NBA.

Chris stroked the check and allowed me to bond out Kendu. He looked at me and smiled. I smiled. My boy was stroking fifty-thousand-dollar checks like it wasn't shit.

We finished filling out the paperwork, and Keith went to go get Kendu, giving me and Chris a chance to talk.

"Got dough like that, son?" I asked.

"They only givin' me a little change this first year, but what nobody know about is the seven-million dollar signing bonus on the low." Chris smiled. "Corey is a blessing to the hood, son. The niggah is for real, showing the world that mad talent rest on these Tidewater streets."

"Seven million." I shook my head. My boy had made it. This street shit was a thing of the past for him.

Kendu came walking out with a big-ass smile. He was out on bond. He showed us love and gave Chris an extra-tight squeeze. They walked over and had some words with the lawyer.

Moments later we walked out front, where Chris still had a car waiting.

"What's up, son? I got you. My whip across the street," I said.

"Going back to Cali, Prince. Missin' today's practice gonna kill me. I'm out now. Keep this niggah out of trouble. Here y'all go." He handed me and Kendu a check.

Kendu looked at the check and smiled a grin I'd never seen.

I looked at mine. I had the same wide grin.

"Kendu, stay away from the game and streets. Prince, don't let him fuck around. We don't need that street money. Kendu, if you beat this shit, you know you've been blessed and you need to chill. That's enough to buy a nice whip, get a condo, chill, stay in, and fuck bitches. Stay out the streets. I got you, my niggah. We've held each other down for too long. Prince, I know you got shit to pull together. Be safe, my niggah, be safe. I ain't trying to lose none of y'all niggahs. I love y'all cats," he said smiling, knowing cats like us don't talk like that.

But it was love between brothers.

He broke out, and me and Kendu headed for the Quest.

We rode in silence to the spot, so he could gather his thoughts. Once inside the duplex, I put two dubs of haze in a Backwoods and sparked.

"So what the deal, killah?" I passed the Back.

"You wild, son," he said humble.

"Niggah, stop playin' soft. You did those fuck-ups and didn't think twice."

"Prince, I feel good. Fuck them niggahs. I'm rich, bitch!"

We laughed.

"Got to find me a spot to chill. I gots to stay on the low for a minute."

"For sure. But you know and I know there's no way in the world you can chill with a quarter of a million in the bank."

"I know, son. I want to get the whip and shine hard, knowin' the man can't fuck with me."

"Move to the other side. Denbeigh. Half an hour away. Fuck around in Hampton and Newport News. You need to be coolin', anyway."

"True."

"I'ma find some shit over there too. I need a change."

"How many houses you got, Prince?"

"Six. Three townhouses, two condos, and that house I was lettin' Brit stay in."

"What about the house with wifey?"

"We were gonna sell it, but I might just buy her ass out now and rent it out too."

"You been fuckin' with that real estate shit on the low for a minute."

"Fuckin' with that niggah, Dee. You know my brother Black? Well, he had a brother name Dee, God bless the dead. Black was the hustler, his brother, the businessman. Niggah used to say buy good jewelry the real shit, you rock it, and if you ever get down, sell that shit and get back up. Real estate. Niggah say buy up everything because this shit gonna go through the roof. He never said when, but I know his peoples got mad shit."

"Right. Do your thing, son. All my mind on is beatin' this shit and I'm out. Find me a six-month lease with somebody. I ain't from here no way," Kendu said bluntly.

"Right, but I am, my niggah, and I ain't goin' nowhere. I'll visit niggahs, but I'm gonna do my thing. Right here born in VA, sling in VA, probably gonna die right here in VA." I gave him a pound. "You a'ight, man?" I asked seriously.

"Naw, but I'm gonna be, believe that." He pulled hard on the Backwoods and stared into space.

Chapter 20

Flight followed Precious into the house. She was moving slow, eyes red and puffy from crying. He wrapped his arm around her shoulder and guided her into the place they called home. She went and sat down. Flight went over and poured her a cranberry and Grey Goose. He walked over and handed her the drink. He then twisted the top to the forty he'd pulled from the refrigerator.

"You gonna be all right, baby?"

"Yeah, without my brothers I just don't feel safe. It's just hard to feel safe."

"But I'm here, Precious. I'll never let anything happen to you."

"I know you will try, but will you love me unconditionally? My brothers loved me and would give their life for me. Now Caddy gone and all Russ can do is bob his head. He all fucked up," she screamed out, crying again.

He walked out over the table and pulled the brick out that Vic had given him right after the funeral at the church. He broke it down and weighed it out. *Thirty-six ounces. This niggah on point.*

There was a knock at the door.

"Get that. Should be Moe," Flight said, knowing none of her peoples or his, except for Moe, knew where they lived.

Moe hugged Precious. "Shit gonna be a'ight."

"Thank you," she said softly.

"Don't hug my baby no more. We might have to walk behind *your* ass," Flight said.

"Shit!"

"That shit ain't funny," Precious said.

"You talk to Herb, niggah?"

"Naw. He lost his privileges again."

"That niggah be fuckin' up," Flight said.

"Naw. He was standing up for his. Herb just can't walk away."

"He'll learn, or they'll teach him," Flight added.

"Actually, last time he called, he said he'd changed his life to Christ. He said he'll be home in a couple months and he was gonna live a completely different life."

"I feel him. I need God, church, something. I feel like I'm about to lose my mind." Precious sipped on her "crangoose."

"Niggahs always get religious when they locked the fuck up," Flight said.

"I talked to him. He seem for real, but you know Herb, religious or street, he ain't nobody to try," Moe said.

Flight went to the room and changed his clothes, kissed Precious, and burst. Him and Moe were pulling in the Park thirty minutes later with a brick of hard, ready for distribution. He gave nine ounces to two of the young'uns out the park, who him and Moe decided were next to take their place. Then they gave nine to two cats from Diggs Park across the street.

Flight gave four and a half to some young'un from Broadlawn that he carried across the bridge.

Then he had Money, thanks to Moe. This was Moe's partner that he'd met through his brother, Herb. Money would buy the rest of the hard. Thirteen and a half ounces gone and looking for more, Money was a selling niggah. Everybody knew him as loud and friendly, but they knew he was prepared for jail and would never tell. His grand-pops was fifty-eight and still hustling weed and liquor. Old head had three bootleg houses. His pops, thirty-eight, and uncles, thirty-five, and thirty, were in and out of prison. They all sold drugs and vowed that was all they were going to do. Money fell in the same boat. He was prepared mentally to do time and come back pre-pared to go back. But as long as they were free and on the street, they were going to get it.

They stood outside by the big oak tree that sat in the middle of Oakley Park. Niggahs began coming up one by one, rolling Dutches, Optimos, flavored blunts, until Flight sent somebody on a 7-Eleven run. The Vietnam vet and respected fiend returned with eight forty-ounces and Flight's change.

Flight took his change. He looked at one of the young'uns who hit the old head off with a little some-thing.

"Look at that niggah," Moe said to Flight.

"Yeah, sad, but fuck him. I'm getting this money now." He smiled at Moe.

Time after time they kept looking at Truck. His mom had sat him in the doorway in his wheelchair, allowing him to view the land that he used to terrorize with a black hand. Now he watched with a dark stare. He tried to make his body move, but he had no control, as he thought about Caddy's death and wished the same for himself.

Chapter 21

Three months had passed, and things were going well. Me and Tee Tee were doing fine. She was giving her all, loving me, being there for me, trying to be the woman I could love, cherish, and one day marry. We had something strong, but I kept feeling that it was going to end. No matter how many times we made love, or how many times I held her and tried to give her all my heart, something kept holding me.

My mind was also filled with the fact that Zaria had me in court, and I'd been down to Princess Anne's Juvenile and Domestic courts three times. They ordered me to pay four hundred and thirty dollars a month. Because she'd taken me, I refused to pay.

By the third time the judge made me empty my pockets. Told me if I didn't have the three months and the month that was now due, I was going straight to jail for six months or until it got paid. This shit had gotten critical.

I handed one thousand seven hundred and twenty dollars to the clerk.

Zaria left out and I followed.

She said to me, "You need to just pay this shit on time before you get locked up, you got it?"

"That's what you about? Fuckin' niggahs, having another baby, so you can get the next niggah, huh?" I yelled out in front of strangers. "Triflin'-ass bitch, all you doin' is fuckin' for dough. You's a nasty, triflin', stankin', ignorant-ass bitch." I shitted on her as if she was the next bitch and not the mother of my son, the same bitch that I once loved, the same woman that had stood by me for four years of my life, and who my world revolved around. Now here I was wishing death on her ass.

She yelled back and stormed off, looking beautiful, sexy, and dressed to perfection, her hair waving in the air. She had that "I-want-to-kill-your-ass" look on her face that I'd seen a thousand times, but today I didn't give a fuck.

A week later I was at the shop and two Virginia Beach police cars rolled up. They came inside, cuffed me, and threw me in the back of the police car. Zaria told them that I'd threatened her and some more shit. I got locked and tried to bond out on my own recognizance, but the half-ounce of haze in my pocket with a fresh pack of Backwoods made my bond five grand.

Luckily my cousin Keith had given me a bondsman he'd attended Norfolk State with that worked the Beach, J.P. Paige. I called J.P. and was out in four hours. But the hassle of being booked, fingerprinted, and placed in a holding cell until I saw a magistrate was fucked up. I knew now never to cuss her ass out again and to pay the little four hundred and thirty dollars. Even though I had no reason to hate her, or she me, we stopped talking. I stopped all communication with her and my son. The sight of her made me sick.

On the other hand, the time I spent with Anita was genuine. She was everything I wanted in a woman, and she could hold her own. We went out to expensive restaurants, we walked along the beach in the brisk air arm in arm, and sat up late looking at movies until she would fall asleep in my arms.

Some nights I would watch her put together events promoting her work. It was a complete turn-on that a woman could go into a world of her own and make things happen. I saw intelligence, strength, power, and confidence.

Something in her eyes kept pulling me in, but she kept slowing me down. So many nights I could feel our bodies connecting. I knew she wanted me, but she wasn't giving in.

"Slow down, Prince," she would say. "Let's not go too fast."

Damn! It's been two months, I thought, but I didn't press the issue. I guess I would have, if I wasn't getting pussy, but I was still chillin' with Tee Tee on a regular, going home to her most nights.

Then I had helped Lecia rent a spot for $625. I gave the security deposit and rent, then took her to Grand Furniture and let her pick out a bedroom set, comfortable living room set, and dining set, all for two grand. I gave them five hundred down, one-twenty a month, which she could handle.

She worked as a shampoo girl for a stylist who had major clientele. So three hundred for a five-day week, tax-free, gave her enough to hold her shit together. She didn't have a man because everybody wanted to lock her down, but as much as I ran, I never had time to sweat her and she had time to do whatever she wanted. I made myself available when she did call, and what started as a friend thing had elevated to her staying in, cutting off her crew, and blowing my phone up all night if I didn't respond.

I knew she was young and would wild out if she got upset, but I couldn't stay the fuck from over her house. Didn't hurt that I also had a key.

Every time I went by, she had on something different, something sexy that she chose to place on that banging body. And the head was "straight monster." She let me fuck her however the hell I wanted, hard as I wanted, long as I wanted, and she'd come right back at me. This kept me at her spot quite a bit. A few movies and a couple of times out to eat made her feel she was my girl. I never said anything different, as long as my key worked.

Being with Anita was different. She made me talk, made me open up to her. She didn't knock my hustle, especially after I shared my dreams with her. Instead of her just saying, "Yeah," and looking at the dough, she showed me how to research and find the shit I needed to really get my shit done. But it was more than just her help and the way she assisted me. It was her softness . . . her look of innocence.

I stared into her eyes, as if I was searching for something.

"You have a condom?" she asked.

"Yes," I said, reaching for it.

"Give it here." She undid my jeans, pulled out my dick, put the condom on, and began sucking it.

What the fuck! This beautiful, lively-ass woman was sucking my dick like she wanted me in her life forever. I leaned back and enjoyed her making love to me.

When she stopped, I took her in my arms, held her close, and fell asleep.

I was awakened to the breakfast cooking.

She'd made herself a scrapple and egg sandwich, and a bacon, egg, and cheese sandwich for me, telling me it was on the table with juice and that she was going to take a shower before heading out.

She came out the shower and went in her room.

I got my sandwich and walked to her door and opened it, just when she was letting the towel drop. "Please, if I can't hit, let me admire."

She laughed and continued as if I wasn't there. She lotioned down and walked over to her cherry wood chest and pulled out the bottom drawer. Next thing, she was pulling up the high-cut panties, then placing those breasts inside of the matching bra that fastened in the front. She sat down and pulled up her stockings carefully, not to snag them. Then she disappeared into her closet.

When I placed my eyes on her again, she was fully dressed in a beautiful skirt suit and blouse, with matching heels.

After playing with her hair for ten minutes, she was out the door. She threw her briefcase in the car, turned to me, kissed me, and was out.

As I headed to the spot in Norfolk to handle something before heading home, I reached for my phone to take it off silent. *Damn! I missed twenty-two calls and twelve messages.* I scrolled down. Lecia had blown up my shit as usual. Then I saw 395-8000, three times, then my baby-momma number twice. *Fuck her.*

I looked in my rearview mirror and saw the flashing lights. I looked at my speedometer. I was doing sixty-two in a forty-five-mile zone. My head was somewhere else.

I pulled over. Fifteen miles over. *He could carry me to jail.*

He walked up, asked for my license and registration. He walked back to his car.

After a few minutes, another patrol car pulled up, and another. I knew after they pulled up my name, the bullshit I'd been in when I was on the come-up and making a name for myself in the streets was going to haunt a nig-gah again. I had like twelve assault charges, and two were on police, not to mention the murder charge I'd just beat.

What they failed to realize was, I wasn't that young niggah not giving a fuck anymore. I was that father who was trying to build something.

I eased my hand in my pocket and pulled out the half-ounce of haze and put it under the seat.

Two officers walked up and handed me my registra-tion.

I tossed it on the seat.

"Will you turn off your car and step out, sir."

As I stepped out, they asked me to lock up my car, and I did just that.

"Did you know your license was suspended?"

"No, sir."

"Well, records show the DMV sent you a letter, but we need you to sign this, saying we notified you that your li-cense is suspended. This is not admission of guilt," the officer in charge said.

"Our computers show that there's a warrant out for your arrest. We don't know what it's for, but a judge in Virginia Beach issued a capias for your arrest. We're not going to have any problems, are we?"

"No, sir." I thought about how Zaria had me fucked up again.

They cuffed me and placed me in the back of that tight-ass car. They booked me when I got downtown, and I went in to see the magistrate for bond and release. Vir-ginia Beach said I was supposed to be locked up. The van going to the Beach was gone, and unless they could get in touch with someone to give them some other informa-tion, I was going to be locked up right there in Norfolk.

I immediately got on the phone, called my sister, and told her where I was and what was up. Told her to get in touch with Zaria and get those papers she got from child support saying all this shit was caught up. "No need to come down," I told her, "because they aren't letting me go until they get word from Virginia Beach."

Then I called Tee Tee.

"What the fuck you done got into? What bitch you done got in trouble behind now?"

"Shut the hell up. My shit on the side of the road, off Ballentine. Call Dundee or El and go get my shit before they tow it. After they drop you at my shit, come down here and get my personal shit. I got a feelin' I ain't comin' home until next week. Virginia Beach gonna close up and ain't shit gonna happen until I get in front of a judge Monday. Handle that shit. Love ya."

"I love you too. It'll be alright. You ain't shit, but I love you."

I hung up feeling good that I had somebody to call on and she could get shit handled. I loved and needed her more than I was willing to accept. That was it, no more calls.

I sat down and chilled until they came and got me. They made me strip down to my boxers and a T-shirt. They took me on upstairs to the 2nd floor and put me in 24B, where I remained in this unsanitary hole, along with forty other muthafuckas sleeping on two-inch foam and a bubble in the mat for a pillow. I had a raggedy-ass sheet for cover.

The night went well. Saturday went well. Talking to Tee Tee got me through.

Sunday was hell. I was straight on edge, ready to get the fuck out of this cage. I had talked with a few niggahs while playing cards, so everybody knew I repped LE.

Lake Edward was shitted on because it was mostly Norfolk families from the projects who'd moved there, since it was a step-up and still affordable.

Virginia Beach said we were on the border, and the way we acted we needed to be in Norfolk, so they ain't claim. Nobody ever had nothing good to say about Lake Edward niggahs, but they had to respect the Lakes and every niggah raised out that bitch.

Sunday's card games got intense, especially since they were hesitant about turning the TV on. I was playing with this one cat who said he was from all over, meaning he was from nowhere usually and he's nobody. The fussing started, and things escalated.

"I'm done," I said.

This niggah looked at me and told me I didn't know what the fuck I was saying.

I ignored him.

Then he said, "Niggahs know when to shut the fuck up and go." He had everyone's attention.

"Ain't a muthafucking niggah walk this earth can tell me what to say out of my goddamn mouth." I looked at him sternly.

"Fuck you, wannabe fake-ass niggah. You ain't shit," he said, backing from the table and flexing.

Soon as he opened his arms, I tore his head off followed by a three piece as he folded on the gate, scrambling and trying to grab me. I put his arm and neck together and began to squeeze. Deputies came running, and other cats broke it up.

We were both carried to medical. When shit was alright we were brought back down and written up for a loss of all privileges and some other shit.

I was so scared they were going to give me more time in Norfolk, but they moved me to another cell, where I stayed until Monday morning.

I got to Virginia Beach too late to get on the docket, so I spent another night down Princess Anne Jail in Virginia Beach.

Tuesday morning I went to court. My moms, sister, and Tee Tee were there. They had the papers to show the judge everything was paid.

The judge said, "Pay your child support on time, young man, and this type of mistake won't happen. You just spent four days in jail for nothing."

On my way home I had to stop at the Department of Motor Vehicles and find out why my shit was suspended. Child Support people had sent a flag to the DMV and suspended my shit. I had to go to the Child Support office and sign a paper for them to lift the flag. I paid eighty dollars for a reinstatement fee, ten dollars for some new license, and was back in the world, HATING MY BABY MOMMA!

I went to my house off Bonney Road. I came in and stripped. I hadn't showered in four days. I stayed in the shower 'til the hot water ran out and went through three washcloths.

I came out the shower, and Tee Tee had a Backwoods rolled with my haze. Her and Dundee knew if I didn't have a weed charge, then it was somewhere in the Quest. I smoked the Back and sat back looking at BET.

She went in and showered, came out, and stood in front of me naked.

I handed her the slow-burning Backwoods that she'd rolled, and told her to hit it like I was going to hit her. I guided her to the room and laid her back on the bed. I took my Backwoods and hit it hard three times before placing it in the ashtray.

I lifted her legs and stared down at that beautiful pussy all trimmed up and looking inviting. I buried my face in there and licked and sucked like I missed her. I fucked slow and hard, then hard and harder.

I didn't know if it was her or just some great pussy, but I was satisfied. I got up and went to the bathroom to take a two-minute shower and brush my teeth. "Where's my phone?" I yelled.

"Here," she said with an attitude. "You can have it now. I'm done with you."

"Shut the hell up. Don't make me go back. I just came home."

"You ain't crazy, for real," she said, knowing I was capable of some unreasonable shit.

I turned my phone on—same number of messages and missed calls. *I'll find out who number she got and who she called later.* I checked all messages, erasing Lecia shit even before she got started. Then I heard Zaria's voice real low. I couldn't make it out. *Fuck her.* I just went through all this shit because of her.

The next message was slightly clearer. "I need you, Prince. Virginia Beach General." I checked the time of the message and the call. She was calling from the hospital in the late night, early morning. She had me worried about my son.

I threw on some Girbaud jeans, a white Tee, white DC's, Breitling watch, platinum dog tags, kissed Tee Tee, opened the garage, and me and my 350 hit the streets headed to Zaria's house to see my son and tell her how she had fucked me. *Stupid bitch!*

As I got closer to the house, it hit me that she was probably at work. I chanced it, and to my surprise, she was home.

I walked inside, using the key I still had. It was real quiet. I walked in the den and saw an ashtray full of cigarette butts and a bottle of Absolut. She sat on the couch in a robe, looking as if she hadn't moved in days.

"Where my son?"

She jumped as if I'd startled her.

"He was with my moms. Then when she brought him back, I needed a break, so I took him out the Lakes to your grandma house. Taking kids over there was the thing. Grandma didn't do shit but drink, but she would never let nothing happen to those kids or let a soul fuck with them."

"You had me fucked up for four fuckin' days, man."

"I know, but that wasn't me. It was the courts."

"Yeah, but you gave them the authority, so it's your fault. Don't give me that shit."

"I'll go to the courts and drop it tomorrow. I'm sorry, okay," she said sadly.

This shit was too easy, not my baby momma.

"Fuck is wrong with you? Ain't you pregnant? Fuck you smokin' and drinkin' for? You don't even smoke. Tryin' to give my son a fucked-up brother or sister. You bein' stupid. What's up?"

When she looked up at me, the sight of her face brought tears to my eyes from anger. Her eye was almost shut and her mouth was twisted from the swelling.

"He came here Thursday night after leaving Upscale. He was all fucked up, talkin' all loud. I tell him to chill, LP in the next room. He still goin' on. I tell him I'm gonna call you to come get your son. I didn't want him to hear all the shit he was saying. Then came the "I-must-want-you, who-baby-is-it, was-I-sure-it's-not-Prince's shit." I said, 'Fuck you, bitch-ass niggah,' and he punched me with his fist," she blurted out. "I fell against the wall, and he punched me in the stomach. Then he kicked me again in the side."

My anger grew as I fought back tears.

"I think he snapped and forgot who I was or some-thing. After all that, he called me *bitch, whore,* and some more shit. Then he grabbed my hair, looked me in my eyes, and called me a pretty bitch. Then he shattered my jaw." She grabbed her face.

I knew I caught three-quarters of the story. I was sure she'd left out the part about how much shit she talked back, and what really started shit. If he came here after the club fucked up, he came to fuck, not argue, so she probably provoked the niggah.

Her jaw and lip were swollen and bruised, but her shit wasn't shattered. She damn sure wouldn't be talking that clear and that much.

I kicked off my DC's and laid my T-shirt on the chair, letting my chain fall on my wife-beater.

"I lost the baby," she added. "I spent Thursday night at Virginia Beach General. I had to call an ambulance."

"LP came out while all this shit was poppin'?" I said ready to explode, but I was thinking and realized she was fucked up and needed my support, not for me to beat up on her with words of slander or tell her she made a mistake. She needed healing and to get her head straight.

I sat down next to her, pulled out my Backwoods, and rolled some more haze.

"Go take a shower," I told her. "Get yourself cleaned up and lookin' like something. Put on something comfortable and come relax on the couch." I walked to the bedroom bathroom and started the shower, walked back out and started cleaning off the table and dumping the ashtrays and shit.

After I finished straightening up and sat down to spark, she came back in the den wearing an off-white silk pajama set, tie pants, and a tank top. Her hair was combed. Her breasts shined through the top and caught me as always, but there was nothing she could do to her face and heart, but give it time.

She came and sat under me as I leaned back and smoked.

I picked up my cell and called Grandma's house. "Who there, Grandma?"

"Dundee just left, and I think Larry in front," she said.

"Tell El I said bring my son home."

"A'ight, baby. You comin' by later?"

"I'ma try."

"You take care of that child support, boy?"

"Yes, ma'am. Tell El, Grandma."

"A'ight, because you know they ain't playin'. Let me go call Larry. Bye."

I looked in the phone book and called a locksmith to come change all the locks. She needed to feel safe.

I leaned back, held her, and smoked. I couldn't help but feel somewhat responsible. This was my baby's mom, and if I'd kept treating her right, then she wouldn't have made such a bad choice.

I guess I had to be there. All that she'd put me through was now forgotten. She needed me right now. Plus, nobody beat her ass but me, and that's because I cared and knew how to do it. *Never fight a bitch like a man.* The anger grew in me again.

I pulled on my Back. "You say Upscale is that niggah club?"

Chapter 22

"Herb's Homecoming"

Moe sat in front of Indian Creek waiting on his brother in his new cream-colored Lincoln LS. Thoughts of his brother's long track record and getting in different shit all the time, swirled in his head. He'd been gone for a minute this time, and last they talked, he was on the right path.

Moe smiled at his big brother, a three-time felon.

Herb gave his brother a pound and climbed in the car. Never did he smile.

"So what the deal, man?" Moe asked.

"I'm a'ight. I am truly blessed. God worked a miracle."

"Blessed, huh? Yo' ass blessed to be free?"

"No, I am blessed in the Lord."

"I heard that. So where we goin'?"

"Home, so I can take a real shower. I ain't did that in five years," he said, thinking about the five years he sat wasting his life.

They arrived at their mom's house.

"Where Moms at?"

"Work, fool. This ain't no special day to take off just because you got out."

Herb ignored him and ran upstairs.

After he came out the shower, he rambled through his shit. Then he saw the bags on the floor. One bag had five new white Tee's. Another had a grey Enyce sweat suit. He looked for a sneaker bag. He removed the box from the Foot Locker bag, and opened it. Crisp white DC's. He threw shit on, never checking the rest of the stuff.

Moments later he was downstairs ready to burst. "Let's go," he said.

"Where to?" Moe said going out the door.

"Precision Cuts. Gotta get right."

They climbed in the car headed to Newtown Road.

"So tell me, what's poppin' on the streets?"

"Brit on the run."

"Yeah, for fuckin' shorty up. I heard."

"You remember those Norfolk niggahs, Caddy and Truck? Well, Caddy dead, and Truck can't do shit for self."

"I knew that sooner or later. You can't keep robbin' and getting' over on niggahs. Some niggahs ain't with that shit."

"Dropp came home and gone again."

"He was in there with me. I saw him."

"It ain't too much more."

"So what you doin'? Comin' up, ain't you?"

"Me and Flight took Caddy and Truck clientele, plus our own. We comin' off."

"So why you ain't got your own shit yet? What you movin'?"

"Two bricks. Two weeks."

"How much?"

"Twenty-two."

"Niggah rapin' y'all. I know I ain't been gone that long. No more than eighteen. Gotta shop, Moe."

"I hear ya, but everybody ain't got mad connects. Gotta roll with what you can," Moe said.

"Things gonna be a'ight," Herb said. "God's with us, so nobody can be against us."

Herb got out the car and walked in the barbershop. Cats who knew him and knew where he'd been showed mad love, passing pounds. Others just watched. He came and sat down in Brada's chair. He knew he could holla and get a cut.

By the time he'd finished his cut, he had a deal set up. Brada said he'd front him a half a brick at eleven grand. Good lookout on the front, but Herb knew he'd never call. He walked outside, where some cats had gathered while waiting on their cuts.

Niggahs came over and gave Herb pounds. Herb looked like money, getting in the Lincoln. It made him look like he came home to some change.

They broke out.

Herb smiled a relieved smile as Moe made the left on E. Hasting. The streets were crowded with kids hanging and young niggahs getting money. Everybody was out.

Moe parked and jumped out. Niggahs knew it was time to celebrate.

Chapter 23

I pulled up, parked, jumped out, and threw the niggah a fifth of Henny. Then I lit the fifty-dollar Backwoods packed with "ghandi." Everybody hit the bottom of the Henny, Herb cracked it, and the celebration began. He hit it hard, then passed it to his brother. Moe passed it to me, I passed it to El, he passed it to Dundee, and Dundee passed it to Poppa, and it disappeared. Poppa passed on the Backwoods because he hadn't seen his PO yet.

Moe had to burst. He had business with Flight, so he left Herb out Lake Edward.

Herb grabbed me and whispered in my ear, "I know you gonna show me love and help me on my feet."

Niggahs be talkin' their ass off. He knew I'd never fucked with him, and at this point, it was out of the question.

"Niggah, you know I got you. I can't front you because my shit fucked up right now, but I can do a half for thirteen and a whole joint for twenty-four. Get at me, baby," I said.

"You crazy than a bitch, Prince. Big-head muthafucka. Common-ass, dirty, dingy-ass son of a bitch," Herb said.

I knew he was gonna joke my ass and talk shit, so I burst. I wasn't fuckin with him today.

I came to find out that Herb hollered at Poppa later the following day, and Poppa told him to relax and he would hit him off in a couple days with some work.

Poppa wanted Herb's brother, Moe. He'd heard dude was coming up, but he didn't know Flight and didn't trust him. Now he could let Herb take those chances putting young niggahs on.

The skies had darkened, but the corners still held mad niggahs doing their thing.

Herb stood out talking, joking, drinking, and seeing the changes. But there was only one, the niggahs trying to play the game.

Moe pulled up. He didn't feel like fuckin' with LE niggahs tonight.

Herb gave niggahs pounds and fell into the passenger side of the Lincoln, and Moe hit Newtown, headed out to the Park. He pulled up beside Flight's truck, as he was parked up front watching niggahs get his money.

Herb walked up and gave Flight a quick pound. He'd never had a lot to say to Flight. He'd thought he was an arrogant-ass niggah, because he could ball, and the bitches liked him. He walked away as the niggahs who knew him showered love for his homecoming. He talked to niggahs and glanced around at his surroundings.

When two ladies walked up and began talking to Flight and Moe, Herb walked over to the car. He knew Moe was ready to leave anyway, plus, he wanted a closer look. As he approached the Lincoln, his eyes met Precious, and hers met his.

Moe introduced Precious and Rosalyn.

"What's up?" Herb said with no smile.

"Nothing," they said simultaneously.

"So what y'all doin' tonight?" Herb asked. He knew he wasn't the finest niggah, but bitches loved his well-defined body and his serious, quiet way.

Flight put his arm around Precious and pulled her close. "This me, Herb, this me." He smiled.

"Better hold her close, niggah," Herb said seriously. "You know I just got home."

Everybody else laughed, but Flight.

Moe finished talking and jumped in the whip, and they were out.

"So what's up, Herb? Tryin' to take my man babe?"

"Who is shorty?"

"That's Truck and Caddy's sister. The other girl Rosalyn. She would've got you right," Moe said.

"Bitch all in my face. I'll take your man girl, gay-ass niggah. Should've grabbed his girl and put her in the trunk and took her home with me. Bitch-niggah won't do shit."

Moe listened as the Herb he knew all along resurfaced.

"What happened to letting God guide you? 'Cause I know God ain't told you to put that girl in the trunk and fuck her man up."

"My relationship with God, nobody knows. While I sat in the penitentiary, nobody can say who became my friend and who helped me through. Now He got me."

"I hear ya," Moe said.

They sat in silence for the rest of the ride. Herb lay back, fucked up from the consumption of alcohol that he wasn't used to.

Chapter 24

For days Herb continued to catch up on the streets. Moe hated dropping his brother off out the Lakes. He knew it wouldn't be long before trouble eventually found Herb.

Herb had finally got with Poppa. He had made his calls, saw niggahs in the club he fucked with over the years and ran into old shorties who let niggahs know he was home and shit was on again. Now his cell was ringing with scrambling-ass niggahs who were buying work at high prices, but knew Herb could and would beat prices and front shit. Herb was that type of niggah. He knew a muthafucka wasn't gonna beat him or even take it there.

Poppa had fronted Herb one of those thangs and let him know that the same niggahs was still cooking for cats.

Herb stopped out Newpointe Condos and gave these two cats a kilo of cocaine. He sat playing PlayStation while they cooked it and turned it into forty-five ounces of crack. When they were done, he took his thirty-six ounces, they kept nine for their services, and he was out the door, headed to Lake Edward apartments to check this girl he'd met. She had two kids, was from Alabama and was living in the apartment with her navy boy husband who was stationed at Little Creek Amphibious Base. Dude had gotten caught up fuckin' with these Norfolk girls and left her ass cold.

Herb had ran into her, walking from Food Lion. He gave her a ride in a fiend's whip he had on loan. They talked, he listened, she cried, he held her.

He'd known her for about eight hours. Now they were alone in her apartment, kids 'sleep, chillin'.

Third day he'd been home and hadn't had no pussy. He made his move. He asked her to show him her room, and she did. She never knew what was coming.

He shut the door, pushed her on the bed, pulled her shirt up, and grabbed at her breasts.

She tried to push him away, but he was too strong and forceful.

He unleashed her bra and threw her titties in his mouth and gulped like never before. He grabbed the sweats and pulled them off, then her panties. Herb dropped his jeans, never removing his shoes or shirt, leaned over and threw his dick in her.

She lay there scared, excited, and mind running. Shit was moving so fast. She told him, "Get a condom," but it was too late. He was in there, fuckin' her hard, flippin' her over, hittin' every wall, until he exploded.

He rested for about two minutes on top of her until she felt him swell inside of her again, and the same routine repeated itself.

"Sorry, if I got a little rough. I hadn't fucked in years." He smiled.

"Well, I haven't been fucked like that in years," she said.

"I need a spot to stay out here. Hold me down, I got you."

"I been married since I was eighteen, Herb. I'm twenty-three now with two kids. I can't be running around with different men. I need to know you're not playin'."

"Games and bitches I don't got time for. There are things that got to be done. So if you say you got me, it's me and you, shorty." He leaned over and kissed her tittie, then he threw some more dick in her.

Damn! This niggah ain't no joke. He put it down, she thought.

This bitch pussy good as hell. I'm chillin', Herb thought, as they drifted off to sleep.

About four in the morning, the phone rang several times and stopped. Then it rang again.

"Better answer that and tell them you don't live alone no more. Calling here at this time can get you fucked up."

She picked the phone up slowly. "Hello."

"Hey, you ain't 'sleep. I'm coming home tonight, so get those panties off," her husband said. He was used to stopping home even after leaving her. She still needed his support and he held it over her head, so even after he left her ass, she still let him, hoping he would come back.

"No," she said.

"No, hell. I'll see you in a minute. I'm on Baker Road."

"No more. Don't come over, and call during the day, not like this. Bye."

"My key still work. Can't tell me shit, bitch," he said hanging up.

"Who was that?"

"My husband. He said he's on Baker Road coming here."

"Here we go." Herb got up, put his shirt, jeans, and

Timbs back on. He walked to the living room, T-shirt in hand.

"I'm done with him, Herb," she said, jumping up and putting on her robe. She stood in front of him looking in his eyes as he stared in hers. "Herb, I am being totally honest, since we talked earlier. He has put me through hell, fighting me and running women. I am done. He left. I want him to stay gone. I want you here," she said, about to cry.

By this time, the keys hit the door.

She moved closer to Herb.

Dude look at Herb in a rage, back to his wife, and then at Herb.

"I know you upset, dude, but your next move is crucial." Herb was scared. He didn't know if dude had a gun, and he didn't want to go back to prison. He stood there as dude cursed his wife and made threats.

Then all of a sudden, he reached out to grab his wife.

She stepped back as she saw her husband spin and his jaw crack from the left that ripped through his jaw. Then the right that shattered his nose and mouth. He hit the door and crumbled.

She stood in amazement. Nobody had ever done that. He was the crazy one.

Dude got to his feet, looked at his wife in disgust, took the keys off his ring and threw it at Herb real hard, and ran out the door.

Herb had been there ever since, chillin'. He seemed happy with her.

He arrived back at his apartment and began making calls and breaking shit down. Then he was out the door. He picked up the phone and called Moe. They hadn't spoken since last night. "What up, man?"

"Nothing. Makin' moves. What you doin'?"

"Gettin' ready to do this."

"So why you don't come my way."

"Let me see what's up with Flight."

"See what's up. I'm safe and I'm cheaper. What's to think about?"

"Let me see."

"Holla, man. Keep that shit in the family, son," Herb said. "You know I need that."

"I know. Got you."

Herb had made his runs and was sitting in the chill-out spot on Margate Avenue out the Lakes. This was the spot that niggahs hung at to pass the time. You didn't go there unless you fucked with Poppa though.

This was a three-bedroom. Karen and Tonya, two dike bitches, each had a room, but shared one most of the time, and Poppa had the other. Nobody ever went upstairs, and the house stayed immaculate, except for the excess tobacco that always seemed to end up on the floor, table, or other areas.

Karen and Tonya kept it like a real home: food cooking, liquor, soda, Kool-Aid, big-screen, PlayStation, and nice furniture. Shit was laid and respected. No shit was brought there or kept there. Poppa, Dundee, Herb, Sykes, Ponic, and Big L all sat smoking, playing games, and talking about nothing.

Herb's phone rang. "What up?"

"Where you at?"

"On Margate."

"Come on out now and take a ride," Moe said.

When Herb walked outside, he started down the street. He knew the routine. Then he saw Flight's truck coming up the street with Moe on the side. Herb jumped in the back. To his surprise there was Precious.

She looked at Herb, fresh butter Timbs, new faded

Sean John jeans, and fresh white Tee, no jewelry, not even a watch.

"So what's poppin'?" he asked.

"So what you do for us, Herb?" Flight asked.

"Beat what you gettin' it for now and give you better shit."

"My number twenty, and things are good. Can you beat that?" Flight asked.

"Naw, not the price, but I'm bringing you soft, and if you cook it up yourself, you can bring back an extra nine to ten ounces and shit still off the chain, guaranteed.

"Well, my shorty cook, so we straight," Flight said.

Herb looked at her and smiled. He needed this bitch. He could put her ass to work. Flight was young and in love and didn't know how to use this bitch to her full potential.

"So when we gonna do this?" Herb asked.

"We still got to see Vic," Moe said.

"Come on, son. Y'all niggahs ready?"

"Naw, we were seein' Vic with half, seein' him with the rest."

"Then I guess y'all niggahs need to get y'all weight up. Drop me back off." Moe stared at Herb. He thought Herb would do the same for them.

Flight stared at Moe. He thought his brother would at least look out for him.

Precious looked at the niggah built like Truck, and hustled like Caddy. He was straight up about that money like a niggah should be.

Herb told Flight to stop at the corner of Margate and Lake Edward Drive. He jumped out. It was killing him not to say something to Precious.

"Yo, I don't know about y'all, but is Vic y'all friend?"

They stared at Herb.

"You know how I do. If you need a hand holla. 236-1360." He stared at Precious. He closed the door and headed down the street.

Flight and Moe began talking as they made their way Uptown, Norfolk. Precious was in the back wondering why every time a niggah gave her his number, she couldn't remember, but Herb's number was indented in her mind.

Chapter 25

I was sitting down at Princess Anne Municipal Center with Anita, getting my business in full gear. She had gotten me incorporated, and now I was giving my business a physical address and name. There were some empty spaces up by Newtown Road, but this venture was big-time and I felt big-time. I was making money, and I was going to make plenty more. The shop and other ventures were all going under the corporation. I had a plan. I could either start building on a low-scale or on a larger scale, doing communities. I wanted to get everything in order, then pull this together. This was the turning point in my life.

I looked over at Anita and gripped her hand and smiled. She was used to dealing with these white folks, I wasn't. I looked into her eyes. They looked sad. Through all of my joy, I couldn't see her sadness.

"What's wrong?" I asked.

"Just tired. I really feel tired," she said.

"Workin' too hard. You need to take a break."

"Can't right now. Too much to do and not enough time," she said.

"Shit. You better slow the fuck down. If you die, I guarantee they'll replace your ass. You are replaceable."

"Am I? It's that easy?"

"To them, baby, not to me." I gave her a quick peck on the cheek.

"Way to clean it up." She gave me that beautiful-ass smile that I wanted to see.

We finished up and headed to the shop. She had to get back to work, so she kept going.

I walked inside, all barbers working, clients in the chairs waiting. I walked to the back, bum-ass niggah washing cars, and cars waiting to get done. *That's what the fuck I'm talking about.*

I ran upstairs to the studio. This new niggah that Dundee turned me on to was a worker. This engineer, producer, rapper was making my job a hell of a lot easier, balancing out the shop. This studio was doing its part. Since he came in, he broke down everything individually and they all had a price. From fucking with niggahs who been tryin' to make it in this music shit, that's all they talked about, so when they're around, I listen and catch mad shit; one niggah knowing a little more than the next.

I walked in while a session was in progress, and he got these niggahs in the seventy-five-dollars-an-hour booth. Plus, these cats came in with just rhymes, so he hittin' them off with his beats.

I went to the office and got a contract, one of many. I showed Guttah through the glass. He nodded and assured me they'd already signed it. Cats needed to know that if you got picked up from our music that you spit on, we got to do at least two tracks on your album. These days niggahs was hungry, and you never knew who was going to make it.

I sat back watching these niggahs waste seventy-five dollars and fuck up my niggah beats with that weak shit.

They left, and here came some more niggahs ready to spend money. As they entered one by one I realized we gettin' ready to have some fun. I wasn't gonna make shit. These were niggahs from out the way. They were wannabe rappers, today's little hustlers, and dream scramblers— all good dudes—trying to come up on what seemed to be a dream. But as long as I got the keys to keep these doors open, these cats had a place to come and bring their dreams together. All these cats from out the way, all rep Northwest Virginia Beach, Area 41, Newtown Road. The Lakes!

When you entered I had a sign up—no profanity, no smoking, and no drinking—then a price list of all services. I walked inside the seventy-five-dollars-an-hour booth and Ashy Knuckles rolling Backs, Lites Out sipping Goose, Ponic smoking and drinking talking loud, cussing.

I said something and he was ready to fight me in my studio, so I had to call him out. "Chill on all that noise, Ponic," I said.

"Nobody don't tell me when to talk."

"Chill out or get out."

"Put me out, put me out," he yelled. "You can't do it. You can't do it. I done beat your ass two times, and I know you ain't fuckin' with three."

"You a fuckin' lie. Oh hell naw, niggah. You won in the fourth grade at Bettie F. When we fought in the sixth grade, I won that shit. I beat yo ass."

We were older than Ashy, Lites, and Guttah.

The door opened, and Squirmy and Twon came strolling in.

"Twon was there. Didn't I fuck Prince up in the alley?" Ponic yelled. "Didn't I beat his monkey ass?"

Niggahs laughed.

"Who won Twon? Tell these niggahs," I said.

Twon stood confused. "When?"

"When we were twelve and I threw his ass over the fence," Ponic said.

Twon started laughing. "Only these niggahs will argue and fight over dumb shit. Man, I ain't in that shit." Twon waved his hand and reached for the Back Ponic held.

"Naw, this *P* shit." Ponic passed me the *L* and the pint of Remy.

The arguing was over. Niggahs started arguing about who had the most dough, Master P or Puffy. Lites had turned on some shit that Guttah didn't find acceptable, until everybody got quiet and started feeling the beat.

As the Backs got lit, the Optimos got passed, and the Dutches got bust open, more niggahs started coming in: Young Hop, Tre, and Tall Man. Before you knew it, the place was packed, niggahs gambling, smoking, cussing, and lying all about money and pussy.

I guess I was feeling different now. These weren't Brit's bum-ass niggahs hanging around. These were niggahs I knew well, and they all knew me. But everybody in there knew that me and Ponic argued and even fought, but couldn't shit come between us and he always had a niggah back. Only thing with Ponic, growing up, he stayed in shit, always assaulting somebody. When it was time to fight, this niggah was ready, so it kept him in shit. I eased back from hanging every day. Then when I started hustling, I ran by myself all the time.

Guttah got up and put on a new beat. "Peep this shit."

This shit instantly hit everybody, as heads started bobbing and niggahs closing their eyes shaking their heads. Then Squirmy started flowing. I didn't know the niggah had skills. He freestyled, dropping some sweet shit. Niggahs yelled, giving him love when he finished.

There was banging at the door downstairs. I went down

to open it. Time had flown by. Detail shop was closed, all the barbers had gone and cleaned, and deposit-slip Jamil had left. It was Dundee.

"Where's your key?" I asked.

"At my house. I got my shorty car."

"Niggahs got some fire coming out of this bitch. Your man creating some hot shit, and doing a hell of a job."

"Man been around forever. He just always fuck with that money and hoes. Don't never get in a lot of shit. He about his work."

"I see," I said walking back up.

As soon as we walked back in, niggahs started passing pounds to Dundee, except for Ponic. They gave pounds and hugged. Ask me, they were happy to be free at the same time. Rare occasion.

They had started the beat over, and Guttah was singing his hook for this song he'd made.

The more things change, the more they stay the same fam
Catch me out the Lakes living like a caveman
Record exec try to turn me into a slave man
But I'll be gangster til the end of my days man

Shit was slow and mellow.

Then he changed up to some shit he'd called a crowd hyper. Music was hitting hard, and niggahs prayed for somebody to ride this shit, not spit on it, but ride that bitch, and Guttah started.

Look, dog, this shit is not a game, and that shit around
    your neck is not a chain
I'm causing a lot of pain
Think about what you doin'. Don't force me to pop that
    thang
Run for a block and change . . .

Everybody hype as hell, letting the best rip it. We started yelling, "Ho! Ho! Ho! Ho!"

The more I fucked with the studio, the more I realized, I loved that music shit. My mind started running. *I get enough dough, I'll sign Guttah and put him out independently, until somebody pick him up.* I laughed to myself. I was high as hell and drunk off that Remy. Nothing was impossible to me.

It had gotten late and everybody was headed out of the building. Kendu had pulled up with one of his boys following him. He was pushing a new black 2003 BMW 745il. This shit hadn't even hit the streets yet. His niggah followed in the convertible 'Vette. Both had two decent bitches riding shotgun.

Kendu jumped out the whip, as I stood in front waiting for Dundee, Ponic, Twon, and Squirmy.

I walked out to the BMW. Shit was nice, real nice.

He told me he was tired of laying low. The lawyer told him that he would probably walk, and he took it as coming from the judge himself. He had rented a two-bedroom condo in Columbus Station in the downtown area of Virginia Beach for a thousand dollars a month and he'd paid a year up to a private owner.

He was draped in new shit, on a natural high enhanced by the trees. Jewels gleaming, my niggah was shining, walking around with a murder charge. His shorty had jumped out and was talking to his partner, probably some goofey-ass niggah, picking up the change that Kendu left around for being a yesman. These two bitches had bodies to kill, but cuties they weren't. He was hanging out and wanted me to swing, but my time was going to be spent with Anita this evening. Maybe I'll fuck tonight.

I was in the whip hollering at Kendu, waiting for the rest of those niggahs to come out. Dundee and Ponic came out with Guttah. Twon and Squirmy was out front looking at the two bitches giggling and playing, trying to catch their attention. I laughed as I drove off, headed to see Anita.

Squirmy had said something relating to the bitch who had her thong showing, and Kendu saw him pointing as he walked back to the BMV he had parked, still running, sounds pumping, looking sweet as hell.

"Niggahs peepin' our shorties, son. Let's go before we have a problem," Kendu said jokingly to his man trying to shine in the Corvette.

His man laughed. "Niggahs better know."

"Come on, girl," Kendu said to the girl with the yellow thong. He looked over at Twon and Squirmy. "Get your own, niggah. All you need is one of these." Kendu patted his car with a big smile. He was showing out for the girls, just playing like he knew these cats weren't gonna say shit because they were, and looked, easygoing.

Kendu stood talking to his man as Twon and Squirmy climbed in the car that was parked by the niggahs who'd just come out of the studio.

Lites asked Squirmy. "What them niggahs say?"

"Something about get our own bitches."

"He said that?" Ashy asked.

"Niggah say that we needed a whip like his," Twon added

Niggahs smirked at Kendu's boldness in front of his peoples. They all had seen him around and let him flow because he'd rolled with me.

"He said that too?" Young Hop asked.

Ponic strolled up talking with his arm around Dundee's neck, showing love, and for support so he wouldn't fall.

"I'ma ride with Dun," Ponic yelled out to whoever was waiting on him.

"Godddamn, Ponic, I could have been gone, man," Tre yelled.

"Niggah, you could of carried your ass. You know how many times I done walked back to the Lakes," Ponic said loud.

"Yeah, you say that shit now."

"Fuck all that. Who them bitches?" Dundee asked.

"They with those niggahs. Niggah drivin' the 745 said niggahs need to get they own bitches and stop looking at theirs," Ashy said to Dundee.

"For real?"

"I know he ain't say that," Ponic added.

"And the niggah said we had to have a phat-ass whip or bitches wouldn't look at our ass," Young Hop added, knowing it would get to Dun and send Ponic over the edge.

"Let's go," Dundee said.

They climbed in the car to leave. As they rode past the BMW, they both stared at the bitches. Inside they both were hating the fact that those niggahs tried to shine on their team.

Dundee looked at the bitches and then at the dude in the 'Vette. "Y'all tryin' to share those hoes?"

"Especially your bitch, son, the one with the dirty thong," Ponic said staring at Kendu.

"Keep those low-budget-ass hoes, unless they suckin' dick," Dundee added as he began to pull off.

"Fuck y'all niggahs," Kendu said, not loud, but loud enough for Ponic's ears.

"Back up, Dun. Bitch niggah think 'cause he shot somebody he gangster." Ponic opened the car door and walked around to Kendu's side. "Fuck you say, niggah?"

Before Kendu could get a word out, Ponic slapped the shit out of him and pulled his .45 and put it to Kendu's head before he knew what the hell was going on. He made Kendu and his dirty bitch get in the Corvette with his man and pull off.

Ponic jumped in the 745 and took off, burning rubber down Virginia Beach Boulevard. He flew past dude's 'Vette and slammed on the brakes. Then he took off again, driving shit like it wasn't his, with three carloads of niggahs following.

Ponic pulled into The Lakes, driving the 745 when his phone rang. It was Dundee telling him to pull that shit onto Baker Road and leave it. Prince had called Dundee after Kendu called him, talking about calling the police. Ponic pulled over and parked in front of the apartments, leaving Kendu's shit unlocked and running on the side of Baker Road.

Chapter 26

I was on my way to see Anita and these niggahs called me with all that bullshit. Something told me to stick around, but they knew better than to set all that shit off around my business. Kendu let that "killer shit" go to his head, then call me when a niggah take his shit for playin' hard.

I pulled in front of Anita's and dialed her home phone. I hated standing in front waiting for a bitch to open the door.

I strolled in, and she got shit dim, wearing a pair of grey sweats, Virginia Tech football T-shirt, and socks. She hugged me tight as if she didn't want to let go.

I told her about my child support situation, and how they had me fucked up for days.

She didn't really put up a fuss like Lecia. Lecia was having a fit, thinking she was too fine and her pussy was too good for a niggah to put her off. But I wanted real love, from somebody with a future, so I had my mind focused on Anita.

She walked in the living room.

I walked in her bedroom.

She followed. "What's wrong?" she asked.

"Tired, I want to lay down," I said direct. "I ain't going nowhere tonight." I removed my clothes and climbed in her bed with my boxers and wife-beater.

This was the first time I was so forward, but I was tired of the slow shit. I could tell she liked me, wanted me, and had the hots for a niggah, but something was holding her back.

She laid down beside me.

I held her and began kissing her.

My hand slid up her T-shirt. She moved it.

I moved it to her thigh and then to her vagina. She moved my hand.

I pulled her to me and began grinding, pulling her close, so she could feel how hard this dick was. As I grunted, I moved on top of her, grinding 'til my dick hurt. I moved to the side, began rubbing her stomach, and quickly slid my hand in her sweats under her panties and pushed my hand between her legs.

She jumped as my finger found her soaking wet pussy. She tried to get away, but I kept fingering her until her tight pussy gripped my finger, while she tugged at my hand saying, "No! No!"

I was in rude form now. I reached under her and pulled the sweats down to her knees.

She threw her hands in my chest hard and her knees to the side so I couldn't have easy access and yelled, "No." "Please, Prince, put on a condom. Please, Prince," she begged.

But I wasn't trying to hear it. I pushed my head in and stiffened my dick to enter from the tightness and her resistance. I began pumping.

She began shaking her head, as that pussy allowed all my dick to enter. The warmness, tightness, and wetness

sent a feeling through me like it was going to explode—
the best feeling in the world.

I held her and fucked hard, and she began to cry. My
dick got harder and I exploded in her. I never released
her, just held her tight and lay on the pillow. We fell
asleep to her whimpering and tears falling.

I was awakened by the alarm going off and her breaking my grip. She went into the shower and I followed.
We showered without a word being spoken.

After we got out and dried off, I walked up on her and
pulled her to me, my dick rising between her legs, while
hugging her from the back. I pushed her to the bed and
pushed my dick in her again.

Again she told me to get a condom.

I stopped. "Get me a condom."

She got up and went to her nightstand and pulled out
a condom and something else. She walked in the bathroom. She returned and lay back on the bed and opened
up.

I eased inside of her. It was not the same feeling, but
her giving me her love turned me on. I fucked, and I
fucked harder and harder. The wetness finally worked its
way into the picture, and I came, dripping sweat.

She gripped me so tight, shaking with tears in her eyes.

I couldn't understand this woman, but I felt her close-
ness and her distance. I began to figure out that she was
scared to love again, afraid of being hurt. All I could do
was show her over time.

She walked into the bathroom, and I heard the shower
going again.

I couldn't resist looking in her nightstand to see how
many condoms she'd gone through, not giving me no
pussy in all these months. I peeked in the bathroom to see
her washing through the clear shower curtain. I eased the

nightstand and opened the door. *Goddamn!* There were boxes of condoms and flavored condoms, which was probably the kind she used when she sucked my dick. She had dental dams, finger cots, and rubber gloves. What the hell were these gloves for? She got me.

I shut the door and peeped in the bathroom again. She was rinsing off. I ran over and pulled the drawer open to the nightstand and saw several envelopes addressed to Anita Bailey, five from EVMS, C3ID, Center for the Comprehensive Care of Immune Deficiency, and two from ACC, Ambulatory Care Clinic, Sentara Norfolk General. *What's goin' on with this girl?*

I still heard the shower running, so I opened one of the envelopes from EVMS. It read:

February 23, 2002
Patient: Ms. Bailey came in for regular visit.
Reason: She complained of kidney stones, diarrhea, unexplainable weight loss.
Diagnosis: Symptoms of HIV
Cause: Kidney stones are associated w/Crixivan
Diarrhea is associated w/Viracept
Hyperbilirubinemia is associated w/Reyataz
Gave new prescription: Take one pill, once a day
Sustiva-one a day-(containing Truvada and efavirenz) is normally taken at bedtime and may cause nightmares, vivid dreams, confusion, inability to concentrate; Emitriva, one a day; Viread, one a day.

I quickly put the paper back and shut the drawer. I walked to the shower.

She kissed me and kept going with a smile.

As I showered, my mind was running. I dried off and was brushing my hair and opened the medicine cabinet. There it was again—Sustiva-one a day, Emitriva-one a day, Viread-one a day. I locked them in my head. I was going to find out what this shit was.

I came out and got dressed without a lot being said. We walked out, kissed, and she was on her way. It was early, I looked at my phone to turn it back on loud from the silent mode it had been on since I'd entered her house. Seven missed calls, six from Lecia, one from Kendu.

I called Kendu. "What up, son?" I asked.

"You ever talk to your peoples?" he asked frustrated.

"Yeah, I left you a message. You were probably on the phone. I couldn't keep calling you. Your shit was on Baker Road. I don't know about now. I'm headed that way. I'll meet you."

"Where?"

I could hear the anger in his voice.

"Yo, I ain't take your shit, I'm trying to help you."

"Yeah, but you run with those niggahs who did," he said and hung up.

I pulled on Baker Road and saw the BMW parked in front of Lake Edward apartments. I pulled behind the 745 and waited on Kendu.

He pulled up in the 'Vette driven by his man from last night. Kendu jumped out and checked his car. Keys still turned forward in the ignition, battery dead, and out of gas.

We went to get gas from the Shell on the corner, came back, and I gave him a jump with the Quest.

"Your peoples fucked up," Kendu said. "They gots to get theirs."

"For real, son," his man added. "Dude drivin' the BMW pulled a sawed-off out on a niggah."

"That shit won't be let go."

I wrapped up the cables and headed to the van.

"You ain't got shit to say, Prince?" Kendu asked all hard.

I started walking back and pulled out my phone. I was tired of all this bullshit, like I did this shit. I pressed on speed dial.

"What?" Dundee answered.

"Yo, Kendu and dude with the 'Vette up here on Baker where y'all left the car. They say they need to see you and Ponic," I tried to explain before the phone went dead. I hung up.

"Look, I didn't have shit to do with last night. I don't even know what went down," I said to Kendu and his man, who was standing in front of me on the sidewalk. "From what niggahs tell me, y'all was poppin' shit, tryin' to shine for them hoes and shit got out of hand. So I figure y'all know it was wrong and got got. But shit is a'ight. Nobody hurt, leave it alone. Go 'head home now! Don't be in my hood tellin' me y'all gonna do up niggahs I been knowin' all my life. Me and all them niggahs been knowin' each other since we were crawlin'. Our mommas all hung, partied, drank, and shit. We stayed over each other house night after night. Now all of us take care of our moms, and after twenty years how close you think we are? You my man, Kendu, but these niggahs is family. So I want y'all to squash and handle this shit now," I said.

"So just stand back and stay out of it," Kendu said. "I'll handle it my way."

"Damn right. Move the fuck to the side when the bullets fly. Straight to a niggah dome," Dude said, giving Kendu dap.

"What?" I said not believing what I'd just heard. *Did he just say he'll shoot my cousin in the dome?* My hand jumped. I started to steal this niggah, but I saw two cars flying around the corner, running the red light at Hampshire Lane and Baker Road.

The BMW wagon shot to the front of the 745 and

stopped. Dundee and Big El jumped out, both wearing jeans, white DC's, and wife-beaters.

The Mazda 929 sitting on dubs pulled beside the 'Vette, so close, that you couldn't open the driver's side door. Young Hop and Ashy got out the front, burners in hand. Ponic jumped out the back quickly, jeans sagging, Timbs, no shirt, gritting.

They all walked up.

"Yo, put them guns away," I said. "They ain't got no guns. Do y'all?"

Kendu stared hard at me. "Naw."

"My shit in the car," dude said.

"A'ight, Ponic, this niggah got a problem with you that he wants to handle, and, Dun, dude said if he didn't handle shit with you now, he was going to put one in your dome."

"Goddamn!" El said.

"Whoa!" Ashy said.

"I'm askin' y'all niggahs to give these niggahs a pass on their life and treat 'em like they from out here," I said.

Everybody stepped back.

Dundee looked at dude and stole his ass, but dude regained his composure by grabbing Dundee and taking him to the ground. He had about sixty pounds on Dun. Dun broke loose and scrambled up, but not without a few blows from dude. Dundee glanced around and saw the empty deuce-deuce. He grabbed it and swung with all his might, busting dude in the head. Dude hit the ground hard, holding his head.

Ponic looked at Kendu. "Squash this shit, man. Sorry about everything. I was drunk last night." He stepped to Kendu and held out his left hand.

Kendu reached out with his left and shook Ponic's hand, but the right uppercut dropped his ass into another time. Ponic threw four more blows on Kendu as he tried to raise to his feet.

Inside I felt bad. I knew how hard Ponic hit. I knew this niggah was an animal and loved to scrap. As Kendu tried to raise up, Ponic scooped him up and slammed him to the ground. He did this three times, each time screaming, "I am a beast!"

Ashy and Young Hop watched in laughter. It was humiliating, but I couldn't laugh.

The third time Kendu just stayed down, and Ponic stood over him catching him with blows.

I grabbed Ponic and stopped him. "Get in the car, Ponic. He done."

Kendu got to his feet, barely standing, fucked up and staring at me. It was a different kind of stare, it was a look of gratitude. He was thankful that I pulled Ponic off his ass.

Dude finally got to his feet with a gash in the head and said, "I ain't done. I can take a killing, not a beating."

We all looked at this simple-ass niggah just before El tore his head off. Before dude could fall, El grabbed him by the back of the neck and belt, picked this niggah up with brute strength, and went running toward the Corvette, throwing this niggah headfirst into his windshield. We heard a loud thump, like his shit had split open, but it was the windshield shattering and his head stuck in the glass.

His body shook, jumped, then he lay still.

El looked at Ponic. "If you a beast, what am I?"

"You a monster who better get the fuck out of here." I dashed to my car as we heard the sirens coming closer.

In seconds everybody was out, including Kendu.

Chapter 27

My phone rang. It was Freddie Mac, my realtor. He had found me some land and wanted me to meet him.

I called Anita. She came and picked me up out the Lakes after work and took me to meet him. We rode out to Chesapeake off Cedar Road, pulled into a new complex of big homes and drove to the back, where the bulldozers were developing the land.

After the land was developed, I would buy so many acres for three hundred grand, produce six lots, and sell each one for one hundred and twenty five thousand. I'll spend one hundred and twenty building custom homes that would sell for five to six hundred grand. I would see at least three hundred grand off six homes. It was a done deal. My peoples would be ready, contractor, plumbers, framers, tile company, brick layers, concrete layers, roofers, painters, carpet men, hardwood floor people, and landscapers.

All this was in order, thanks to Anita. While on her work time, she sent out these jobs to different companies and got bids. Best price and production time had to play together. All I had to do was let Freddie Mac do his thing, bring people who'd already purchased lots to my downtown office in Virginia Beach, and choose their design.

Freddie Mac knew it was a go and already had the Purchase Agreement ready for me. I signed and gave him a thirty-thousand-dollar check for earnest money, so the mortgage company and the seller would know I was serious.

I was in deep thought as Anita traveled down Interstate 64 headed to the beach. She seemed to be in deep thought also. It was as if we never talked too much, but her presence lifted me, changed my mind state, and she made me feel good.

A Backwoods full of that "purp" would make me feel a hell of a lot better, I thought.

When we reached the Lakes, niggahs was still sitting at Grandma's house on East Hastings in the same spots.

I kissed Anita and promised to hit her in a minute.

She just stared at me when I pulled back.

"What's wrong?" I looked into her sad, weak-looking eyes.

"Nothing, baby. Be careful, okay."

"Always, baby, always."

She pulled off.

I walked inside. "I just went and made a million dollars and y'all niggahs still in the same spot."

"Well, you can give me five grand to pay these child support people, so I can stay free," Big L said, jumping up going to the bathroom.

"Shit! If you can leave this bitch for two hours and make a million, why do anybody got to get a job? I ain't doin' shit," Ponic said.

"But be a beast," his son said. His baby moms knew where he was and had dropped him off right to him.

I walked outside. Standing in front, I would see the fiends slowly driving through, catching their morning blast. I watched the young cats, fifteen, sixteen, walking up and down the block trying to be cool, trying to find weed, wanting to be hustlers. *They needed to be in school*, I thought.

Ponic, Ashy, and Twon all came outside. "That shit was crazy this morning," Ashy said laughing. "I can't stop laughing every time I think about that shit."

"Niggah gettin' his ass whipped is one thing, but El destroyed that kid." I shook my head. "I haven't seen a niggah get fucked up like that since we were twelve."

"When Black snatched that old head out his car through the window and stomped his ass into a coma right there on the curb," Ponic said, pointing. "Niggahs was like twelve."

"I was out there. Every time he kicked the niggah, his head slammed against the curb with a hard thump," Twon said. "I always wanted to stomp a niggah ass out like that."

"Black woulda killed that man if Brit didn't stop him," I said.

Nobody said anything. I guess they saw the sadness that draped over my face when I mentioned my brother's name. I was close with my peoples and Dundee was my closest cousin, but Brit was the big brother that always held me down. This business shit was him. I just wanted to have fun and enjoy life, but here I was being serious all day, day-in and day-out, because I had nobody to trust.

I remember when Brit had did a bid in ninety-four. He told me then, "Niggahs don't love ya. See what they done to me? So when I go away, fuck muthafuckas." The niggah Fishbone had set him up, Lo, and a couple other old heads. That was the only time I'd been without him . . .

and now. Hustling, sleeping late, running hoes was all me, but this business shit was where the money was, so if Brit wasn't here to follow it through, I had no choice. These streets would forever call my name.

"I'm gettin' ready to head home. I'll holla," I said, walking to my van.

Talking about my brother had me kinda feeling funny. If he was here I wouldn't be so stressed.

I picked up my phone and dialed Lecia. "What up, baby?" I asked.

"You know the deal, Prince. I thought I was going to lose my mind at the shop this morning, so I came home on my break. I got to be back at the shop at three-thirty."

I looked at my watch. It was twelve-fifteen. "Check you in minute."

I walked in the small apartment, no sign of her. Peeked in the bedroom, no sign. I opened the bathroom door to find her taking a steamy hot bath in the middle of the day, scented candles burning.

"Please join me," she said once, and I was in.

We played, we talked, we fucked, and she carried her ass back to work.

I threw on my shit and rolled a Backwoods. I sat looking at BET, smoking, until I received a call. This was the call I'd been waiting on. This was that real shit.

I jumped up and headed to Bonney Road. I was there in half an hour when Brada called telling me he was turning on my street.

I opened the garage so he could pull in.

He came inside and handed me the book bag. I had seventy-five thousand sitting on the table for him. This shit was smooth. He was comfortable and I felt good.

I never thought this cat had connections like this, but I

guess that explained the four-hundred-thousand-dollar mini-mansion him and his wife had out in Denbigh, outside of Williamsburg.

Brada headed out and I followed.

We met at my new spot, I guessed, because it was safe and neutral territory. He knew I wasn't gonna get him in my new shit, and he was right.

I arrived at the duplex and began weighing shit out. I hadn't sniffed in a minute, but somebody had to give the shit a rating.

One and one, then my head went side to side as I tried to shake it off, but something had a hold of me. This shit was decent.

I bagged shit up and started making calls. Niggahs was waiting. I met Chris' man, young money-gettin' niggah from Tidewater Park. He bought a whole joint for twenty-five grand.

Then I met Kendu's man. This niggah was real thorough. Money was always neat and never off. He got his brick and I got another twenty-five grand.

I called this young niggah from Oceanview that I'd been serving. Boy was sixteen, movin' half a brick with ease and payin' thirteen grand, five, no front.

I was sitting at the white strip club when the white pickup pulled up. Chauna, a white boy I'd known since we played football at Bayside Middle, lived in a trailer park out Chesapeake. He always had his thirteen grand, five in all twenties and fifties, never anything else. If I hadn't known this boy since Bettie F. Williams Elementary, I would think his money was funny, but I knew his shit was a family thing. His dad and brother also helped him move his weight, so they were all in together.

I broke out and headed to the crib. I had made my seventy-five thousand back, so it felt good to place that back in the safe in the score spot. I shuffled the papers and folders back to camouflage the safe, then I shut the chest. I ran out and jumped in the Z.

My body raced as if I was coked up, but I wasn't. I had the gritty face, but I wasn't mad, just serious. As I hit the interstate at Rosemont headed to Norfolk, I punched her. In no time I was running a hundred. Ten minutes later, I was exiting on Brambleton Boulevard and made the right on Park Avenue.

I glanced over at the shopping strip where 7-Eleven, Kappatal Kuts, Nail Shop, and 360 Gear sat. Bitches were roaming around, but nothing was really jumping. I punched her again, getting a wheel up to about forty, never noticing the police on the left with the radar. I was focused to the right, where Norfolk State University sat, and you could always holla and put dibbs in real quick.

I spotted two cuties, one was carrying a book, so I figured they were NSU shorties. I stopped, they stopped. "Yo, what the deal? My name Prince," I said as they walked closer to the car. I knew they would stop and talk because my style was crazy. I wasn't a bullshit perverted-ass niggah. My style and tags said, *Another cool-ass Norfolk niggah gettin' it.*

"My name is Amaia, and this my friend Prayyiah," she said with that Spanish northern accent that flowed naturally and soft. It wasn't hardened up to make fuckin' sure I knew she was from New York.

I looked into her soft eyes, clear caramel skin and those glossy petite lips, down to her neck where the thin gold chain rested with the word "BRONX" hanging. Her hair was pulled back in a lengthy ponytail with little waves disappearing to the back. She wore a Baby Phat coat that puffed at the top, but stopped at the waist to show her small waist and the slamming shape in the jeans she wore.

"Y'all go to the state?" I asked, making sure they

weren't up here walking from Booker T. Washington High School, being grown.

"Yeah, I'm a junior, and my girl workin' on her CPA. She graduated last year," Amaia said, her cuteness turning me on.

"Prayyiah don't talk?" I looked at her, then Prayyiah.

Prayyiah frowned her face. "Not to strangers."

I looked at her expression. I glanced at her tight jeans, about a size seven I gathered, small waist being hugged by the same type of coat as her friend, but hers was Rocawear. She stood with her hands in her pockets. Her pretty brown skin was flawless and looked smooth. Her thick arched eyebrows sat perfectly over her dark brown, slanted eyes. I looked at her long, dark hair fallen on her shoulders and into her hood, except for the piece that kept blowing across her face.

Her eyes were saying, "Come here, Prince."

I couldn't take my eyes off her. Nothing could break our stare. Nothing could stop this feeling.

Except the police who pulled behind me.

"Damn!" Amaia eased from the car as the police walked toward the driver's side.

"Yo, I know y'all ain't gonna let me get a ticket for nothing. Come on," I said.

"We goin' to McDonald's," Amaia said.

"See you in a minute, Prayyiah," I said, letting her know she was the one.

The police didn't have to ask for my license, registration, or insurance card. I handed it all to him when he walked up. "Hurry up, man. I got to catch them shorties."

"Do you know how—"

"It don't matter. Just write it. I got shit to do. I make real money, son."

He walked back to his car and returned moments later. "Sign here and here. It's not an admission of guilt . . ."

He gave me my copy, license, registration, and insurance card back.

I threw it on the seat and took off. He didn't give a fuck. Norfolk police were like that. In Virginia Beach I would have been in the back of the police car and my car towed away, just for being smart.

I pulled in McDonald's, Prayyiah and Amaia were coming out. I jumped out the whip.

"So when we gonna hang out? Talk, drink, smoke, shoot pool, whatever."

"I don't know, tell us," Amaia said.

"We don't smoke, we don't shoot pool, so there goes that," Prayyiah said.

"So I guess y'all alcoholics. So be it. Let's drink. That ain't even my thing."

"So we are supposed to just go drink with you?" she asked with that funny expression again.

"No," I said quickly. I could tell I startled her. "You gonna have a drink with me. Fuck the bullshit. Take my number," I said.

She had a stern look like she had attitude, but she held her phone up in her hand.

I gave her my number. I said, "Now call me at seven-thirty, and I'll tell you where to meet me. Got a car, right?" I frowned.

"Yes."

"Yes." *Little proper-ass smart-mouth girl, you better know.* "Nice meeting you Amaia, what is that?" I asked.

She said, "My name is—"

It was long and drawn out. Sounded like four names. "Godddamn!" I laughed. "Do you know what she said?" I asked Prayyiah.

Prayyiah looked at her and said something in Spanish. They began talking back and forth.

I stared in amazement. This pretty brown thing had

impressed me outside of her beauty and her degree that so many hoes hide behind. They think the degree brings respect; a man respects the fact that you got a degree. Now make him respect what the fuck you do with it.

I don't know what they were saying, but I got tired of that shit. "Look, seven-thirty, and leave that smart mouth home," I said, getting back in the Z.

Chapter 28

The day was getting away. I stopped by the duplex, ran inside and got three bags. One was the extra brick my peoples brought back on the four bricks, and another one I kept as powder. I tossed the three thangs in the trunk of the Z like it wasn't shit and took off. First stop now was to Bigg.

I'd known Bigg for a while. He played ball for Norview High School and threw out his knee. He stood about six four, three hundred twenty pounds and walked with a limp. He lived in a house out Camalia Acres, in the Norview section of Norfolk. He had spots throughout Norview—Oakmont North, Wellington Oaks, Norview Gardens—and he moved weight. The brick I dropped at his house was gone before I hit the interstate headed to Ballentine with his twenty-five G's.

I got off on Ballentine and turned into this new section of Norfolk. I navigated my way through this beautiful neighborhood that only housed the upper class. I pulled into Professor Clark's driveway. I reached in the backseat and got the powder. The exchange was quick.

Professor was almost fifty, but kept several girls half his age hanging around his home, mostly former students. All I knew was, he was willing to pay thirty grand for this shit I never touched, no cut, straight to him.

I left Ballentine and headed out to Little Creek Road. I had met two young niggahs, these boys were like fifteen, sixteen. They lived in an area called Texas Lane. All streets that go in and out are Texas-related. They had a street called San Antonio Boulevard locked. This shit was hidden from the unknown. This was a section in Norfolk between Tidewater Drive and Little Creek Road with the homos, crack addicts, heroine addicts, female and male prostitution, and a killing every two days.

I was dropping off twenty-seven ounces to three niggahs, thinking I better get twenty thousand four hundred back, or they'll be doing the counting.

I pulled the Z on the interstate headed for the shop. I hit Jamil's phone, so he could hit the alarm button to unlock his car.

Ten minutes later he had my last nine ounces under his passenger side seat.

I walked through the back to see how the detailing part was doing. Not much, not a sunny day. I walked inside and Jamil handed me the deposit ticket in an envelope, along with some more papers with the sixty-eight hundred, times three. It wasn't because I didn't trust him, I just enjoyed counting my money. This was the only thing that I truly loved.

I placed the cash in my pockets. It made me feel like I could buy anything I wanted and, almost, anybody. I was walking out when I heard music coming from the money booth. I walked in. Guttah was leaning over on the board. He'd fallen asleep. He had designs of album covers and a list of songs that he'd made and produced himself. This niggah had an album almost done and ready to put out, yet here he was finishing his shit on my time, equipment, computers, and everything. I had this place ready to make money.

"Been in here a minute?" I asked.

"Yeah, got to put in work, if I want to make it. At least make it out The Lakes," he said.

I could hear the struggle in his voice. This niggah was older than me and had been around a minute longer.

"Never make it out The Lakes, that's home, even when you do make it, never lose your right to come out The Lakes and stand by the green tank and smoke, drank, and lie about how you fucked the night before. If you lose that, then you gonna lose some of self, and then you can't spit that shit you spit, and you might lose your edge you got over everybody. Those hot-ass beats you make? You nice like radio niggahs nice, and your beats fire like Dre make, not that bullshit Pharrell and Kanye West make. You make that shit somewhere else, not at this muthafucka. I want some Murder Musik shit, feel me?"

We gave each other a pound.

He still had a look of despair in his face.

"So you handle it, son. Make it, put it out, and make somebody offer you a million, niggah," I said hype.

"Yeah," he said slow. "But it's hard getting it out, Prince. You know how long I been at this shit, man. Twelve years, man. I got two kids. They need shit. I live with moms and my girl, bills both places. They don't stop. Mom's rent four days late, just paid my girl shit and the late fee. Cable off, Moms sitting crying, child support gettin' ready to lock me the fuck up if that ain't caught up." He shook his head.

I pulled out my Backs and rolled one. I could tell he needed to talk, and this medicine was the best.

"Man, I'm twenty-five and no whip, livin' day to day,

and I don't want to fuck with that shit no more. I'm done with that drug shit. Been around that shit all my life out The Lakes, you know, Prince."

"Damn right. We're products of our environment, but we tryin', man. We tryin' to turn around."

"Yeah, but my hole gettin' deeper. I need dough."

"Give me a second," I said, walking out into my office.

I went and called my niggah Sherm. He'd been fuckin' with this music shit forever. I told him I had somebody I wanted to put out through my studio, Triple Play Records. He sent me over a standard contract and let me know to make hot shit—make him hot and you never know. I waited for the contract to be faxed over. I made several copies and changes to my advantage. This cat had hot material, but couldn't get it out. Shit was frustrating to him.

I called Dundee and he was up there in minutes. He had just showered and was starting his day.

I told him my plan to sign Guttah and Young Hop. We agreed I didn't know shit, but both of those niggahs were hot, and it would be fun. I had the dough.

We walked in with Guttah. I asked him to play me the beats he'd made. He played me thirty beats that he felt was hot. Me and Dundee felt seventeen beats. I was prepared to offer two hundred a beat and laid thirty-five hundred on the table.

"Now this is for those beats, unless you got something else to do with them. You've had them a minute. Now, this says we goin' seventy percent to your thirty percent. After I get all this done up and put out there, if somebody offer a million, I roll with seven hundred grand to your three hundred. If nobody offers anything, my loss. You can keep the thirty-five hundred, the ten grand advance, and the 350Z." I tossed him the keys.

He smiled, initialed everything, and signed the contract. This was our first artist. He scooped the $13,500 and bagged it.

"Go take care of shit, son. Come back in two days with a clear head, feeling and lookin' like you down with Triple Play, niggah. We rich."

I walked down and got all my shit out the 350, pulled out the papers and signed the title over. It was his. I was getting ready to get on some new shit. Making eighty grand a week off the street, I had no choice.

Dundee drove out to the townhouse in Kingsville Greens. I went inside and went to the closet, pulled back the carpet and lifted the safe from under the house. I placed fifty thousand in the safe and thought about the other twenty grand still on the street.

I went in the room and showered. I came out in my boxers and sat down on the couch.

Dundee was looking at ESPN.

I grabbed the remote and turned to BET.

"Fuck you doin'?"

"I don't want to see no sports shit," I said.

"Man, I got shit to do. I'm out. You straight?"

"Yeah! The Ac in the garage. She comin' out. Yo, where that haze?"

"Niggahs got it. One fifty a quarter," he responded.

"What up?"

"Get a whole joint," he said. "I got half."

"Go ahead. I got you."

"Man, fuck that. Give it here."

"I ain't got pants on, Duke. Come on, you actin' like that over two hundred."

"Naw, three hundred," he said, getting my pants.

I pulled out three bills and gave it to him. I sat there after he left, smoking the last of the haze.

At 7:30, my phone rang like clockwork. "Hello."

"I'm punctual," she said.

"I see."

"So tell me something about yourself, so I'll know who the hell you are."

"What you want to know, Prince?"

"Where you from?"

"Virginia." She answered as if she thought I was from somewhere else.

"That's tellin' me a lot."

"Bellamy Woods. I went to Tallwood because my mom was the principal over there. My mom replaced Mr. Morgan."

"Following Mr. Morgan is tough. That principal was the shit," I said letting her know that I knew of the principal who made his name by changing Bayside around. The school was known for producing some of Virginia's worst, but he'd come in and made a big change, before me.

"Yeah, but my mom is about her work: bachelor's from Virginia Commonwealth University, master's from Old Dominion University, doctorate from the University of Richmond."

That damn sure explains the big-ass house out Bellamy Woods. "What your pops do? Nothing? Mom's got all that, ain't no need for a niggah to do nothing." I started laughing.

She didn't think it was funny.

I didn't give a fuck. You cute, but don't get it twisted.

"No, my dad works for the planning commission for the state. He works in Virginia Beach, but goes to Richmond quite a bit. He's also a minister."

"I heard that. Where he go to school?" I asked, like I gave a fuck.

"Virginia Tech and Regency."

"House full of smart-ass niggahs."

"Know what, you're an ignorant bitch, just like my brother," she said with an attitude and hung up.

I had her number on my phone, so I hit her back. "Look, shorty, you can get mad and talk shit, but don't hang up on me. That's rude and ignorant. Makes me think you can't come up with shit to say out your educated mouth to this twenty-one-year-old niggah from the Lakes that never had a chance to finish school," I said like it was unbelievable.

"Are you finished?"

"Are you on your way?"

"No, I got some other stops to make," she said.

"I'm in Kempsville Greens, down the street by—"

"I know."

I gave her the address and hung up.

Forty-five minutes had passed when the doorbell rang.

She came in and sat down.

"This my shit," I said, waving my hand around, referring to the house. "Check it out if you like."

She sat down as I looked at a new DVD I'd gotten called *Shottas*. I sparked my Back and hit it, then I asked if weed bothered her.

She said it did.

I took another pull and I asked her why. Then another, while she answered.

"Well, this what I do, I don't want this relationship startin' off with no secrets. Do you got a man? Are you fuckin' somebody? Do you fuck with girls? Talk to me."

"No man as of a month ago. I fuck my ex-boyfriend from time to time. No commitment. I just feel safe with him. I've thought of fuckin' a girl, but never have, and if I did, she would be really fine like Amaia."

She had my attention. I mean, all of it. Her answers

blew me away, and the way she blurted it out so strongly after looking shy and innocent had me gone. "Damn!"

"You shouldn't smoke."

"Do you care or doesn't like the smell?"

"Actually the smell doesn't bother me, but I don't want to smell like weed."

"Then you better roll down the muthafuckin' window. Come on, let's roll," I said, throwing on my Timbs, grabbing my white Tee and blue Flight jacket, and fresh-rolled Backwoods.

"We walked out and I hit the garage door opener. I tried to start the Acura, but the battery had died.

"I'll drive, and nobody smokes in my car." She smiled as if she had me.

I smiled. She looked so fuckin' cute and innocent.

"Yo, give me a jump. I'm gonna leave it runnin', to charge up the battery."

"You just gonna leave it runnin'?"

"Hell yeah! This Kempsville. Ain't no niggahs thuggin' out this bitch. All y'all got is money around here and the surrounding area. That reminds me," I looked in her eyes as she sat in the car. "What the fuck took you so long? You stay not even ten minutes away if you still live at home."

"Yeah, I'm still in school, not making much money at this part-time job. I'm barely able to make this car payment, so I stay at home, hating it after being away for four years."

"I can believe that. So what, you're twenty-three?"

"Twenty-two. My birthday in May. May eighteenth."

"Heard that." As the words came out my mouth, I realized she looked like Amerie. This girl was really pretty with some intelligence.

We got the Ac started, and I told her to park her car. I jumped in the passenger side and lit my *L*.

She jumped in and pulled off, driving like that shit was hers. I liked that.

"Where to?" she asked.

"Cheesecake Factory."

It took us about ten minutes to get to the garage downtown. We parked and walked across the street to the restaurant. We sat at the bar during our forty-minute wait. She ordered apple martinis and I ordered Grey Goose straight.

She was on her second when our table became available. She was becoming a little more talkative. I noticed her movement when she expressed herself. I listened to her use big words, or should I say, words that weren't in my everyday language.

"You need to stop talkin' like you in school or at home. I'm from Bayside. Never graduated. Street niggah, baby, but I can read and comprehend every muthafuckin' thing I read, and I don't know what some of that shit mean."

"It means—"

"I don't give a fuck. If you gonna use a big-ass word, go to the part of your brain that holds synonyms and pick one. Shit!" I smiled.

"So I'm supposed to lower myself to your level."

"Yeah, I keep it simple. Let's eat."

We ate, talked, and had an after-dinner drink to go. This was her third apple martini. I knew, from taking girls out, three was crucial if made right.

I paid the bill and we were out.

She handled her liquor like a pro and never swerved.

We got back to the house. I asked her about her choice of music.

"Everything."

"I know you fuck with the white shit. What you mixed with anyway?"

"My dad is black and Asian," she said.

"Um . . . I bet you spoiled. Got the perfect life, no problems." I touched her face.

She was beautiful, no make up, just beautiful.

I looked into her eyes and stared deep. She reached out, touched my face, leaned to me and kissed me.

I wasn't too fond of girls kissing me in the mouth, but I wanted to kiss her. I wanted to hold her, and as the thought came, she eased her way into my arms. I reached over and pressed play on the CD player. The new shit with Ashanti and Ja came on the mixed CD.

We fell back, and she lay on my chest, and held on to me as I hugged her.

"You and your peoples real close?" I asked.

"Me and my brother are, when he's home. Me and my mom stay on the outs, and my dad ain't around enough to get close to."

"So it's just you four there?"

"Yeah, my brother moved out when he was seventeen, but every time he get locked up, when he get out he come home for a minute. He just did two years, so he there now."

"How old is he?"

"Twenty-five. I got another brother twenty and a sister sixteen. They live out Churchland. That man got two families and we ain't supposed to know. Since my mom started her job at Tallwood, she has mad meetings with the football coach, who also teach P.E. We refer to him as *Coach*. I know my brother know. My dad got to know."

"How can he say shit? How long they been married?"

"Twenty-seven years."

"Damn!"

We sat, talked, hugged, and kissed until three in the morning. I had turned my phone on silent, because I could tell it was irritating her. We had taken our affection to another level. I was trying to fuck.

She stopped me.

I didn't mind. I was enjoying her. Her touch, her kiss, her beauty and those eyes. I was into her. Not once did I think of Tee Tee, Lecia, or Anita.

She ended up laying in my arms on the couch until the next morning when she had to get to class. She kissed me, told me she really enjoyed herself, and was out.

I lay there with a feeling that I never had. I was happy.

I reached over and grabbed the piece of *L* that was left from last night and lit it. As I took a deep pull, thoughts of Prayyiah filled my head. I could actually see her living in my home, driving my whips.

I had never wanted a house, just phat condos.

She made me see a house and doing yard work in the evening. "Giving her two babies," I said out loud and burst out laughing. The haze I was smoking was no joke, and shorty had me high off life.

I checked my phone. I had four missed calls. One was Tee Tee, one was Anita, one was Chris, and one was a strange number with a 770 area code. Only Anita and Tee Tee left a message.

"Just wanted to talk," Anita said. "Miss you and I love you, Prince."

"I know yo' ass ain't at the studio," Tee Tee said. "I rode by. Don't start that bullshit, Prince. It's fuckin' four-thirty in the damn morning, son of a bitch!"

Yeah, I gots to get away from her ass.

I ran to the room and showered, changed my drawers and wife-beater that shorty probably slobbed on while laying on me. I then threw the same shit back on.

I grabbed my phone and hit Chris. He was busy, but wanted to make sure we booked our hotel room for the

All-Star game in Philly at the end of the month. I told him to book me two rooms along with his. He had me. We agreed to talk later.

I grabbed my L and thought, *If she's the bitch I think she is, then my plans include her. I got to let some of these bitches go. I can't keep jumping from girl to girl. I can't keep making girl's emotions go up and down. I can't keep hurting girls. I can't live three and four lives.* I wanted to focus on one. Love one and see what happens. Prayyiah was a weakness.

I took the last pull on the L and dropped it in the ashtray.

Before heading out the door, I went by the couch and kneeled down. I put my hands together and bowed my head. I took a minute to clear my mind of all the bad shit, the bitches I desired, the niggahs I hated and the haze that I desperately needed. Something began to cover me. I opened my hands palm up.

"Dear Heavenly Father," I prayed, *"I come to You as humble as I know how, realizing you are the Almighty and no man comes before You. I know I don't live the perfect life, but I ask You to never let anything happen to my family because of how I live. Protect my son, protect his moms, protect my moms, protect my sister, my nieces and nephews, my cousins, especially Dundee. And God, please protect Brit. That's my brother and only You know how fu—miserable I am without him and scared that he can't look out for self. Bring him back home, God, and give us the strength, knowledge, and capability to beat his charges.*

"God, You know I always ask that You take care of me, let me keep my health and strength because I got sh—things to do. I'm sorry for slipping up, but Lord, You know me. So I'm not questioning how long You plan to let me run these streets, but allow me to get some things done and make some money, so I

can leave my family right. Just allow me to stay on this earth
long enough to leave my peoples straight. And, God, please
help me to make the right decisions in everything I do. Please
guide me and lead me, for You are the only man I will follow
and fear. Amen."

I jumped up, grabbed my keys and headed for the Ac.
I drove up Baxter Road, hit Independence, and then the
interstate to see if these niggahs got my muthafuckin'
money.

"Let's get poppin' early," I yelled.

"Yo," he answered.

"Ready to see me, baby?" I yelled hype.

"Come on through. You straight," they replied.

I headed to Little Creek Road and pulled in front of an
apartment building on San Antonio.

Dude ran out and sat in the car, threw me a paper bag
and dipped. Three stacks of sixty-eight hundred.

I hit the road headed to my crib when my phone rang.
"Yeah," I said.

"You got missin' in action last night, huh?"

"You ain't even call."

"My sisters came over. We bullshitted 'til about three-
thirty, and they stayed over."

"Should of called. I would of come through and dam-
aged all y'all. Put it down."

"Come damage this, come put it down over here and
we'll see."

"I'm on the way."

"For real, Prince."

"Be there in fifteen minutes."

Just the thought of her in some sexy shit made my dick
hard, but the ring of the phone and my baby momma's
number coming up disturbed that.

"What?" I answered.

"Why you actin' nasty?"

"Because you fuckin' with that same niggah."

"Prince, that's my business."

"What about when he beat your ass in front of my son and really fuck you up, huh?"

"That ain't gonna happen."

"You's a simple-ass muthafuckin' bitch to have a degree. The choices you make don't make no sense to me. Your momma ain't even fuckin' with you, I bet."

"Well, I'm pregnant again, and we gettin' married. I already moved, and I'll let you know where, when I feel it's right."

"You know what—"

Click.

I had some real choice words, but she never caught them.

This day got off to a hell of a start. It was about noon and I had done more today and made more money today than niggahs made in a year.

I picked up the phone and hit the 770 number back. I didn't usually call numbers back, but this one had me wondering.

A girl's voice came on the other end. "Hello."

"Who dis?"

"Leah, Prince."

"Where you at?" I asked. She was the last person.

"ATLANTA. Me and Brit," she said and got quiet. "I've been down here a minute, but I'm ready to come back home. He scared he can't beat that shit we got in. I'm his wife, so I don't have to testify, and I'm not pressing charges, so I know he can beat it. I'm not supposed to call you, but I'm ready to come home and Brit scared." She started crying. "I'm lonely down here without my peoples, but I love Brit and I ain't fuckin' up or leavin' him again."

"Where Brit?" I asked.

"He at work."

"Work? Doin' what?"

"Work at some place in Sandy Springs."

"And where y'all live?"

"Marietta."

"Give me the address."

Chapter 29

Big Herb was standing in the living room of the two-bedroom apartment in Ash Brook that he and Precious shared. In the last several weeks, things had changed. Moe had decided to step out the game. Herb was all about getting money and was coming strong on niggahs, building a team, putting them in places to get money, until he eventually began stepping on toes.

When Moe and Flight took too long getting back at him, he chanced dropping half a brick on a young niggah out Oakley Park named Sterling, just to take their clientele and make them feel it where it hurt—their pockets.

Flight was going through Precious' phone and saw Herb's number. She said it was in there for his back up, in case he forgot it. Flight was in a rage. He made her call it and put it on speaker phone. He had pulled his nine and put it to her head. All he could picture was Big Herb fuckin' Precious.

"If he answer like y'all been talkin', all he gonna hear is the gun goin' off and your brains hittin' the wall. I don't believe you fuckin' wit' my man's brother." He slapped her ass.

She picked up the phone as it rang.

"Who is this?" Herb answered.

"This is Precious," she said, the cold steel pressed against the side of her neck.

"Who the fuck is Precious? I don't play games, baby. Wrong niggah." Herb hung up.

Flight stormed out the apartment mad. His mom, who had gotten out of rehab and for once was doing good, came out when she heard the slam.

His mom had just told him earlier that she'd made up the whole story about his dad being from Lake Edward and his family was some notorious people. She'd heard mad stories about Black and his family just like everybody else in the neighborhood, and every girl wanted a ballin'-ass niggah to be their baby daddy. She couldn't tell him the truth. That her and his dad got caught up in some bullshit, and he had to do ten years. He did two years, snitched on some real niggahs, and came home.

He started smoking, and people said he had got turned out in prison, but she didn't believe them until she was coming from Park Place and saw this niggah in women's shit walking up Church Street. When she pulled over, he took off, walking up a one-way where she couldn't follow. She let it go and hadn't seen him since. She didn't know why she'd decided to tell him the truth that day, but as a part of her recovery there was a lot she had to clear her mind of. Telling him the truth was a start.

Precious was sitting on her bed when her phone rang.

It was Flight. He was screaming on her as he drove out the Park. "What the fuck were you thinking?"

"You got things wrong, Flight," she said, not wanting him to think some shit that wasn't true.

"I'ma carry this shit straight to Herb. Fuck that shit!"

"I know I ain't did nothin'."

"Right, bitch, you just like them other stankin' hoes out the park. Just want a niggah to take care of your dumb ass."

"No, I don't. I've learned to do for self, and my brothers always took care of me," she said, tears in her eyes.

"You don't do shit now. And fuck your brothers. One of them six feet, and the other should be, sit around all day bobbin' his muthafuckin' head and shittin' on hisself."

"I cook up shit for you, I bag shit for you. I even serve dudes you send to the house when you ain't here, and you got the nerve to say I don't do shit. Then you say fuck my brothers, and they made your ass."

"Niggahs ain't make me. Fuck them niggahs. They wasn't shit. Yo' momma ain't shit. I don't know how the fuck I thought you were different. I wish I could come home and you be gone," he said.

He was waiting for her to yell back, but those words had cut too deep.

She lay down on the bed, closed her phone, and cried. She was alone. Caddy was gone, Truck was fucked, and her moms was still moms. Going back home wasn't an option.

She had drifted off to sleep, when the ring of her phone disturbed her. She thought it was Flight calling back. "Hello," she answered.

"Can you talk?" he said.

Her eyes popped open and she sat up on the bed. She walked to the window to see if Flight was home. His car was still gone.

"Sorry about earlier. Flight saw your number in my phone."

"It dawned on me about ten minutes ago. I realized you were the only Precious I knew. I hesitated calling back."

"Timing is good. I'm glad you did, Herb," she said and began crying. "I'm a good person, I don't use guys, that ain't me, and, and, and—" She started crying harder.

Herb had only met her twice, but he felt he wanted to hold her and tell her that things were going to be all right.

"Fuck is you cryin' for? First thing, you may not be bad, but why was my number in your phone?"

"From when you said it gettin' out the truck that day, it's been in my head," she said softly.

"Then that's where the fuck it should of stayed," he said harshly.

She took it as if he were telling her something, not fussing.

"I would think something too."

"Right, but he know how I hold him down, cookin' shit, baggin' shit, sellin' shit, but he say I ain't shit, down me, and my family, and my brothers gave him his start," she said through cries.

Big Herb's mind was going a mile a minute. *Cook, distribute, sell, and I'll have that bitch driving too.*

"He said he was gonna come to you and ask you about this."

Big Herb laughed. "Girl, you crazy as hell."

"What?"

"Nothing. What you doin'?"

"Sittin' here," she said.

"Meet me at Varsity."

"Where's that?"

"Out the Beach, off Bonney. Second Independence, right on Bonney. Got it?"

"Yeah."

"I'll be there at 9:30," he said. "See ya."

"Okay, I'ma erase your number, since that shit in my head. What kinda club is this?" she asked. "Herb." She realized he had hung up.

She jumped up, asking herself why she was meeting Herb, if Flight was gonna be there. This wasn't good, this wasn't right, but he did say he wished he'd come home and she'd be gone.

She gathered all her shit and threw it in her car. She began crying, not over leaving Flight, but over where she was going. She tossed all the personal shit in a bag: curlers, her hair oils, and lotions which almost cleared the dresser.

Flight's mom saw her going out the door. "Wait, Precious, let me talk to you."

"No, thank you. Your son said some things that hurt too deep, and he said he wanted me gone. So here's his key and tell him anything I left throw it in the trash."

She got in her car and was driving, listening to Beyonce's CD. She pulled up out the park. She was glad Flight wasn't there, as she backed up and began unloading the three bags.

Truck sat in the door, looking at his sister come up the walkway. Other people saw her dragging shit and began making little comments. Her mom sat in front playing spades, smoking her Newport 100's and drinking Budweisers with her three friends, Auntie Vera, Mary Jane, and Ms. Evelyn.

"Hey, Auntie Vera, Ms. Evelyn, Mary Jane."

"I knew your grown ass be back. What he do, whip your ass?" she said, sipping her beer.

"No," she said.

"He better not had," she yelled standing up. "Because I'll fuck that niggah up. Tell him, Vera, I'll fuck him up, fuckin' with my baby," she said hugging Precious.

"Damn right. Slap a muthafucka, so he know you ain't no soft bitch," Vera said.

"See, Vera, don't tell her that," Mary Jane said softly.

"Cut his ass, girl. Cut him good. He might beat your ass, but before he do it again, his motherfuckin' ass will think," Evelyn said.

"Learn that motherfucka somethin' " Mary Jane laughed.

"Glad you're here. Feed that muthafucka in the door. Maybe he can say more than *mama*."

They all laughed and continued their game.

She walked inside without a word. "Hey, Russ." She leaned over and kissed him.

"What's up? Talk to me," he said.

"Niggah on some high horse shit. Talkin' shit on the fam, you know how y'all do. I'll be okay." She smiled, so he wouldn't be upset.

She walked back outside to the car, pulled the other two bags out, and sat them on the sidewalk.

A young, light brown dude with two long ponytails, in a red bandanna came running up. "What's up, Precious?" He grabbed one of the bags.

"Nothing up, Sterling," she said, nonchalantly.

"Don't act like that toward me," he said. "I ain't the one puttin' your ass out."

She looked at him.

"I'm just jokin'."

"What you doin' hangin' over there with them niggahs?"

"I'm from a new breed of niggahs. I'm gonna be smart about things and staying in school. I'll meet niggahs from all over claiming BLOOD," he said seriously.

"That's why you wearing a red T-shirt, bandanna,

claiming BLOOD. Y'all niggahs are fools. Y'all niggahs gonna start killing each other over colors too." Precious looked at her friend of ten years.

"Naw, girl, it's bigger than that, but I'm on my last year of school and I got plans. I know niggahs out Park Place, Titas Town, and out Suffolk. We all connected. I got niggahs comin' now buyin' quarters and halfs. I'm goin' through four and a half in like two days on my time. I work from two to eight and I'm done. If I had the weight, I could take over this shit," he said, knowing Precious knew cats.

"How you gonna take over anything?" she smiled, taking Sterling as a joke.

"You see how many people over there?"

She started counting slowly. "About thirty nothin'-ass niggahs."

"How many claimin' red?"

She stared again.

"About nine."

"That's all I need, because they'll die for me, and me, them. It's not for me to explain or for you to understand. Just hold me down if you know something." He looked in her eyes, seriously.

They walked up to her house and walked in.

He looked at Truck. "I'm the one you and Caddy should of put on. I'm the one," he said and walked out.

As he walked out, Precious's mom said, "Better go on, Blood."

They all laughed.

He smirked too. *Simple-ass people will see*, he thought.

Precious told Truck everything that Flight had said, how it started, everything she was doing for him, and that she was going to meet Herb. When she saw the tears drop down his cheek, she knew why. Caddy was gone, and he was no longer Truck. He was just Russ.

When Precious ran upstairs, Russ called his mom in and told her everything. She made a call for him and walked back out to drink her beer and finish her game.

Precious ran and jumped in the shower, came out, and lotioned down. She looked at the time and saw it was already eight. She pulled out her tan Liz Claiborne jeans and a brown sweater shirt that buttoned down the front with fur around her wrist. She stood in the mirror doing her hair, making sure it fell perfect on her front shoulders.

She walked over to her bed and found her brown panties and brown bra, threw on her clothes, and her brown boots she'd picked up at DSW. With makeup, this seventeen-year-old could pass for twenty-two easily.

When she walked downstairs, Truck was staring out the door at what was going on. Flight had pulled up with Moe.

She kissed Truck's forehead and was headed out when she saw Flight and Moe. Her stomach churned.

"Be careful," Truck said.

"A'ight. I'm going to my car and I'm out," she said, walking out the door.

"She leavin' out again? If that was my child . . . Whoa!" Auntie Vera said.

"Her ass wouldn't leave outta here," Ms. Evelyn said.

"A jealous man is a fool, girl," Mary Jane added.

"Be careful and bring your ass home tonight. I taught that bitch how to handle herself, goddamn. I raised that one right." Her mom stood up. "And I dare a bitch to say I didn't. Where's my cigarettes? That's where I fucked up, right there." She pointed at Truck and sat back down as she lit a Newport 100.

"You did fuck up on that one," Auntie Vera told her.

Flight saw Precious walking to her car. He had been home and realized his hopes had come true. She was gone, and it hit him hard. He was upset earlier, and yes, he was jealous, but he didn't really expect her to leave. He thought she had nowhere to go and never figured she would go back home, a place she once called a hellhole.

He broke into a stride headed toward Precious. She was looking fine as hell, and it was fuckin' with him. "Where you goin'?"

"Why? We're not together."

"Look, we need to talk, I'm sorry about—"

"Fuck all that, Flight. I'm done. I'm free. Put mother-fuckin' space between us niggah," she said walking off.

He snatched her by her coat and pulled her back.

"Get off me, Flight," she said snatching her arm.

He reached out with both hands and snatched her by her collar and pulled her to him, her boots barely touching the ground, causing her purse to drop. "Bitch," he said, "I'll slap the shit out yo' ass if you pull away from me. You ain't goin' no goddamn where." He cuffed her closer.

Her mom was coming down the sidewalk.

Sterling stepped up. "Get off her, man."

Flight looked at him and his partners that all had red on in some way or another.

Moe stepped up and grabbed Flight. "Come on, man. Chill. This ain't the way."

Flight looked at Moe for a minute and felt shit was his fault, because Herb was his brother. "Get the fuck off me," Flight said, holding Precious by one hand, looking on at Moe, then at Sterling.

Before anybody could say another word, a black figure dressed in a black Dickies suit stepped on the sidewalk. By the time his right Timb hit the concrete, the .45 was out and sitting on Flight's chest, while his left hand rested on the 9mm in his waist for any unexpected shit.

Satan wanted to kill this niggah so bad. "It won't be

said again, my niggah." He pulled back the hammer, but it was too many people and he heard Precious's voice.

"No, no, no," she said, easing over to Satan.

Flight had instantly let her go when the long barrel touched his Bear coat.

"Go 'head and go, baby girl," Satan said. He put his gun away and stood there, waiting for Flight to do something.

Then Moe told Flight to come on and drop him off, and they walked off.

Satan stood there until they crossed the street. Then he walked up to see Truck.

Precious arrived at the Varsity at nine-thirty. She had fixed her face and clothes at the stoplights on Campostella. She looked fine, but her insides were eaten up. She dialed Herb's number as she walked to the door. By the time she reached the door, they asked for ID. She stood there as if she'd forgot it.

Herb came up. "She with me," he said, and they let her in. *Damn, she's a banger*, he thought.

Just like a lady, she hugged him with both arms under his and placed her palms on his back. He hugged her back, and she felt good, smelled good, and looked even better.

They walked back by the pool table, where he introduced her to Poppa, Twon, Dundee, and Squirmy, shooting pool and already running a three-hundred-fifty-dollar tab.

She came in and sat at the booth closest to Herb.

"What you drinkin'?"

"Hennessy, straight," she said.

Niggahs looked at her like, *Damn!*

She sat talking to Herb and sipping as they shot pool and gambled. She told Herb all that had happened.

It was going on twelve o'clock when Moe came in and saw Herb standing on the wall with Precious standing in his arms, her ass pressed against his dick as he waited his turn. Moe shook his head at both of them. She hunched her shoulders like whatever, and Big Herb just smiled, walked over and gave his brother a pound and they hugged.

"That shit ain't right, Herb," Moe said low in his ear.

"Fuck that niggah, son. Bitch niggah don't know how to handle her. I gots this now," Herb said slow.

Moe could smell the Henny. He knew when Herb was fucked up. He watched as Herb took his shots on the table.

Herb missed. He turned to Moe, who was looking at Precious. "Tell me, Moe, is she a keeper?"

"Look, man—"

"Again, Moe, is she a keeper?"

"Yeah, niggah." Moe remembered that Flight said she had one niggah one time before him and he was teaching her. "She chill, real chill."

"You done with this shit, son. This hustlin' shit gettin' grimy, and you don't need to be around it. You didn't tell me I had brothers out the Park like that."

"What?" Moe asked.

Herb pulled his shirt up on his phone showing his red rag hanging out of his back pocket on the right side.

They all noticed that shit, and Moe just noticed that Herb wore more red boldly.

"Fuck is that?"

"Niggahs belong to something. We're a family, and it's gonna take over, starting with the Park. You need to stay away from your man, cut your ties." Herb looked at him.

"Already have." Moe looked at Precious. Him and Flight had some words when he'd dropped him off. Moe ain't appreciate how he came off, he let him know.

Flight said nothing, his mind totally somewhere else.

Moe walked over to Precious, and they began talking. After a few, they were kicking it like old friends.

By two, everybody was headed out the door.

Herb walked Precious to her car, his arm wrapped around her. He knew he had one of the hottest bitches in the club.

She leaned back against her car, and he fell in her arms.

"So when I'm gonna hear from you?" she asked.

"Oh, you not stayin' with me?" he asked surprised.

"Am I?"

"Yeah. Follow me," he said and walked off to where Poppa and them were parked. "Who got the hook-up?" Herb asked out loud to his team.

Nobody knew offhand.

Then Squirmy asked to hold Herb's phone. "My niggah I went to state with was working at the Courtyard. I don't know if he still there," he said, dialing his number.

After a brief conversation, Squirmy looked at Poppa and said, "$40, and he waiting on you."

"Bet. Y'all know where I'll be." He gave everybody a pound.

Moe gave a hard pound and pulled Herb to him. "You do know she only seventeen, right?"

Herb looked at him. "Should of told me before that last Henny."

They laughed as they broke and went their separate ways.

When they arrived at the room, Precious was feeling nice, and she was feeling Big Herb. She took off her coat, kicked off her shoes, walked over to Herb, and began kissing him.

He removed his shirt and wife-beater and stood in his jeans and Timbs. He pulled her close and grabbed her ass. "Yo, get that shit off," he said.

She removed her clothes, and within minutes he had her ass up standing on the side of the bed moving in and out. He closed his eyes as her tightness grabbed at his dick. Her moans got louder as her pussy got wetter.

He was only going five minutes when he bust on her back. She lay flat on her stomach, wondering what she'd done.

Herb left no time for thinking. She was on her back with legs in the air. He'd kicked off his Timbs, came out of his State Property jeans, and was on her. The more he pounded, the louder and wetter she got. This turned him on even more.

She realized, that night, that there was a beast that dwelled in men, and when he came out, her kitty cat was no match for Herb. Through the night her body would go through hell, but she loved every minute of it. She fell asleep tucked in Herb arms. He squeezed her as if she was going to leave and she loved it. They slept until housekeeping knocked.

"Are you checking out?" a voice asked through the door.

"Are we checking out?" Herb asked, not moving.

"Naw," she joked, "we stayin' two more days."

"Look in my pocket, and go take care of two more nights," he said and rolled over.

She did as she was told and came back up, crawling under Herb. She wanted some more of this twenty-six-year-old man, and Herb gave her exactly what she wanted.

Afterwards, he showered and dressed. She was lying there looking at TV naked. He stared at her. She was too fine. She would definitely have a place on his team.

"Where you shop and shit?" he asked.

"Anywhere. Mainly the mall, but if I'm trying to

stretch some money, Ross, T.J. Maxx, Marshalls, Lern-
ers."

"How much for outfits for two days?"

"One fifty. I could probably find some shoes."

He tossed her two hundred and told her he would
holla later. He was getting ready to be out, when she
came to the edge of the bed on her knees.

"Take him out for me right quick," she said, staring at
his zipper, never looking at him.

He did as he was told.

She sucked his dick for two minutes. As he was getting
into it, she stopped. "Go ahead, Big Herb, handle your
business. I'll be here."

"If not, I know you better answer your muthafuckin'
phone." He tucked his hard dick away and headed out
the door.

They ended up staying in the Courtyard for four days,
then Herb asked Moe to get an apartment out Ashbrook
for him. Precious would probably be there too.

Moe smiled. This young girl had Herb going.

They went from the hotel to the apartment, then Herb
rode with her to get her shit from her moms. If anybody
needed to see him or her, now was the time.

They pulled up out Oakley Park, where niggahs were
hangin' out, tryin' to get money, including Flight. He
looked when she turned in, but quickly turned his head,
actin' like he wasn't payin' attention.

She parked and got out. Herb got out and adjusted his
.380 that sat in the waist of his black Dickies. He pulled
his shirt so his rag would show, then adjusted the red
bandanna on his neck. He looked over at the crew of niggahs repping their colors, which were the same as his.

Sterling threw a sign and Herb threw one back. Then
Sterling came across the street, followed by two niggahs

draped in red. They all showed love, but Sterling hugged Herb almost like Precious did, but brought his right hand around and grabbed his red hat. "What's popping?"

"Five popping, four dropping, all day!" Herb said.

They began talking. The niggah excused one of the cats that had walked over. Herb turned and excused Precious.

"This my man, Blanco. He from a set out Grandy Park. This is my right hand, and we need more work. You hit me off once to hurt cats, but I'm ready to take over."

Blanco stood there, never saying a word, but the red Dickies shirt, red bandanna wrapped around his head, red hat that was tilted on his head, and the red Converse on this black-ass niggah—who had his entire fronts and bottoms gold—said enough.

"What you need?" Herb asked.

"Half to start."

"Both of us. We ready. If you want us to blow, kick this shit the fuck off. You'll get paid," Blanco said.

Herb looked at Blanco.

"We been waitin'. They waitin' on us. We all over. Be the man to bless us."

"Okay, here's my number. Call me later." Herb began to walk off then he stopped. "Yo, I may need to call on my family."

"That bitch niggah who never deserved to be put on," Blanco said. "Just tell me when, just tell me when," he added, showing his golds.

Herb smiled and walked up to Precious' house. Her moms and Auntie Vera were sitting in two chairs out front, smoking cigarettes and talking.

"Precious found her a man built like Russ," Auntie Vera said.

"Probably been locked up like Russ. You been locked up, boy?" her moms asked. "How long you been home?"

"About three and a half months," Herb answered.

"I hope you mean to do good by her," Auntie Vera said.

"Yes, ma'am," he responded.

"I tell you this, muthafucka, she only seventeen, and if you mean good, all right. If you gon' use or abuse her, go on 'bout your business," her moms said.

"That's not my intentions. Just here to make her happy."

"We ain't got no beer, girl," Auntie Vera said.

"Can I get y'all to get me some beer before you go?"

"Sure."

Precious came to the door and asked Herb to grab a bag. She was walking out the door when her moms hollered, "You bring my cigarettes and beer back."

"No," she yelled.

"I already told her we would," Herb said.

"She asked you? Damn! She don't give a fuck."

"Shit all right." Herb laughed.

Chapter 30

Herb stood back as his girl finished working her magic over the stove. He then walked over and weighed out the thirty-six ounces, taking eighteen ounces and putting it in two separate bags. He walked outside and put the bags under her passenger seat.

She had just finished cooking up three kilos of powder and turned it into four and a half. She came over, kissed him, and headed out the door.

It had been weeks, and he was still feeling her like the first time.

She was happy, climbing in her car, headed out the Park. She knew the routine—go out the Park, park the car, and leave it open. Sterling would get the work from under the seat and leave the money.

Truck would sit at the door and watch everything go down. He didn't feel Herb was truly using Precious, because she made money every time she cooked, dropped off shit to Sterling and Blanco. He would even get money for looking out.

Herb had his street shit running perfectly and steady building. Sterling and Blanco were off the chain. Sterling the laid-back money-getter, and Blanco, that wild-ass money-getter. Both were respected and powerful, and now feeding niggahs. Their team expanded throughout Tidewater. They had already moved into Oakley Park, and Flight was feeling it. Grandy Park, Park Place, and Titas Town were theirs also.

Weight was being moved, and everybody's pocket was seeing it, especially Herb's. He was sitting on a nice piece of change that he kept all in the apartment closet, in shoe boxes and coat pockets.

Herb and Moe were sitting in the apartment sipping Hennessy, when Precious came back in with a dirty yellow Western Union bag with twenty-three thousand. He was now buying straight from Poppa. No more fronting. The new grey Navigator sitting on twenty-threes in Oasis spinning wheels let everybody else know what he was getting.

Precious ran in and ran back out. "Call me. I'm going out for a minute. Need anything?"

"No," Herb said. "Don't get lost."

"No," Moe said.

She blew a kiss at Herb and was out the door.

"So you goin' to Philly?" Herb asked.

"All-Star game, fuckin' right," Moe said.

"Look, Poppa and Twon talkin' about havin' a boat cruise. They ask me the other night if I was gettin' down. I want to get down, but I don't got time to watch that money or sell tickets and shit. If you gonna do it, I'll go in."

"Sounds good. I'm about smart money."

"So get with Twon and them. See what it's gonna cost, and give me the details."

"Bet."

Herb got up and threw on his white Tee and white DC's, wrapped his red bandanna around his wrist and headed out the door, to his apartment out the Lakes. He wasn't spending much time there, but the apartment was convenient, and he didn't want to leave shorty fucked up. After all, she'd looked out at a critical time in his life.

He was rolling down the boulevard when his phone rang.

It was Sterling and Blanco. They were letting him know that the Park was hot. They had just laid down a niggah who was supposed to be a snitch, but he was part of Flight's crew. They were getting real touchy because their clientele had died down to almost nothing, so Flight was on some bullshit.

"Just give me the word, baby. Give it to me," Blanco yelled.

"Y'all niggahs crazy. Give me a second. Let me check something."

Herb hung up and called Precious. She had become his road dog. She rolled out with him, and they did more hanging than any girl he'd ever fucked with.

"Hey, baby."

"What up?" he asked.

"Nothing. I'm in DSW looking at shoes, me and my girl."

"I need to talk to you about something. Now."

"Where?"

"You know where I'm at. My office."

She left the store quickly, headed out The Lakes to Margate, Poppa's spot. When she arrived, she hit his phone. She knew better than to knock on the door.

He came out and climbed in her car. "What's up, baby?"

"Word is your man tellin' on the family, bringin' cats down. Two of Sterling's peoples got knocked off. They say they had to lay a niggah down already."

"I heard. My moms called me. Told me some niggah got shot three times in the stomach. He died before they got him to Norfolk General."

"For real? Well, let's put it like this. I don't want to let that shit go down, but he's threatening to hurt the fam, and what we built. I don't want to kill your man for personal reasons."

Herb's phone rang. It was a 646 area code. His mind began to race. "Big Herb," he answered.

"What land you claim?" the voice said.

"Blood land."

"What's poppin'?"

"All day, Rohan."

Somebody went over his head. For him to get this call, somebody was looking out for somebody in Indian Creek, who was looking out for somebody on the island.

"Got a problem."

"No problem," Herb said.

"No, I'm not askin' you, I'm tellin' you. Handle it today."

Herb was getting ready to say something, but the line went dead. He looked at Precious. "Forget our conversation," he said, opening the car door.

"No, Herb. Finish, please," she begged. She knew what was going to happen. "You don't have to do this," she yelled.

"Look, you don't understand this shit. This is way bigger than me. I've been in and out of jail and prison since I was sixteen. I've touched so much *hard* that my hands should be numb, but I have never seen or had over five grand of my own at one time. I go to prison, and niggahs accept me as I am—nothin'-ass, wild-ass muthafuckin' niggah, with nothing but my knowledge of this game, the heart to handle my business. Shit got easier this stretch, and through my family, we got seventy grand. If this get fucked, one family falls." He tugged on his rag.

She turned around, saw Herb dialing his phone. She rolled out, making her way up the street in deep thought. She didn't know what to do. Herb was her man, and she had fallen for him and the lifestyle he'd provided for her. But even though Flight had shitted on her, cussed her out, put her out, and within a week, moved some bitch with two kids in the apartment, he didn't deserve to die. She had to give him a chance to get away from the Park.

She dialed his number.

"What bitch?"

"Fuck you, Flight. I called to see how you and your ready-made family doin'?"

"We fine, bitch. Livin' good, bitch."

"Me too, flossing in our new Navigator. I'm gettin' ready to buy me an Altima, and since I'm pregnant, we gonna have a four-bedroom house built in Chesapeake." She knew she had cut his ass hard, lying, talkin' 'bout she was pregnant. She went for the kill. "I called because niggahs put a hit on you. I don't like you, but I don't want you to get hurt up. You need to get ghost, niggah."

"Appreciate the heads-up, baby, but the streets been talkin'."

"Be careful. Bye."

By the time she was hanging up, Herb was dialing Sterling's number.

"What's up? Everything straight?"

"Yeah, paper always straight. Who made a call?" Herb asked.

"I talked to my uncle all the time, Quan. He doin' like fifteen."

"Yeah." Herb knew who he was. "So is Blanco with you?"

"Right here," Blanco yelled.

"Handle that?"

"Done."

Chapter 31

A couple hours later Blanco had a young team in the back of a tinted, silver Town & Country. He called Sterling, who was already out the park, to let him know he was coming over the Bridge which meant at least ten minutes.

Sterling had niggahs in place ready to run up on Flight and his team that stood by the tree.

Flight stood talking to his team as if he wasn't worried about shit. The silver van pulled into the Park slowly and came to a sudden stop. The right door slid open, and Sterling pulled his TEC-9 and started popping.

Flight pulled two nines, and the thirty-four shots he had started to fly. The cats that Flight was talking to pulled burners and started shooting, but the guns Sterling and Blanco's team had were too big and outnumbered them.

Flight began to fall behind the tree for cover. Then he saw the cats coming from between the building and back of the Park, and the guy coming up on the opposite side of the van, with a big Bear coat.

When his coat came open, he showed his shotgun and his identity. It was Vic. He turned, and they heard the blast from the shotgun, then screeching tires. He then pointed his guns at Sterling and let his last twelve fly.

The guns stopped.

As the sirens drew closer, everybody who could, broke out.

Blanco, after the blast shattered the windshield and showered him with glass, punched the gas and did a U-turn, almost hitting Vic, running on the curb and across the grass back on Campostella Road.

Within minutes, you had eight police cars with two in a car, two unmarked cars, an ambulance, and the rescue squad.

Everything was taped off and nobody could come in or leave. They found one dead body that they bagged up. Because of all the red, they marked it as being gang related, some new shit in Norfolk.

The other body was Sterling's. He'd been hit two times, only by Flight. He knew it wasn't his time. They put him on the stretcher and took off to Norfolk General.

Flight was driving home when his phone rang. He was still shook from what had just popped off. "Yeah!"

"What up, baby? You all right?" Vic asked.

"Fo' sho. Thought you had forgot about me."

"Naw, baby, we family. We gets money together, and I know you. You ain't with all this bullshit. But when it was time to stand your ground, you called me, and that said a lot about yourself. A lot of niggahs would of fell into that color shit."

"Got my own mind, and I gets my own paper, dolo," Flight said.

"Be safe, kid, and lay low, because the block is hot. The block is hot!" Vic laughed and hung up.

Over in Grandy Park, Blanco had changed up in his

all-black State Property set that looked like Dickies, ditched the van, and was driving his Tahoe, no rims, no sounds, just clean. He stood outside with some family, piecing together what had happened. This shit should have been too easy, but dude was prepared.

He jumped in his Tahoe, headed to Norfolk General, hoping his man was okay. His phone rang. "Hello."

"This Herb. What up?"

"What you think, man?"

"What you mean?" Herb asked, confused.

"I've never been a fake-ass niggah, so I'ma come straight. Old boy was ready. Somebody told him we were coming, and they got my man, probably fighting for his life."

"Damn! I don't know," Herb said.

"You know, only you," Blanco said slowly.

"What?" Herb said angrily.

"Nothing, partner. I'm out," Blanco said, and hung up.

Herb stood on his balcony. He couldn't believe what he'd just heard. His mind raced. Flight must be an on-point niggah, because how would he have known this? Streets don't talk that fast, unless . . . then it hit him. He tried to erase the thought. *No, she wouldn't. No, she didn't. I know this bitch didn't fuck up my life.*

He picked up his phone, dialed her number.

"Hey, baby," she answered.

"Where you?" he asked calmly.

"Leaving Candy Nails, turning on the boulevard."

"Waitin' on you," he said and hung up. He looked at Moe who was laid-back on the couch, looking at BET, and shook his head.

"What?" Moe asked.

"Nothing, man. Just fucked up right now."

Herb walked to the counter and took a swig of his Hennessy, then he returned to the balcony. He was staring into space when he heard the front door. He walked back inside.

"Hey, Moe. Hey, baby." She kissed Herb and dropped her purse and phone on the table. She walked to the bedroom.

He picked up her phone and pressed *Send*. Then he saw *dialed calls*, and hit *select*, scrolled down until he saw Flight. He pressed *view*. *She called this niggah as soon as she left me*. He sat the phone down.

She came out and stood in front of him. "What's wrong?" she asked softly.

He looked into her eyes. "Did you warn dude?" he asked softly.

"No," she said quickly.

"Did you call Flight and tell him?"

"I called him, but—"

The backhand sent her against the entertainment center, screaming. She was then silenced by an open-hand slap to the other jaw.

She tried to run, but he grabbed her by her hair with his left hand, by her collar with his right, picked her up off the ground, and slammed her to the floor.

Her eyes widened as her eyes met Moe, who was getting up.

"Moe," she yelled.

He felt her cry for help.

Herb brought her back up by her hair and collar, the look in his eyes she hadn't seen before.

Moe looked at her as he closed his room door, her petite body off the floor, her eyes wide, pouring tears, mouth open using her last breaths, screaming, "Moe, help me, please." He had to shut his door because the look in her eyes was pure terror, as Herb carried her dangling into their room.

Chapter 32

"Fuck that niggah Prince, and that niggah, and that one tonight. My cousin is a winner," Dundee said as they were leaving the gambling spot.

Some cats were mad, but what the fuck, I had just won thirty grand one week before the All-Star Weekend. Prince realized that he had all the niggahs that kept the city running in his presence, and people just knew each niggah made money.

Tonight it was six players, including me. You had Doughboy from Suffolk, who ran an entertainment company, brought groups in town, but word was that him and Jim Jones of Diplomats were peoples, and he was backed by money.

Terri owned a high-class restaurant and catering operation downtown that turned into a jazz club after nine. His peoples had money, convenience stores, non-profits, and a restaurant business for years.

Pappy owned a club on the oceanfront that catered to a white crowd. They kept a crowd and a live band, with famous artists stopping through. He was known to have money, but he was also known as Teddy Riley's cousin, which opened more doors than usual.

Then there was Gee, little-ass niggah always dressed up and known for having big parties in other cities when special functions were going on. He would have parties and pay big stars such as Jay-Z, Jermaine Dupris, Nelly, Nas, Puffy, anybody, to make a guest appearance and charge two, three hundred dollars at the door. He always came off, but if he didn't he was still manager of The Clipse and the Pharell boy.

Then you had this niggah Shawn Graham. Everybody knew him, but nobody knew what he did. He was always with money niggahs, always kept a phat whip, wore designer shit, and would promote clubs from time to time, but it was never a surprise to see Joe Smith by his side hanging out at any time. Seemed to me that was his man.

And there was me. Nobody knew what the fuck I did for real. They knew I owned Triple Play and they knew I loved to gamble. I bring mad cash because I come to play, but for the cats in here now, they all knew me from that street shit. Me, Kendu, and Chris.

They respected Chris, and they just figured if Chris was my man, I would always be straight, which was true.

"Who bringing 50 to the Convocation Center?" I asked loudly.

"I am," Doughboy said.

"I got an artist. He fire. Can he open?" I asked.

"Too many already askin'. I think I'm gonna let them Money Island niggahs get on," he said.

I pulled out my dice. "I'm Bank. If I hit, my artist open. If you win, I'll pay two grand for him to open."

"Bet."

I rolled two, two, one. I paid him two grand, shook hands, and Guttah was going to open Friday night at the Convocation Center for 50 Cent. *Yeah.*

"Who got it poppin' in Philly next week?" I asked.

"I got a party for ya and a show," Gee said. "Special invite guests, Melissa Ford, Buff the Body, LaLa, Damon Dash, Omarion, Irv Gotti, two fifty a head. And guess what? State Property and Young Gunners performing. That's in stone. What?"

"So I'm good. Guttah openin'?"

"Three openin' acts, Prince. I got two locked, sold for some G's too. Sherman got his boys in, Kenny Wayne and Doom, locked."

"How much those Money Island niggahs give you? Niggahs call themselves a 'boss.' Niggahs money can't touch my money. What? Same as Doughboy, my bank," I said, ready to roll the dice.

"Naw, son. Irv Gotti, Damon Dash, possibly Baby from Cash Money. Come on, son, do yo 'money-shit' on Baby money too, Prince? You shittin' on Dash too, Prince," he said smiling, knowing he had me.

I threw a stack down. "Ten grand?"

He stood there like the ten G's didn't mean shit. "Roll, baby."

I shook the dice and tossed them down—two, four, six; three, one, four; four, four, two. I stood there sad inside, because the two was so low.

As his six, six, one hit the ground, I yelled, "Nobody fucks with a deuce." I picked up my stack and smiled, stuck my hand out like a gentleman, and our deal was locked, just like them Money Island bosses.

"Call me," he said. "I got you."

Me and Dundee decided to go by the studio to give Guttah the good news, and we weren't ready to call it a night. It was late, and I still wanted Prayyiah to come over.

For the last several weeks, she had slowly worked her way into the number one spot. I wasn't spending as much time with Tee Tee, Lecia, or Anita.

Lecia was definitely a thing of the past.

Me and Anita were doing more talking than anything. She was still helping me with my business shit, but she wasn't running like she used to, claiming to be tired quite a bit. I had to run, so I stayed in touch. But more and more days were passing us by.

Now Tee Tee wasn't that easy to dismiss. We were connected in a lot of ways—house, bills, family, and business—was what I kept telling myself, but I loved her. We just had our differences that started to get on my nerves. But no matter what I was doing, I had to know she was okay.

I dialed Prayyiah. She answered on the second ring. She must've wanted to see me too, because she usually called me back, like she busy or something.

I told her to meet me at the studio and that I was waiting on her. It wasn't long after I got there that she arrived. We hadn't been together long, but she never hesitated speaking her mind.

I was upstairs talking to Guttah, Ashy, Young Hop, and Pop G, when my phone rang. "What up?"

"I'm down here. You ready?" she asked.

"Naw, come on up."

"I'm tired, Prince. I'm going home."

"No, you're not. Either come up, or give me ten minutes."

"I'll stay in the car. Hurry up," she said with attitude.

Guttah had produced a beat and was freestyling. Mad niggahs tried to battle or hang with Guttah, but the only niggah I heard that could hang was Pop G. And when they got together only the best came out.

Guttah was hype when he heard he was opening for 50, and was going to do a show in Philly at the All-Star game. I was just hoping somebody recognized his skills and picked him up. He had been working hard. That's why I really wanted to see this niggah succeed. I was ready to put whatever behind him. I made sure he had the best equipment to make and produce the best beats, and he was doing it. I could tell they were finishing up no time soon even though I loved just hanging in the studio, listening to the beats he made, then listening to different niggahs try and ride the beat.

I said my last words and I was out.

Me and Prayyiah reached the crib. She went in the room and laid down, and I hit the television and turned on BET to peep that *Uncut* shit.

After sparking that haze and watching all those bitches in the strip club and in the clubs, I walked in the back and crawled in my bed, and eased up close to Prayyiah. I leaned in and kissed her.

She moved.

I kissed her again.

She turned over and wrapped her arms around me, and allowed me to slide inside of her. I guess being high off life and haze made her body feel like heaven. I actually wanted to say, "Thank you for allowing me to fuck. I really thank you."

I came hard and collapsed on top of her, and she held me close and rubbed my back. I was in heaven for real.

Friday came quick. Guttah had been in the studio twenty-four seven. We were all going to leave from the studio to make sure we all flowed in together to get backstage. Guttah had his hype man, Lites. Then he had his team that wanted to shine and flaunt on stage, so he took Young Hop, Ponic, Squirmy, and Young Twon. The rest of The Lakes would be in the crowd.

I had bought fifty tickets and gave them away out the Lakes, to make sure Guttah came off.

I could see Guttah in deep thought. Everybody else was sparking Optimos, passing Dutches, pulling on Backs, sipping on their drink of choice.

"You ready, son?" I yelled at Guttah.

"No doubt, daddy. I'm a hustler. What you think I'm in it fo'?" he said, quoting one of his lines from his CD.

Everybody got hype.

"Let's head out, we got to ride through the Lakes so I can get that feel," Guttah said heading out.

Everybody walked out and stopped in their tracks.

For finishing his CD on time, I had gotten a black Yukon Denali XL and had it wrapped with his cover. *Back to the Guttah*!

I popped the trunk. I had pressed five thousand CD's to give away. I had also pressed up five dozen *Back to the Guttah* T-shirts, and twenty thousand flyers. I had designed all this shit myself. It was my way of relaxing, but of course my graphic design company charged my record company to keep the books straight.

Big El was holding down the truck. Everybody piled in.

Guttah jumped in his 350 with Pop G driving. I knew they were going to freestyle and smoke all the way to the Convocation Center. Then he would be ready, but not before riding through the Lakes.

"Yo, I'll meet y'all over there," I said to Big El and Guttah.

"Don't forget you got the pass to get us in the back," Big El said.

"Dundee got one too. He gonna meet y'all out the Lakes and then we out." I jumped in the Quest, headed to the house with Tee Tee.

I met Brada, but this time he gives me back ten grand and buys the Quest van. I leave the work there in a safe place, and broke out with Brada, so he could drop me off up the street.

I called Prayyiah, and she met me, so we could go get dressed. Damn right, I was taking her. They didn't get much finer than her, and I enjoyed having her by my side.

To my surprise when she picked me up, Amaia was following her with some dude. I got in the Ac, and she began driving. "I missed you, baby," she said.

"Yeah, I know they not followin' us to my house."

"They were, but I guess not," she said sarcastically.

"Yo, I ain't with that smart-ass shit tonight. Don't get fucked up."

"What?"

I stared directly into her eyes. "I'm not playin'. Handle that shit."

She sent them to get a drink until we returned.

"You happy?" she said, hanging up her phone.

"Naw, because I ain't fuckin with dude. I don't know him. He not goin' with me. And if you say one word, you'll be ridin' with them," I said, getting in the shower.

She removed her clothes and followed.

I was washing my hair, and she soaped down my rag and began washing my back. She said, "I figure if I wash your back, then you'll really know I got it. Sometimes I forget things, Prince, and who I'm fuckin' with."

I turned around, gave her a big hug, finished washing up, and got dressed. I threw on my Evisu jeans, with some Gucci sneakers, and an Evisu T-shirt. I reached over and put on my stainless Breitling, my five-carat bracelet for eight grand, and my five-grand white gold pinky ring. My chain that fell on the Evisu T-shirt made Prayyiah look at me and smile.

She walked over in her Baby Phat jeans, short tight Baby Phat shirt, and boots that complemented the outfit. Her hair fell perfectly over her shoulders.

"Look in the drawer."

She opened the drawer. Nothing. "For what?" She turned around with a funny look.

I was holding a half-carat, white gold, tennis bracelet in one hand, and a ladies Cartier watch in another that I'd picked up at White Hall Jewelry. When she walked over, I placed them both on each wrist.

We were on our way out the door, and I stopped her. "Look, I have some very strong feelings for you, and I just want you to know, I promise to be here for you and always give you the love and respect you deserve. But niggahs need to know you're mine."

I reached in my pocket and pulled out the half-carat marquise cut diamond ring.

She smiled as her left hand went up.

I placed it there, and we kissed. "You know I own your ass," I said. "Don't fuck with me."

"I ain't scared of you," she said, headed out the door.

I opened the garage, and she almost fainted. I saw her mouth drop to the sight of the new Black CLS 500 Mercedes Benz, sitting on chrome "gambinos."

She climbed in, and the soft leather wrapped around her body. This shit wasn't set to hit the dealerships for another year, but my money bought me a different lifestyle, and today was my turning point.

I was tired of sitting back. It was my time to shine.

We rolled out.

She dialed Amaia and they followed. We got by the Convocation Center, and the police let me and the truck

in. I had to get out and let the policeman know Guttah
was performing before he would let Pop G and Guttah in.

We got in and went backstage. G-Unit and 50's niggahs were in another room under tight security. We had
mad peoples rocking our T-shirts and passing out CD's.

The lights went dim, and a bright light hit the stage.
Lites Out, Ashy, Young Twon, Squirmy, and Pop G ran
out on the stage, and the beat came on.

The crowd started yelling as they began singing the
hook:

What ya wanna, what ya wanna do?
You ain't as hard as you think that you partying
What ya wanna, what ya wanna do?

Then Guttah bust on stage.

In my hood, I'm always hungry
Death lives right around the corner from me
But I ain't scared, I'm prepared,
That's why niggahs runnin' from me
You be dead, so I hope your peoples comin' for me

Guttah did two more songs and they gave the signal to
wrap it up.

I walked out on stage and told everybody the album
Back to the Guttah would be in record stores soon. The
crowd was hype and Guttah had done his job. My niggahs
were hype. We had never been here before so I yelled,
"One for the road," and everybody on stage began:

The more things changed, the more they stay the same, man
Catch me out The Lakes livin' like a cave man
Record execs try to turn me to a slave, man
But I'll be gangster 'til the end of my days, man

As the crowd joined in, they gave me the signal to end my act.

I ignored them. *Fuck y'all. This my time and my niggahs' time.*

Then I saw Dundee come past security iced-out, mad ice draped over a black Sean John sweat suit, white DCs, and white Tee. He had Ponic and Poppa with him. They ran on stage and hyped shit up more. I know we had a hundred people from Lake Edward and probably three hundred from Bayside in the crowd.

I felt so good inside, a feeling of greatness, a feeling of belonging, it wasn't my fly shit, it wasn't the bulge from the ten grand in my front left pocket in 100's, or the two grand bulging in twenties in my right pocket, but it was the fact that I was from the Lakes and looking at all these niggahs on stage happy, smiling, going crazy, singing, repping The Lakes.

Guttah finished, and they left the stage, with the crowd still singing the hook. We all went to the back, everybody hype and hollering. Banks was in the back ready to go on. He had his hands full. Getting that crowd back was going to be a job after what Guttah had just dropped on the Center. I was telling Doughboy that I appreciated the love, that was a definite look-out. Then we heard Squirmy getting loud, and that wasn't in his character.

"Get the fuck out the way now."

"Who the fuck they talkin' to?" Dundee said.

"Talkin' to you now." Another security officer stepped up because he was close enough to hear my cousin's question. "Move."

I made my way over. "You about to make shit get critical." I stared up into his eyes. "Respect. Remember respect."

"Set this shit off, *P*, set it off," Ponic said ready.

Other security and people backstage came closer.

"Yo, baby, we all family over here. Nobody, and I mean nobody, from my family will leave here hurt. We'll destroy this bitch," Poppa said coming closer.

"Shut this shit down." I gritted on this big-ass niggah in front of me. In my mind I knew I could fuck him up. The one and one had my body racing and my mind said, *Fuck him up. Set it off, Prince.* But deep inside I knew that once I caught this niggah jaw, my hand would go straight to the loaded black .380 that sat in my waist.

Doughboy walked over and said something to security, and they eased back. He looked at me and said, "This my money, son. Same money you'll be tryin' to get next week."

I gave him a pound and left, and everybody followed. Banks was bombing out, anyway. We had done our thing, and that niggah was out there trying to get the crowd back.

We walked outside and jumped in the whips. We were driving up Hampton Boulevard, wildin' out, when the new Platinum Range Rover pulled up beside me. The window came down, and Dundee threw up the *L* sign with his right hand.

"What the fuck?" I looked past Prayyiah. She was so busy staring at the Range, I had to hit her ass, like my shit wasn't bangin'. "Girl, you ridin' in the hot shit. Better get your eyes off my cousin."

She began laughing. "That shit phat as hell," she said smiling.

"I know," I said, knowing my cousin was getting it with Poppa.

It wasn't too much to do, so we ended up at Picasso's, our home club, on Newtown Road, across the street from The Lakes.

We pulled in the parking lot, music blasting from the truck, while niggahs acted the fool, passin' out CD's and

T-shirts. Me, Dundee, Poppa, and Big El were standing by our whips talking when my phone rang. "What up, baby?" I yelled.

"What y'all niggahs doin'?" Chris asked.

"Not a thang, son. We just ripped the Convocation Center. My new artist, Guttah, opened for 50 and them G-Unit niggahs. And when I say F-I-R-E, son, I mean, niggahs was fire."

"Signed who? Fuck you doin'?" he said.

I walked away from the others. Nobody needed to know my pocket. "Son, I'm doin' big things with your gift and my change—music, building homes, real estate. In three months, man, I should have a mill." My eyes watered.

At that moment, I stopped, blacked out my surroundings and prayed.

God, I truly thank You for what You've done and what You are going to do for me. Put Your arms around me and protect me from all harm for I am Your child. With You on my side, who can touch me?

"What?"

"Yo, I'm gettin' down. I'm going to buy into the music shit, the studio shit, like forty percent, so give me a number when I get there. And the next project on those houses, I'm goin' half, me and you," he said.

"Yo, that's all I needed to hear, because I was gonna get an office building downtown and an apartment, two-bedroom, for eleven hundred."

"Downtown Norfolk," he said, not sounding too enthused.

"Naw, man, Virginia Beach, across from Pembroke. It's that new shit, son, phat shit. High-rise, city living."

"For real? I trust you. Get me an office, man, phat office, phatter than yours." He laughed. "Is the two-bedroom, two-baths phat? That's all they got?"

"Naw, if you got half and gonna be chillin' there, shit, they got three bedrooms. Loft shit. Two masters. People come clean that shit and all that, twenty-one hundred a month."

"Do it. I'll be home next week Wednesday morning. Have me a spot to stay, a phat-ass office, and a bad bitch."

"Done, son."

"Yo, man, just to say, I'm glad I got a niggah that's about business. I can relax my mind and know I'm not gonna go broke. I got off this year, but I'm not gonna know my salary for a sec. I pray—"

"We gonna be straight, and you gonna be straight. That's your shit, son. Nobody balls like Chris. Niggah, you done shook niggahs on the courts of VA. Now on the courts of the NBA, they gots to see you, son," I said, giving mad encouragement.

"Yeah, you right. I just wanted to say, you could be like these other niggahs, beggin' they ass off. I flew some cats out here. Somebody stole my Rolex, stole my earrings. Kendu ain't laying low. He call the other day. He done went through two hundred-fifty thousand. I had to tell him no. Kinda fucked me up."

"You know him. We'll build him a house close and keep an eye on him. He beat that shit, and now he think he unstoppable. But I think he slowin' down. I tell ya about that later." I laughed.

"Shit. I heard about it already, niggah. But y'all ain't have to put dude away. His mind gone. Kendu say he gone crazy."

"His momma should of prayed for him and told him to stay the fuck off Baker Road," I yelled.

"See ya Wednesday. We in Philly Thursday."

"No doubt." I hung up.

I was in deep thought. My mind went to Brit. I missed

him. I never thought I'd be doing like this, and he wasn't here. I was gonna try calling him later.

Prayyiah was looking at me, questioning who I was talking to.

I walked over to my peoples, where they had the sounds pumping. Guttah and Pop G pulled up in the 350Z. They jumped out. Guttah had a big smile across his face as he exited the car, giving me a pound and hug like niggahs do when they're truly glad to see each other.

"Fuck it up, son. You fucked it up."

"Did my job, my niggah, and I'm ready for Philly," he said cool and calm.

Pop G eased over and showed love. I could feel the burner when he hugged me. "I'm ready, Prince. For real, niggah, you know I'm real, and you know my skills. I'm ready," he said, no smile.

I knew he was serious, and I also knew some shit came with him also. He was real to the streets, and he got dough. Straight grinder. I knew he wasn't carrying the burner for fun.

"We'll talk Monday. Catch me at the studio on Monday. I want you on my team." I smiled. "Oh! Think of a name for your CD, and I need to hear some fire so you can do a song All-Star weekend when we light Philly up Norfolk style."

He responded by handing me a CD.

I gave him another pound for being on point. I liked that. I handed it to Prayyiah.

"One minute, cutie," I said returning to my team as she gave me another "I'm-ready-to-go" look.

My phone rang. It was Tee Tee. I ignored it.

I talked with niggahs for a little longer and figured it was time to burst. I decided to check my messages first. I had five messages.

First: "You need to call me back."

Second: "You need to answer your phone."

Third: "You need to get home now. I'm starting to get worried."

Fourth: "You need to get home, Prince. It's an emergency."

Fifth: "Somebody done ran up in this bitch and tore my fuckin' house to pieces. You need to dump whatever bitch you with and get the fuck home. Now!"

I hung up and pressed two for speed dial.

"What, fuck?" she answered.

"What's going on?" I asked worried, but calm.

"Somebody broke in here and tore up the place."

"You know where to check. Check."

She knew where I would keep shit. She returned to the phone. "It's gone. Nothing!"

My heart dropped. "Something you wanna tell me?" I said.

"What? Prince, I know you," she screamed.

"Look, either you or Brada. One of y'all muthafuckas or both. You roll with your peoples," I said, starting to get aggravated.

"Something is wrong with you," she said.

"I'll be that muthafucka in a minute."

I jumped in my car and took off. Niggahs knew something crucial had happened for me to leave like that. Me and Prayyiah rode in silence all the way to the crib. I dropped her off to the Ac and kept going.

I arrived at the townhouse and walked in. The place was in shambles as I looked in the secret spot. "Somebody gots to die over this shit." I pulled my .380 out and put it to her head. "You and that niggah goin' away from here," I said loudly. "Y'all must be out y'all goddamn mind."

She looked at me with tears in her eyes. "Much as I've been through with you, Prince, when will you trust me? After you kill me?"

"Goddamn, Tee Tee," I said. I believed her. That left Brada as the only other person. He had gone back. He was the only one who knew for sure something was in there to tear shit up like that. I had to think things through.

I started cleaning up shit with Tee Tee. It took about two hours.

I sat down and rolled a Backwoods full of haze. Tee Tee sat down next to me. I had all kind of shit going through my mind. I wanted to trust her because she was more than my girl, she was my friend and I wanted to make sure she was always all right.

"You need to find a new spot tomorrow," I said. "And nobody will come over there, not even your family. So make sure that's what you want to do."

We sat in silence, and she fell asleep in my arms looking at BET.

The morning came, and I thought thinking things through would help me deal a little more rationally, but no matter what I tried to do, I couldn't believe this niggah robbed me. I couldn't let this shit go.

Tee Tee got ready to leave. She had some apartment hunting to do today. I told her to drop me at the Ford dealership on the boulevard. They had the 2005 Mustang. The old-style Boss was coming back, and this wasn't even supposed to be sold. I paid ten grand above retail for the manager to pull it off the showroom floor. I needed something to run around in, and it had to be fast.

I went back to the house and called Two Men and a Truck Moving Company. They came and packed up everything. All I needed was an address.

It was after two when Tee Tee called me with a new address. She'd found a condo off North Hampton back in
the cut, and we moved that day.

By four o'clock, I was more than ready to see Brada. I
was headed to Baker Road, coming up North Hampton
doing about eighty miles per hour, with my loaded .38
laying on the seat. I picked up the phone and dialed
Brada's number.

"Yo, baby, can I get that?" I said.

"What?" he said.

"You know, what you got out the crib."

"Fuck you talkin' about?" he said, playing dumb.

"Come on, Omar, don't make me show you this ain't a
game."

"You must be out your mind, comin' at me like that,
cuz."

"We'll see, son."

I pulled up in front of the barbershop and walked inside. They had a nice crowd for Saturday. I walked over
to his chair. "Let me holla at you, partner," I said.

"In a minute," he said and kept cutting.

My calmness turned to rage inside. I gripped the .38
that was in my pocket. "Naw, muthafucka. Stop what the
fuck you doin' and go get my money."

"Or what, niggah?" he said loudly, stepping from behind the chair.

Sherm, the owner, stopped cutting and stepped between
us. "Not in my shop, Prince. Handle that shit somewhere
else, man," he said real low.

Brada was standing there as if he was really gonna get
down with me. I turned to walk out, but the thought of
this niggah thinking he can fuck me pissed me off. *No,
sir!* I pulled the .38 out and turned around.

Brada's customer jumped out the chair as the .38
sounded like a cannon within the four walls. One bullet

shot through his right shoulder and the second, his thigh, as he fell to the ground.

"Niggah, you better get me my money, or I will see you at your fuckin' house," I said to him in a low voice. Then I walked out the same way I came in, jumped in the Boss, and was out.

As I rode down Newtown, I passed the police flying to the scene. I made the light at the boulevard, and I was history. My stomach was churning as I left but now I didn't feel shit. *Muthafucka better be glad I didn't take his life.*

I hit the interstate headed to Norfolk, and was at the duplex in minutes. I sparked and I sniffed. The haze settled my body down to a perfect speed.

I then realized that I was that muthafuckin' niggah. I sat at the computer looking at nudeafrica.com. I went to the free section and was flipping through the pictures when the phone rang.

It was Dundee. "What the fuck, cousin? Everything a'ight?"

"Yeah, everything's fine with me, shit."

"Well, you know me. I'm up here wit' Ponic." He walked in the barbershop asking if anybody knew anything about what happened. One person saw something, but after Ponic told me to look at dude and told somebody else to remember his face, I think everybody got the picture the barbershop full, and nobody saw nothing."

"That's what I'm talkin' about. Dundee, that niggah sold me five of them thangs, then went back and ran up in the crib and stole them back. That's what's up," I said.

"All I need to know was that it was a good reason, fam, and not over no bitch."

"Naw, good shoot, partner," I said.

"Hold on."

Ponic said, "Yo, Prince, all I got to say is you holdin' niggahs down. You feedin' niggahs now. Niggahs see what you can do for them. You too big for this shit here. Next time call me. You hear me, *P*? Call me, niggah. I likes this shit, and I know you got me." He passed the phone back to Dundee.

"Stay low, and I'll let you know what's up," Dundee said.

"Yo, Dundee is that Quest still up there?"

"Yeah."

"Let me holla at Ponic," I told him.

"What up, *P*?"

"There's a spare key to the Quest van up there on the right side by the front tire. Bring me that van when shit clear. I got you."

"Where to?" he asked.

"Norfolk, Industrial Park."

"Bet."

Chapter 33

My phone rang about two hours later. It was Ponic driving the Quest headed down Princess Anne Road. I told him to make a left on Azalea and go down by the Pepsi Company. By the time he arrived, I was there. He parked and I got out.

"Help me search this bitch for money and drugs like we the police."

"Think shit in here, *P*?"

"Yeah, the niggah robbed me yesterday while we were chillin', doin' the show."

"Damn!" Ponic said, not believing what he had heard.

As we rambled through the van, I heard a loud yell.

"Yeah, this what you lookin' for?" Ponic gave me a gym bag filled with five kilos and a hundred grand.

We tossed it in the Boss and left the van sitting unlocked in the Pepsi parking lot. That shit was in that niggah name.

I dropped Ponic back out the Lakes, gave him twenty grand for bringing the van, and threw him one of those thangs for the come-up. I went back to the duplex, weighed shit, bagged shit, jumped in the Boss, and handled business as usual. Except now, I wore my vest and carried the loaded .45 on the left, to back up this little brother, the .380, that sat on the right. These Tidewater streets wasn't no joke.

Monday morning I was up and running. I was calling Anita and wasn't getting an answer. I called her job, and she wasn't in. I decided to go downtown and handle things myself. I let them know I wanted the three-bedroom, and I wanted office space: a receptionist area, at least two offices, a copy room, and a break room. I wanted the layout of perfection.

Any business bringing in millions was not to be taken lightly. The leasing agent, after completing all the paperwork, gave me my keys, then she gave me my first piece of mail. Nobody knew I was coming here or even doing this, except Anita.

For sure, it was a letter from Anita. I threw it in my pocket until I reached the car. I sat in the Benz and removed the letter from the envelope.

> *My Beloved Prince,*
> *It is with a heavy heart that I write you this letter. It breaks my heart to know that what started out so beautifully could now be coming to an end. There is so much that I need to tell you. I just don't know where to begin. How do I tell the man that I have been praying for all my life that we may have no future together?*
> *I have prayed and longed for a man like you. Never in my wildest dreams did I imagine you really existed. There are no words to completely describe how you make me feel. From the first time I met you, I knew this was real. I've heard people say when you meet "the one," you'll*

know. I always thought they were lying. I didn't believe it was possible until you came into my life. I truly love and adore you. I love everything about you. More than that, I actually like you as a person. You are my best friend. Nothing and no one matters when we're together. Just seeing you excites me. A kiss from you is pure ecstasy. I love having your soft, beautiful lips pressed against mine. I feel so safe in your arms. I feel your love and compassion when you wrap those life-size, strapping arms around me. And when we finally made love, oh my God! I know I give you credit, but not for the reasons in your head. When you pulverized every inch of my body that first night, you made me feel and experience things I've only read about. When we made love, it wasn't just about sex. It was so much more than that. It was like we connected on a deeper level, something almost spiritual. You made me feel like I was floating on a cloud. Damn, I never wanted that feeling to end. Most of all, I fell in love and felt that you loved me back.

You are the first man I've been with and totally trusted enough to even get close to me. See, all my life I've seen how the men in my family treated the women they've been involved with. None of them were ever faithful. It was as if they felt it was their God-given right to run around and do whatever the hell they wanted to do. These are the men who had wives, but kept a girlfriend on the side. They had babies all over the place. They stayed out all night and beat their wives and girlfriends whenever and wherever they pleased. No child, especially a little girl, should see that nonsense when they're growing up. Seeing that craziness as a child turned me into a cold and untrusting woman. I figured that all men were like the ones in my family, and I swore that no man would ever treat me like that. I would hurt them before they hurt me. I've had my share of relationships, some good and some bad, and I've made more than my share of mistakes. Some mistakes will cause me a lifetime of pain, suffering, and loneliness.

My darling Prince, there is no easy way for me to tell you, so I'll just come out with it. What I've wanted to tell you for so long is that I now have AIDS. I'm not sure if you know exactly what that is, so let me explain. When we were first together, I was HIV+. You may not have contracted it. Later my VL count dropped, but now AIDS. We've always used protection after the first time. AIDS is caused by HIV, which is the Human Immunodeficiency Virus. A person can contract HIV through blood, breast milk, semen, and vaginal fluids. You can't get HIV or AIDS from hugging, touching, or sharing food. I didn't shoot up. I wasn't promiscuous. I never thought something like this would happen to me. Crackheads, prostitutes, gay men become HIV+, not a woman like me. Hell, I'm an educated sista. But now I'm a statistic. That's the thing about HIV. The virus doesn't discriminate; it doesn't care who it infects. Because I didn't protect myself, I'm one of the over 900,000 people in the U.S. who are HIV+. Some days I still have a hard time believing it. I was in shock when the doctor first told me. I called that man everything but a child of God. I made him repeat the test like three or four times. There was no way in hell that I could be HIV+! No way! It was like I was living my worst nightmare. Then I got mad as hell. I was almost certain who had given me this. My now ex-fiancé. If only I knew then what I know now.

I started to go back over our relationship, and the things that didn't make sense back then suddenly started to make sense. I thought about the medications with the names I couldn't pronounce. I remembered all the visits to the doctor, all the nights I used to wake up to wet sheets because he had night sweats. What I remember most is that toward the end of our relationship, my ex insisted on using condoms. His excuse was that he saw blood in his urine and the doctor said that blood could also be in his semen. He said the doctor told him to use a condom while he was waiting for the test results. I asked him if he was fucking around on me. Of course, he said no. What cheating man is going to admit he's cheating? I knew he was lying, but I wanted so much to believe that he was being faithful to me. This was the man I was going to marry, and I wasn't ready to let him go. I couldn't let him go. Do you know what that son of a bitch had the nerve to say when I confronted him about being HIV+? He said he was sorry. I went off. I wanted to kill him. He said he had been too scared to tell me. He didn't want to risk losing me. He said he couldn't bear to live if I wasn't in his life anymore. He said losing me would be a fate worse than death. I didn't understand what he was talking about until I met you.

Prince, I would never do anything to hurt you. I love you more than life itself. I would die for you. I would never intentionally infect you. That's why I kept pushing you away even though I wanted you so bad. I was so hot, so wet for you, but I was so afraid something would happen and I would possibly infect you. I would never, ever want to give this disease to you. Prince, you can't imagine what it's like to be HIV+. People still feel that anyone who is HIV+ deserves to be infected. They say people who are HIV+ must have been engaging in some type of nasty, dirty, or abnormal behavior. Some even say HIV/AIDS is God's punishment for immoral behavior. This type of thinking led me to the decision to keep my status to myself. I feel ashamed that I became infected, that it's my fault. I've isolated myself from friends and family. I don't want anyone to know my secret. I've been afraid that my friends, family, and community will ostracize me once *they find out I'm HIV+. Being HIV+ is an unbearable weight that I carry. I go to great lengths to prevent anyone from finding out I have it. I live my life in fear, fear of being found out. Some people have lost their family, friends, and loved ones when they disclose they are HIV+. For that reason, I choose not to disclose that information anymore. It's sad to live your life in fear. It's lonely to live your life without experiencing love. How sad is it, that this is now my life?*

The doctor says that I can live a long, healthy, productive life if I take care of myself and take my meds like I'm supposed to. But there are some days I just don't want to take anymore meds. I get so tired of the pills and doctor's visits. Some days I pray for death. I figure it would be easier than the life I'm living now. What I wouldn't give for a normal life again. A life without HIV meds, a life without CD4 counts, and Viral Loads, a life without worrying if my cough is going to turn into pneumonia and kill me. I know the doctor means well with his words of encouragement, but he isn't me. He doesn't live my life. Prince, I know this is a lot for you to take in. I wish I had the nerve to tell you in person, but I just couldn't. I couldn't bear to see the look on your face. I didn't want to see the sadness in your eyes. If I could take away your hurt and anger, I would. I never meant to hurt you. I don't know what the future holds for me. I don't know what the future holds for us. Just know that I will always love you.

Loving you always,
Anita
P.S. Please go get tested!

I sat there feeling sick. All of a sudden my body felt weak. I thought I might throw up, or shit on myself. I cut myself two days ago. It was healing, but not fast enough! *Oh! My God, what the hell this bitch done gave me?* I'm thinking this sweet, fine, educated bitch was good to go, and she just as nasty as a muthafuckin' bitch smokin' that shit.

I reached down and took out my dick. It didn't look like AIDS was on it. It still looked the same to me. My breathing sped up, and my eyes watered. This wasn't real. This wasn't my life.

Then my mind went to Prayyiah. I sunk down. Then to Tee Tee. I got scared. Then to Trecia. I began crying and beating my steering wheel. This shit wasn't fair. These girls all felt they were fuckin with a cool-ass niggah with dough. And here I was, nasty muthafucka walkin' around this bitch with AIDS.

I fell on the passenger seat and cried. I didn't know what to do. I was lost and confused. For the first time in my life, I was scared. There was nothing nobody could do, nothing my money could do, nothing my guns could do.

After crying like a girl on the front seat of my new CLS 500 Mercedes Benz, I realized the only person I could talk to was Anita. I had to go tell her about her nasty ass, and why she allowed me to fuck her and make myself nasty, because that's how I felt. I didn't feel like no baller, didn't feel like I was the shit and any bitch would be glad to have me in their life. That I was that niggah.

I felt any woman in their right mind could see the nastiness on me and go the other way. I screamed at the top of my lungs, beating myself for fucking that girl. "God, why her, and why me? I ain't did nothing to deserve this. God, I ain't did nothing to deserve this."

As the tears flowed, I had to pull over. I took several deep breaths and regained my composure. I called her cell again, and a lady answered, "Hello," the pleasant lady's voice said.

"Yes, can I speak to Anita?"

"Well, she can't get to the phone, but may I ask who's calling?"

"Prince. My name is Prince," I said, wondering what was going on.

The phone was silent. Then the voice returned. "Prince, this is Anita's mother, Ms. Bailey. She says for you to come by. She's at Leigh Memorial, room 424."

"Okay." I hung up. "This girl almost dead, shit probably runnin' through her entire body, takin' over."

I began to feel sick again. I prayed, "Oh God, don't let it be gettin' me. Don't let it break me down, Jesus, please."

I arrived at the hospital. My mind was in a daze as I put out the Backwoods full of haze, leaned over, hit me a "one and one." I shook my head, wiped my nose, and went inside.

I felt like people were looking at me funny. I reached her room. Her mother was there, aunts, uncles, church friends, and three girlfriends that had graduated with her from college.

I walked in, and her moms introduced everyone to me. I looked at Anita lying there. She looked weak, and her face looked much thinner. Thoughts of cursing, fussing, and possibly trying to kill her drifted out of my mind.

I finally allowed my eyes to meet hers. I remembered the first time we'd met. Her eyes jumped with excitement. Now they were low, red, and glassy.

At that moment something came into my heart and opened. I knew what she was feeling. I knew she was embarrassed, humiliated, and felt nasty, like nobody even wanted to touch her. I knew because I dreaded facing my family. I wished I would go to sleep and not wake up.

I vowed at that moment to be there for her. I didn't blame her anymore. I allowed the reality to sink in and realized I had nobody to blame but myself. I had no business running up in this girl raw.

I walked over to her bed, leaned down, and kissed her. I took her in my arms and held her tight. She cried and cried, but she never let go, and I never pulled away.

By the time we let go, everybody had left the room. I stood there holding her hand, and I finally opened my mouth to ask what I was aching to know.

"Why? Why didn't you tell me? I know why from the get-go. It wasn't my business and you didn't know me, but after we were intimate orally the first time, after that, I should have been told," I told her in a voice that almost trembled, trying to have a calm conversation and act like I had sense.

She looked away. "I couldn't. I just couldn't,"

"Fuck you mean, Anita? You can suck my dick, put a condom on it, and can't tell me the real reason you put the condom on?"

She began crying.

I was hurt, sad, ready to scream on her, but I didn't want her to hurt no more than she already was. "Damn! I wish all this shit would just go away," I said grabbing my head. "But it ain't, is it, Anita?" I lay my head on her chest.

She held my head and rubbed it. "What's with the vest?" she asked.

"Nothing, for real. Tryin' to make sure I don't die one way, and goddamn if I ain't killing myself another way. I guess I should want the bullet," I said sadly.

"Don't talk like that. That's not the dude I fell in love with. What happened to the strong, confident cat that asked me to sit and have breakfast with him?" She tried to smile.

"He caught AIDS, lost his pimp game," I said, quickly looking at her.

"You don't have AIDS, fool. You might have HIV, and that's a weak *might*."

"What's the fuckin' difference?"

"I got AIDS, full-blown, and I am going to die. That's the difference, asshole. Go get checked. I pray you don't. We did it once without a condom. At that point your chances were real slim. Go get checked."

Some hope came to my heart. I felt a little better, but the thoughts of Tee Tee, Trecia, and Prayyiah stayed in my head. I prayed I didn't fuck these girls' lives up.

I spent the rest of the day to myself. I felt on edge, which would've turned to anger in a split second if somebody came at me wrong, so it was best if I just stayed to self. I sat in the townhouse out Kempsville, sparking haze until I passed out. I couldn't talk to no one, couldn't tell nobody. I didn't even want to look at BET. Watching them phat-ass hoes, knowing I couldn't fuck them, took all the excitement out of the videos. My mind wasn't even on pussy.

Chapter 34

When I woke up, it was five-thirty in the morning. I called my moms about the lady who did a class on HIV and AIDS at her church. She said the lady worked as a case worker at Eastern Virginia Medical School down by Norfolk General and that I could go at anytime and get tested.

I went in early, praying I didn't see anybody I knew. I went in and spoke to the young lady who'd done the seminar for the AIDS ministry at my mother's church.

She took me to the back and talked. She pulled out a kit, which she called Ora-Quick, pricked my finger, and squeezed out a drop of blood to be tested for HIV.

What I thought would take days and a phone call, she said would only take twenty minutes. I sat out in the waiting area for what seemed like the longest twenty minutes of my life.

Tee Tee was blowing up my phone. The shit I'd kicked off with Brada was now a family issue, and nobody knew where she lived now. Prayyiah was wondering if she'd done something wrong and what was up.

Trecia wasn't calling me. I guess she'd found a niggah, who she made feel like she was all that, and he did the same. She needed that in her life. I was gonna miss that bomb-ass body that possessed some of the world's best pussy, with lips that made any man weak if he was chosen. *Damn!*

I was sitting in a daze from the haze that I'd blown on the way there, when the case worker signaled for me to come back in.

My stomach turned, and my breathing got heavy, as I sat down, and she sat across from me. She gave me a speech about safe sex and how AIDS is killing the black community, and how she could tell I was scared of not knowing.

My breathing eased up when she told me my test results were negative. I felt life come back into me.

As the case worker talked, I didn't hear shit. I looked at her pretty lips moving and her clear dark brown skin, then my eyes floated to her cleavage and down to her thick thighs that I could see clearly in her short skirt. I wanted to say, "Shut up. Grab one of those condoms and lock the door."

Instead, I said, "Thank you," shook her hand, and was out. By the time I got down to the CLS 500 and sat down in the plush leather seat, I realized I was back. I was that niggah again.

I headed to the airport to pick up Chris. I was pumping that "Back to the Guttah," floating, when my phone rang.

"Hello."

"How are you?" Prayyiah asked.

"I'm okay, and you?"

"Just wondering if I'm gonna get any time before you go to Philly. When you out anyway?"

"Yes, and tomorrow. Let's do dinner at seven. P.F. Chang's."

"I have to pick up Amaia at seven from work."

"Then come straight there. Bring her with you."

"See you, Prince. I miss you. I really miss you."

"Same here, cutie. See you around seven, and we'll be together for the evening, a'ight."

"All right. I love you, Prince," she said softly.

"Love you too, Prayyiah, for real. Please don't fuck me up," I said.

"Never that, never."

I reached the airport, just in time. Chris was getting ready to cab it when I pulled in front of him and rolled down the tinted window. "Ain't this more your speed?"

"Fuckin' right. This how you pick a niggah up—in some shit that ain't even out yet." He gave me a pound even before climbing in.

We rolled, smoking the rolled Back, full of official.

First stop was Haynes on the boulevard. We went in and purchased two bedroom sets, dining set, living room set, TV's, everything to make a crib phat as hell. Chris slammed the American Express Platinum card down and gave the delivery man five crispy hundred-dollar bills to have our shit to the condo just three miles up the boulevard in the next couple of hours.

We sat in the new apartment, talkin' and blazin' 'til the furniture arrived. They set everything up, and the shit was on, ready for whatever. I was ready to run with my boy, but that niggah fell asleep on the couch looking at ESPN.

I was headed out the door when my phone rang. I looked at the caller ID. It was that 770 area code. "What up?" I answered, thinking it was Leah and something had happened.

"What up?"

"What the fuck you think, big time?"

I caught the voice instantly. Brit was my big brother, but his hustling days had passed him. He rode it while he could, but now it was my time. And until he was here living in one of our homes, I worried and prayed hard that God would watch over him.

"You what's up, niggah. I'm just tryin' to fill your shoes, but those joints too big. Them muthafuckas too big," I said, laughing loud.

Black laughed on the other end.

"Where you at? We can't come to the business?" he said, emphasizing *we*.

I asked no questions. "New shit, son. Moved in today. Get off on the second Independence, make a right on the boulevard, make a right at the Cheesecake Factory, come down by the Funny Bone Comedy Club. You'll see the high-rise, twelfth floor. Park in the garage."

I rolled another two Backwoods, went over to the new bar, and poured me some Grey Goose. Chris had stocked the bar. Hennessy, Hennessy XO, Grey Goose, Belve, Remy, Remy XO, Absolut, Apple Puckers mix, and some other sweet shit for them hoes.

As I was putting down the bottle, Chris woke up.

"Fix me one too, niggah. Henny straight, about four shots. It's that time, baby." He yelled before going in the bathroom.

We were sitting on the couch, looking at the new sixty-inch flat-screen TV hanging on the wall. This AIDS shit was killing me inside. I had to talk to somebody, so I just came out of nowhere and told him, "Bitch almost killed me, son."

"What you mean, man?"

"I met this woman several months back, when I came home from all that shit."

"Anita, right?"

I nodded.

"Yeah, you told me about her. Jag, truck, nice home, good job. Yeah, go ahead."

"Bitch in Leigh Memorial dyin' of AIDS."

"You fucked her raw, man?"

"Naw, one time. The first time."

"Goddamn, man, I'm killin' them hoes out west, son—black hoes, white hoes, Mexican hoes, mixed hoes—but all them hoes get a wrapped-up dick. I don't play, son. We got money now. Bitches love us. They loved us before, but now we rich. We gots to be careful. So you been checked?"

"Yeah." I pulled out the paper that had my results from earlier.

He looked at it and smiled.

I smiled and we gave each other a pound.

"I still ain't fuckin', eatin', or drinkin' behind you. Can't believe you fuckin' them nasty hoes raw." He bust out laughing.

"Shit ain't funny, son. Far from funny," I said answering the knock at the door.

"You right. God just gave you a pass. You only get three," Chris said, giving me a big hug. There was a knock at the door. I went and opened it knowing the phone call I had just got, had me excited. When the figure walked in, I grabbed him like it had been years, but one day was too long. I felt like crying. My brother was right here beside me. I felt complete. I was all right, I didn't have to worry about Brit. He was right beside me on my left side, but that .380 was still on the right.

I looked Brit up and down—Rocawear jeans, new white DC's, and a button-down.

Black walked in and shut the door. I turned my attention to him—black Indigo Red jeans, black DC's, black T-shirt, thick platinum chain, platinum bracelet, platinum Breitling watch with a black face, and at least a half a carat attached to each ear.

After we embraced, I backed up and shook my head. He smiled, looked around, and shook his head up and down, giving me his okay.

Call it what you want, but I not only looked up to this cat, I respected everything about him. To be like Black was every young niggah out Lake Edward's dream. Now here he was, approving of my life. I felt good.

Chris walked up and gave Brit a pound and hug. Then he looked at Black. Chris let him know he played ball.

Then it hit Black. "You nice, son, but you gonna need some help to get a ring. They gonna have to spend some money," he said.

"Yeah, whole lot of inside problems too."

"I can imagine." Brit went to the bar and grabbed two glasses and the bottle of Henny.

"Pop that XO, niggah. We in VA now, baby." Black lit the three dubs that I had stuffed in a Backwoods. "Niggah got XO, and he gonna pop the regular."

Chris sipped on his drink. "He know what that shit cost, that's why?"

"Don't matter what it cost. You want to get paid for it?" Black pulled a knot out his pocket, peeled off two hundreds, and placed them on the table.

Brit handed him the bottle and glass, and Black broke the seal and poured him and Brit double shots straight.

Out of nowhere, Chris said, "Yo, Black, I didn't mean shit the way it sounded," he said stuttering. The weed and liquor had him nice.

"I didn't take it wrong, believe me. I just wanted you to know how much something cost don't matter in my circle. We'll go buy some more. Been like that since eighty-eight, ya know? Sometimes you forget who you in the presence of."

"Now I got a question," Chris said.

Black smirked as he glanced at me.

"Since I got you here, one, they say you made a million a month when you reigned, two, that you are the only niggah from Norfolk to ever have a Colombian connect. And three, niggahs and bitches say that your brother Dee fucked over two hundred bitches." Chris smiled.

"Every time a story's told, it gets more off-track. Those are way off." Black hit the Backwoods hard.

"Shit, I don't know about the first two, but I knew Dee, and he could of fucked two hundred bitches easy. I know for a fact he fucked eighty-five. I saw the bag he wrote hoes name on in the back of the sports bar," Brit said.

We all began laughing. If you knew Dee, you couldn't help it.

My phone rang. It was Prayyiah and Amaia headed to P.F. Chang's.

We were out the door in minutes.

I was hoping Amaia would like Chris, but you could tell she was feeling Black, as she focused on the quiet, black-ass niggah draped in ice, not saying too much.

After dinner and paying a four-hundred-dollar tab, we began walking to the high-rise.

Amaia wanted ice cream, and Chris jumped at the thought. It gave them personal time standing in line at Cold Stone.

Me, Brit, and Black was talking as Prayyiah stood close by. I caught up on what Brit's been doin'. He was actually running around with Black, working as his right-hand man with several of his legit businesses. Black was also into flipping real estate, but ran a promotional and marketing firm. He'd hired people straight out of Spelman and Morehouse with high grade point averages. His strategy had worked, his business prospered, not to mention his bonding company, so Brit was all right.

We all went back to the apartment for drinks, trees, and conversation. I don't know what Chris and Amaia discussed in the ice cream spot, but he had all her attention now. He was showing Amaia his room, while I took the time to introduce Brit to the new love of my life.

Black got a call and stepped away.

I looked at Brit. No jewels, just a nice watch, always laid-back. I didn't know how he let that girl get to him like that. *That's that "fucking-one-girl" shit*, I thought.

Black came back in the room. "Poppa said they got a 'Models & Bottles' at the Broadway tonight. Said that shit goin' to be jumpin'. Niggahs need to go politic."

I looked at Black. I knew this niggah, imitated this niggah, and it got me everything. I knew he wasn't about business. He wanted to go out and shine his ass off, let everybody in Tidewater know that he still reigned.

I was with him. *Let's go lock it down*, I thought.

Chris came out the room. "Y'all ready?"

Everybody looked at him.

I looked at Prayyiah, wondering what to say. I promised her, and I could see it in her eyes that she was already getting upset. I hadn't seen her in days, hadn't fucked her in days, because we'd been going at it for a second. She was definitely catching real feelings.

"Going to the club, Joe, Plaxico, couple other cats called. They on their way to the Broadway." Chris grabbed his coat. "We gonna just politic, grab a few drinks, and we out. Amaia stayin' here 'til I get back. I would appreciate if y'all will go to Wal-Mart and get some soap, utensils, towels, and shit. Use that two hundred dollars on the table, house warming gift, compliments of Black." Chris looked at Black.

Black smirked.

I looked at Prayyiah. "I ain't pressed, but Chris ain't got no whip. You know I'll be back soon," I said, giving her a kiss.

Prayyiah was in a deep stare directed at me, as Black, Chris, and Brit went out the door I was holding open. As I stared back at her, I saw and felt a different stare. I wondered what she could be thinking. "I love you, Prayyiah," I said.

"Just be careful, Prince."

"Always, shorty, always."

Chapter 35

We were rolling down Virginia Beach Boulevard. I knew the CLS 500 was fire, rims shining, floating, but the black two-door Bentley made a statement like no other.

"What that niggah do?" Chris stared at the Bentley. "I know it ain't just drugs and shit."

"Man, you know how long Black been around? Do you know how long that niggah been gettin' money? Since like eighty-eight, son. Niggah made millions. They came in and made a big sweep, and he burst. Ain't see that niggah no more 'til like ninety-nine, and that shit happened in ninety-five. He came back strong. Say he was Up Top, still hustling. Then he came back, made some more mills, always staying in touch with one niggah," I said.

"He still doin' the same shit, ignorant niggah," Chris said.

"Man, he got a mansion in the Beach. He got a mansion in ATL. He got businesses like crazy, and he never here. His brother took his money and invested that shit right. When his brother got killed, that niggah sold mad real estate they had, packed up and moved to ATL. Niggah rich, son, and smart," I said, correcting him.

Chris was my man, but Black and Brit were like daddies to the young niggahs. When they started getting dough, shit got better for the kids out Lake Edward. So saying something wrong could get us on the outs.

"Heard that," he said, as Black made the right on Newtown.

He probably ridin' through the Lakes. Nothing like home, I thought.

When we pulled up on E. Hastings, mad cats were hanging out. It looked like a car show. Big Herb's Navigator, Dundee's Range, and Big El had the Denali out, representing. There were two whips I hadn't seen, a '96 Ferrari, black, aluminum rims, with Georgia tags with *COBB* at the bottom. Behind that was a Cadillac DeVille sitting on twenty-two's, with Tennessee tags, with *SHELBY* at the bottom.

We parked and jumped out. Niggahs were shooting dice, sparking, and arguing about nothing. I saw niggahs I hadn't seen in a while and realized who was what. That's that niggah Lo and Kev who had those whips. They were Black's peoples when he reigned in VA. When he burst, they disappeared.

"So what you doin' out here, Herb? Where that red-flag niggah?" I said, talking shit. It was good to see him.

"I'm dolo, niggah, and I go any muthafuckin' where."

"A'ight, baby," I said.

Niggahs laughed.

"Don't fuck with Herb," Black said. "He was mad growin' up, and he still ain't changed."

Niggahs laughed again.

"I'm ready to fuck a niggah up," Herb said.

"Fuck that," El said. "You out this bitch hidin'. Niggahs with the red bandannas after your ass. Niggahs out here hidin' after claimin' all that red shit. Now you run your ass back to the Lakes for protection."

Niggahs was looking at Herb.

"Fuck you, El. I ain't hidin'."

"Yeah, right. Y'all heard on the news about that niggah runnin' up in Herb man's spot. Shot Herb man. Think they called the niggah Flight. Tied him up and made him watch as he shot his girl and her two kids, dude moms, then bust that niggah again. Say the girl was giving the kids baths. Shorty was holding one of her kids and the niggah shot everybody two times, once in the head. Them niggahs wasn't playing," El said.

Herb was real quiet. He didn't have shit to say.

"You back, Herb?" Dundee yelled.

" 'Cause we don't bang around here. We get money. Broadway, baby," I yelled, and we all pulled out of Lake Edward, headed to the club, with Herb leading in the big pretty Navigator.

We hit Newtown Road and made a right on the boulevard. When we hit the boulevard, everybody flew past Herb. The Lambo Lo had and that Bentley was in the wind, but the 500 Benz kept them in sight. I realized that day that a Cadillac got much power.

We arrived at the Broadway in minutes. I was thinking we could park right in front and hit off security. Shit, we had enough dough to buy the club, but I was wrong. In the front of the club was a black Hummer H2, bright yellow Hummer H2, Escalade EXT sitting on twenty-four's, Benz E55 AMG, Phantom Rolls Royce, which had to belong to Iverson, Joe, or Pharrell. We went to the side and parked by the door where everybody would be leaving.

We pulled in, hitting security with one hundred dollars per car. That or walk from down the street. Ballers don't walk that far.

I pulled up beside a S500, mad niggahs just hanging out and bitches that I didn't even know existed in VA.

"Nothing like home," Chris yelled, getting hype about a group of bitches we'd passed.

We parked, and our clique caught mad attention as we made our way to the crowded door. The parking lot was off the chain. This young cat that was with Plaxico had a Lincoln Mark X convertible on twenty-four's platinum with FL tags, with sounds hitting so hard, the club owner had to come out.

Things were crazy. Mad niggahs were out, not going inside, but seemed to be on the prowl for someone slipping and Black drew mad attention with the Bentley and his jewels. He was shining.

We'd been chilling outside for about ten minutes when Black noticed Bob, the club owner.

"Got to ease in the club," he said as he moved closer to the door. "Don't know all these niggahs. Stay close."

He got Bob's attention. Once their eyes met, Bob made his way straight to Black. The way they greeted and hugged, people knew they were tighter than friends.

"Where the fuck you been?" Bob smiled. "Naw, Black, don't even answer that."

"Just know I'm all right." Black gripped Bob. "Question is, are you all right? Man, I was real sorry to hear about your dad. You know Bob Fields was a dad to many niggahs and was there for me like my dad never was. Niggah, you know."

They smiled about some of Black's early days.

Black handed Bob a bank envelope. "My card in there. I'm always here for ya."

"Appreciate it, Black. Love ya, man."

"No doubt."

"Hangin' out or goin' in?" Bob asked.

"Goin' in for a minute. I got five with me."

Bob told head security to take us straight to VIP, and security opened the way. Black entered, telling security Kev, Lo, Brit, me, and Dundee were straight. Then he turned and kept going. I made sure Dundee was close because we moved fast.

Security took Black inside, straight to the VIP section, which had a separate dance floor, bar, couches, a picture man, and only dime bitches ready for whatever. Special guest was Melissa Ford from BET, and LaLa from MTV. VIP was more laid-back, people talking, drinking, relaxing, and enjoying the night.

Behind the closed curtains, things slowed down. I looked over at Chris, who was talking to Kwan, some Newport News niggah who had just did a song with Nas that was in rotation.

Just then my phone rang. Big El was outside with the entire clique and Poppa. I told Black, and he went to head security, said some words, gave him a firm shake. Then Dundee went with security to get Big El and Poppa.

Moments later we heard the LE sound in VIP. I was like, "Oh shit! Niggahs about to set it off. What?" I looked over at Black and threw my hand up. "Got first round on me?"

"Don't matter, niggah." He smiled. "Let me see what I taught you."

I called for the waitress to come over. Ten bottles of Moet, ten shots of Hennessy straight, and twenty Heinekens." I looked at Black, with Brit, Lo, Kev, and Poppa beside him.

"Make those Henny shots doubles," Black said to the waitress. "How much?" He pulled out a knot of hundreds, which fit comfortably in his hand.

"One thousand, two hundred and thirty dollars," she said, staring at Black's ice.

"I got this," I said in her ear.

As she turned her head my way, she caught the glimpse of the hundreds that I could barely hold. I had no choice, but to pay. I handed Brit a stack of hundreds. "Give her thirteen hundred, while I fix this money." I glanced over at Black.

He laughed. He told the story about how he used to pull out knots so big, money would fall on the ground. Everybody fell out, laughing hard.

Before you knew it, bitches began coming over and dancing for us and the VIP party was set off in our corner. Our drinks came, and niggahs crowded the table in unity.

Black removed a bottle of Mo from the bucket of ice and popped it. He poured a little out and said, "That's for Dee."

Lo stepped up and got a double shot and poured it in the bucket. "Now that's for my muthafuckin' cousin and all the money he spent," Lo said seriously.

Kev took the bottle and turned it up, pouring it into the bucket. "Now that's for my big brother. The shit he said still ring in my ears today."

"You talkin' about the hoes, niggah," Big El said. "Dee was the only muthafuckin' niggah I know that smoked and fucked more than me."

Herb had just made his way in the club, him, Ponic, Moe, Ashy, Squirmy, Young Twon, Guttah, and Pop G. It was one a.m. They had just got in because Ashy and Pop G did business with the DJ outside the club. They went to the bar.

"Ten shots of Remy, ten Heinekens," Guttah said.

"And two bottles of Mo, and some glasses," Pop G yelled.

"Champagne glasses," Squirmy said.

"I don't give a fuck what kind of glass it is," Pop G added.

"Shit, give me a cup, pour it in my hand. I'm gonna get fucked up, believe that."

Cats laughed and grabbed at shorties walking by. The more they drank, the louder they got.

By the third round, around one-fifty, niggahs was in rare form.

"What's in VIP?" Young Twon asked Ponic.

"Fuck VIP," Big Herb said, leaning on the bar.

"Herb drunk. Come on, we goin' in there," Ponic said.

Moe, Ashy, Guttah, and Pop G followed.

Security stopped them, but this guy had done security at the show the other night. He remembered Guttah and showed him love.

Guttah told niggahs he was gonna go get me to get them back there.

When he approached me, I introduced him to Chris. He already knew Black and Brit.

Guttah told us who was trying to come back, but niggahs wasn't trying to leave Herb by himself fucked up.

"I'm comin' out, man," I said. "It ain't shit back here. Fuck these hoes. And that bitch ain't that bad."

"Shit, I saw that bitch. I'll take her."

"Nino Brown, niggah. Cancel that bitch. I'll buy another one," Black said.

"Beans, niggah. You don't know about beans, son."

We laughed, and I walked out front with Guttah and Chris. "Fuck VIP," I said to my niggahs coming out front.

"That's what the hell I said. Somebody order some chicken," Herb said.

I got a waitress and ordered two trays of wings and fries. I turned around and there was Trecia and her clique. They all had on revealing shit, mini skirts with their ass out, shorty shorts, with the bottom of they black asses hanging, and here she was with her see-through shirt and bra.

Trecia stood real close. "Where my drink?"

"Back the fuck up off me, girl," I said. I must've shocked her, but she got the picture.

"So what's up with you?" she asked.

Then Herb said, "Here comes trouble, trouble."

I looked up to see Tee Tee and her one girlfriend MaVette that I thought was into church now.

Tee Tee came up close to me as I stood by the bar. "Why is she all in your face?" she asked me.

"She just talkin'. I don't even know her like that," I said quietly.

Trecia overheard me. "Know me like that? Niggah, you put me in my crib. You still got a key, and you fucked me Friday night, niggah."

I wanted to slap the hell out of this girl for lying.

Tee Tee grabbed the Moet bottle and spun around, busting Trecia in the face. Trecia fell back, and MaVette was on her ass. Trecia's girls jumped in, but that Moet bottle was in Tee Tee's hand and she was damaging bitches.

I grabbed MaVette, and Dundee grabbed Tee Tee, and we all exited the club.

Outside, my niggahs were tripping about the incident. We walked them to the car, me and Dundee. Tee Tee was mad and her girl was mad because she had set that shit off.

"We at the car," Tee Tee said. "Now get the fuck away from me," she said.

"That girl is lyin'. I ain't did shit with her," I explained.

"Yes, you did, Prince. Yes, you did." She looked at me with tears in her eyes.

I felt like shit again.

"I know you put that bitch in a spot, I know you got a

key to her house, and I know you've been fuckin' that bitch. But you didn't fuck her Friday, that I do know. Let that be the reason I whip that bitch ass." Her and her girl got in the car and drove off.

Me and Dundee were walking back up to the club. We saw our team surrounded by shorties, so we eased in the mix, trying to see what was up. The club continued to empty, so we stood checking out everything that exited the door.

"I'm out," Big El yelled.

"You ain't by yourself," I yelled. "Come on, Chris."

As me, Dundee, Herb, and Ashy started toward the cars, a van pulled up, and out jumped Blanco and Sterling. I thought these niggahs weren't real, but they pulled their burners quickly, saying nothing, and pumped nine shots into Herb's chest, and another four hit Dundee.

My legs froze, and my heart dropped, as two hot ones pierced my body. Then I heard eight shots after that. I heard screams, but then they soon faded.

Chapter 36

It would be Sunday before I opened my eyes. I was breathing hard, wondering what had happened. My sister was there holding my hand. The two bullets had fucked me up. One numbed my leg, and the other ruptured my gallbladder, so it had to be removed. I stared at her. I didn't have the strength to talk or ask questions.

People were coming by saying, "His eyes are open." They would talk, and my mom and her prayer partners from her church would pray.

I could hear every word, but I couldn't respond in any way. I tried to move, but nothing happened. I tried to speak, but nothing came out, but my mind kept going. For four months, they say I'd slipped into a coma. I disagree, because I knew everything that was going on.

When I finally spoke, my words were different, my heart was different, and I felt higher than if I had smoked any weed. I was high off life, and all I could do was thank God for His blessings and figure out my real purpose in life.

Once I spoke that morning, my sister had called everybody, letting them know I was out of a coma.

I was sitting up in the hospital bed, speaking real slow, when Big El, Moe, Guttah, Squirmy, Twon, Poppa, and Ponic walked in. I heard them in the hallway, making all kinds of ruckus. The love these niggahs were showing me was outrageous. They got so loud, the nurse came in and said I could only have two visitors at a time.

Guttah said, "The shop is fine, studio straight. Jamil been holdin' everything down for you. I got my next CD ready, and Pop G told me to tell you he ain't stop workin'." Then he left out.

My moms and sister left, letting me know they'd be outside. Everybody else showed love by giving me pounds and hugs.

Ponic was standing there staring, a gritty look on his face.

"I'm glad to see you all right, man," Moe said. "You in my prayers. Soon as you better, man, I want to see you at my church. This life we've lived ain't meant for dogs. We have to live different and think about giving your life to God. It's a new day, Prince. Make the right choices. I know you about money, Prince, but let me give you this.

"Job 36:11 says, 'If we obey and serve Him, we shall spend our days in prosperity and our years in pleasures. But if we don't obey, we shall perish by the sword and we shall die without knowledge.' I lost my man and his family to a gruesome death. Prince, I lost Big Herb." His eyes watered and the tears fell.

My breathing quickened. I didn't know about Herb. I looked at Poppa and Big El. "Tell me what happened that night, El. Don't leave out shit."

"Niggahs jumped out the van, came up, and hit Herb eight times point-blank, he never had a chance. Dundee tried to burst, and they hit him four times. And before you could blink or move, I saw niggahs point the burners on you and pop two times."

"So where Dundee?" I asked.

"Dun gone, son. Big Herb gone, son," El said.

I lay back down. I couldn't stop the pain nor the tears. *Not Dundee. Not my cousin God, why?*

"You fell to the ground, man. It wasn't shit nobody could do. Nobody had guns. They caught us slippin', man, niggahs that's supposed to be trained to go."

Emotions were running high in the room now. We lost family, and that shit hurts, no matter how long ago it was.

"Go 'head, man. Finish."

"You were down and them two kids were gettin' ready to pop your ass again, and I heard burners lettin' off, about eighteen rounds. They came from my left and right. So close, shells was poppin' on me. When the smoke cleared, all you seen was that black Bentley and that black Lambo peelin' out the parking lot. Them niggahs dead too, son. Closed caskets. They got massacred. They say your brother had a nine, and so did Black, but that niggah pushin' the Lambo with the dreads—"

"Lo," I said.

"Dude had a cannon. His .44 shook the club. Six times," Big El said too loud. "Well, after all that, y'all layin' in front of the club, everybody burst because they on paper or can't get tied up with the police."

"So y'all left me on the cold concrete to die?"

Niggahs laughed.

"Naw, man, Squirmy stayed with your ass, talkin' to you, tryin' to keep you up and shit. Niggah rode with you to Norfolk General and everything. He stayed on the phone with me, I stayed on the phone with Poppa, and

Poppa stayed on the phone with Brit. I'm out, son. Got to pick up my kids before they mommas get the child support peoples after me." Big El headed out the door.

Ponic followed him, after Moe said another prayer.

"This shit done fucked him up," Poppa said.

"Fuck anybody up, son," I said, feeling fucked up inside about my cousin, my closest.

Thoughts of Black, Lo, and Brit saving me again showed me The Lakes ain't what it used to be. Those real money-gettin', ruthless-ass niggahs left with the nineties.

I asked Poppa. "Do you think seein' all the shit we've seen and losin' your brother would make a niggah turn to crack, or God?"

"Look at me. Look at who you askin'. I been fuckin' with Black and Lo since like ninety-five, Prince. I did three years in Greenville before that, son. There's nothing I haven't seen, from niggahs tortured and mutilated, to watching niggahs' flesh burn. I'm cold, my heart and soul are cold. Don't reach this point."

"Feel you." I didn't know Poppa been fuckin' with Black that long. *Poppa should be rich.*

Poppa picked up his phone and made a call. He handed the phone to me.

"What up, little niggah?" Black said.

"You know I'm straight, God."

"Damn right. With God looking over, nothing can go wrong. Look, I took some things into my own hands. Me and your man Chris, we sat down and talked. He flew into ATL, and we had a real sit-down. He said he was forty percent in everything?"

"Yeah! On his word, and we like that," I said.

"Okay, so I turned him on to a realtor named Freddie Mac, and we hired your girl Prayyiah to run the company. You had everything laid out, so all she had to do was put it in motion, and with Freddie Mac right there, he listed all your houses. That's his pay. I did some things and got Prayyiah power of attorney so she could sign, and got your man Chris some legal papers so his signature would be good also. I didn't want you to lose what you started because, if you lose, the streets will call. I figured you and Prayyiah like that, the jewels, the ring. She knew about the house at Kempsville Green. Brit said you had to be in love."

"True."

"She knows everything, man—Tee Tee, some other girl Anita—but she past that. Yo, you got two real niggahs, Chris and that young niggah Squirmy, and your girl got your back. Glad you back, and I'm out your business."

"Love ya, man, for real, Black. Thanks," I said from the heart.

"You the only niggah like me. It ain't the money, it's what we do with it. We want to see other niggahs do good and make sure our family straight, bottom line. Out."

So where's my girl? I handed the phone back to Poppa.

"So what he say?" Poppa asked.

"Basically, he said keep my legit business straight and don't worry about the street."

"That's the same thing he told me. Niggah say I should have enough money saved to chill, so he cut me off. I can't get shit."

"I shot my connect. Shit I need y'all," I said laughing.

"Yo, I'll check you out the Lakes," Poppa said, letting the door shut behind him.

Later that day Prayyiah stopped by. Her eyes watered at the sight of me lifting my hands for her to come hug me. She held me like she was never going to let go. We talked about business, but not too much more.

I checked out of the hospital two days later, and she was there to carry me home. We went to Kingsville Greens.

She opened the door, and I walked in and sat down on the couch.

She walked over and handed me a new key ring. "Now here are your keys," she said, "the car key, the house key, the office key, and your apartment key, that you and Chris got. Huh! Don't let another key pop up on this key ring. I met Anita. She helped me and told me a lot on the business end and how she helped you put things together. She died two weeks ago from AIDS. I don't know if you fucked her, but I know you ain't got AIDS 'cause they check you in the hospital."

My head sank. I never had a chance to say goodbye.

"I also met Trecia. Her key is gone, she is gone, and she's paying her own fuckin' bills. And I met Tee Tee. She showed me where y'all lived when you shot a niggah over her gettin' dropped off. She showed me where y'all lived when you got robbed and then you shot her sister's man. Then she showed me where y'all moved to. She was real informative. But all that shit is behind us, and most of that shit was before me. All that's going on now is me.

"When Chris and Black asked me to hold down your shit, I wanted you to see that I had your back, so I sat out a semester, Amaia sat out a semester, and Chris hired Squirmy. He's smart as shit and we made it happen. We finished what you started. Then we started building Prince Cove, seventy homes, six different builders, our project." She smiled.

"And Freddie Mac put us in with a lender who does all construction loans. You sitting on a mil, boy, and your business is just shufflin' paperwork, no more cash. So remember I would never get you for nothing, but I helped you build this, and I'm not going anywhere. Never." She leaned over me.

"Then you need to marry me then," I said, not knowing where it came from. I guess deep inside I was tired. I was just turning twenty-one and had experienced a lifetime of shit. I had two strikes on my life, and I really didn't want to try for the third.

"Are you serious?"

"Yes," I said, staring into her eyes. "I'm very serious. I would like nothing more."

With those words, I decided to change my life. I wanted to get away from all this street shit and start new.

My phone rang. It was Chris.

"You better, baby?"

"Yeah, niggah, I'm straight."

"You know I signed my contract, son. They kept me out here."

"How much?" I asked.

"Six years, seventy million."

My throat choked up. "You straight for life."

"You my man, son. You scared me, but you opened my eyes. This is a turning point in our lives. Nothing but the good life. What they say, son? Money and haze."

I smiled. "Money and haze."

A year later . . .

We finished the housing project and started another. Me, Chris, Kendu, Poppa, and Guttah all lived in the same neighborhood. All the houses ranged from seven hundred thousand to a million, all what we built. Guttah signed a deal with a major record company and picked up Pop G as a ghost writer. His first album went double platinum.

Moe opened a church on Baker Road, in the middle of the Lakes, right in the shopping center with the barbershop, saying, "That's where God called me to minister."

Leah and Brit still live in a beautiful home in Marietta, GA, and just a new baby girl, Leah Brittany.

Chris married Amaia, but seemed to be unhappy.

I was still engaged to Prayyiah. I tried to be faithful and didn't fuck around. No Anita, no Trecia, no Tee Tee, only Prayyiah. And even though Prayyiah made me very happy, and I knew I made the right choice in life, no matter how great life was going, I couldn't understand why

Tee Tee stayed on my mind. I couldn't get through a day without thinking of her. But I left it alone. I'd hurt enough women in my life, and I promised God I was going to change.

I looked at Prayyiah. I smiled and thanked God for blessing me with her.